THE SPINSTER AND THE RAKE

THE
SPINSTER
AND THE
RAKE

NEVER A
WALLFLOWER SERIES

USA TODAY BESTSELLING AUTHOR
EVA DEVON

Entangled Publishing, LLC
10940 S Parker Road
Suite 327
Parker, CO 80134
Visit our website at www.entangledpublishing.com.

Amara is an imprint of Entangled Publishing, LLC.

Edited by Liz Pelletier and Lydia Sharp
Cover design by Bree Archer
Cover art by Photographer Shirley Green and
fotoVoyager/GettyImages
Interior design by Toni Kerr

Print ISBN 978-1-68281-613-4
ebook ISBN 978-1-68281-614-1

Manufactured in the United States of America

First Edition February 2021

AMARA

ALSO BY EVA DEVON

THE WALLFLOWER WINS SERIES

The Way the Wallflower Wed
The Wallflower's Wicked Wager

THE DUKE'S SECRET SERIES

A Duke for the Road
How to Marry a Duke Without Really Trying
Duke Takes All
Between the Devil and the Duke
The Duke You Know
My Duke Until Dawn
No Duke Will Do

DUKE'S CLUB SERIES

Once Upon a Duke
Dreaming of the Duke
Wish Upon a Duke
All About the Duke
Duke Ever After
Not Quite a Duke
A Duke by Any Other Name
My Wild Duke
If I Were a Duke
Never a Duke
A Duke Like No Other

For Esaul, the hero of my heart.
You always believe in me.
I am so grateful I went out dancing that night and
that you decided to come inside.
With two small, seemingly insignificant decisions, a
love so big was born.

And for Elizabeth Pelletier, who during a way too
fun phone call one December night, said the magic
phrase, what if the hero…

CHAPTER ONE

YORKSHIRE, ENGLAND
1795

Edward Andrew Richard Stanhope, sixteenth Duke of Thornfield, always did the right thing, even if doing so wasn't easy.

So, when one of his guests, a young lady whose name he could not recall, tilted off her sidesaddle and plummeted straight for the ditch along the field, Edward urged his stallion forward and leaped to catch her before she would break her neck.

Alas, she slipped through his gloved hands and gravity took its course upon the pair of them. They landed in the mire of an extremely deep and questionable puddle. A general cry of alarm and consternation arose from the mounted onlookers. Great murmurs of concern filled the air, but not a single lord or lady jumped into the fray. No, they observed in genteel horror as Edward and the young lady wallowed in the mud. They were all, save he, apparently above such chivalrous rescue.

Very practical, if not gallant, of them, he had to admit.

Unable to find purchase, Edward was forced to grab hold of her lest they slip about for eternity. Or at least until his man assisted them.

Once safely in his hold, the chit stared up at him with great brown eyes, which happened to match the mud and wet hair streaking down her pale cheeks.

"Are you all right?" he asked urgently. "Have you hurt yourself?"

"No." Her voice was light and feathery, and she batted her long blond lashes up at him. "Oh, your Grace, you have saved me."

Edward stared down at her, attempting to make sense of her expression. Whatever did she mean?

He reconsidered her words and the batting of her lashes. Batting lashes meant flirtation. He'd made note of it before and remembered well. Women batted their lashes at him when they wanted his attention—or rather, the attention of an unmarried duke.

Comprehension dawned.

Edward longed to groan at the young lady's audacity. He refrained. Inwardly, he allowed himself to rail at the antics of determined debutants.

He wasn't generally given to assuming someone was a bad sort. No, he liked to believe that generally people were not manipulative. But from the way she was looking at him and from the way her hands drew suddenly about his neck, clinging as if she'd never let go, Edward had the rather serious impression she hoped to be the next Duchess of Thornfield.

In fact, she was holding on to him so tightly, he wondered if she believed possession was nine-tenths of the law. As though she felt, if she could simply keep a hold of him, she would assume the title.

She was mistaken, of course.

He had no intention of marrying flibbertigibbets who could not sit their saddle. And now he doubted she had been unseated at all. He again stared down at what he assumed many would call a beautiful face. But good looks didn't make one a good duchess by default.

"I'm glad you are well." With his soppy, gloved hands, he attempted to unwind her grip from its prize. Namely, himself. "Please release me so I can get us out of this dank hole."

"Oh, Your Grace, of course!" She unlocked her taut embrace but then proceeded to bring a fluttering hand to her brow. Her eyelids fluttered as well. There was far too much fluttering going on for his liking. "But I find I am most dizzy," she whispered dramatically.

He scowled then immediately smoothed his expression, fighting a surprising dose of irritation. He did not usually suffer the vapors, pretend or otherwise. "I will help you out of the ditch, and that is far enough."

"But could you not carry me to the castle?" she insisted, her voice still holding that breathy note that completely mystified him.

And now, amidst the dales he loved so well, sitting in several inches of good Yorkshire rain water, he was cold. His breeches were wet. His coat was drenched. And to add insult to injury, he was covered in mud, as was she. They were both a right mess; he supposed he should offer further assistance. But that didn't mean he had to be the one to carry it out.

A good north wind whipped down the dale, rustling his guests exceptionally clean riding clothes and exacerbating Edward's chill.

"I will ask my man to take you back to the

house." He gritted his teeth, willing himself not to say anything he might regret or that might support his reputation for being a cold sod. It had taken a great deal of training over the years not to blurt out the thoughts in his head as they came to him. Presently, she was putting all that training to the test. "I'm certain he will find your mother to take care of you."

"Oh, but Your Grace. You are my hero and you must allow me to thank you properly." The young lady leaned forward and had the rather shocking temerity to touch his arm. "Come with me."

Edward eyed that hand upon his forearm. He did not like to be touched by strangers without his wish or approval, even lightly. He arched a brow, then before he could stop himself, he said matter-of-factly, "You look like a drowned rat."

A squeak of dismay exited her Cupid's bow lips.

She was clearly not used to being told the obvious truth. He hoped someone would explain to her that one did not throw themselves into ditches so dukes would go after them.

He had helped, of course, because he really *wasn't* the cold sod everyone thought him to be, but such a charade was not the way to matrimony. At least not with him.

Edward helped her to stand, her riding habit all but pouring water down its heavy skirts. Delicately, he guided her toward his footman, Hobbs. "Take the young lady back to the house. Make certain she is dried out and that her family is found."

She let out several sounds of protest, but Edward ignored them all, stepping away to grab his stallion's reins that he'd had to abandon to rescue her.

Rescue, indeed.

Such machinations were unfortunately common.

It was the life of a duke. People would stuff handkerchiefs down his coat, fall into ditches, and corner him in rooms. Who knew what they'd think up next?

As he stepped forward, he felt an alarming draft and winced. *Bloody hell.* His breeches were torn in a most indiscreet place. Edward held the long tails of his riding coat about his legs, or else half the county would see his nether regions.

Escape. He needed to escape.

Quickly, he swung back up onto his stallion and charged off in the direction of the stables, leaving the riding party without a word. He really had no desire to continue on in this particular vein, regardless, not after such a moment. And soon everyone would be gathering for the ball—he would need to clean and change.

Relieved to be alone, Edward galloped back to the stable block where he knew he'd find a spare set of clothes, though none would fit him. He was far larger than all the stable lads, but this would have to do until he could get upstairs and properly change.

But he also wanted dry breeches so he could avoid everyone, servants included, and find a moment's solitude in his private library. He needed his special chair. It would help calm the tension throughout his body. And he required that calm, if he was to face the evening ahead.

Edward left his stallion with a groomsman, headed for the tack room, and grabbed a pair of dubious breeches. He yanked off his drenched ones and quickly pulled the coarse wool into place. They were ill-fitting and dried mud showed in a few spots, but they would suffice.

As he stared down at the state of his dress, he sighed. Perhaps "rescuing" her had been the right thing to do in more ways than one. It gave him a legitimate excuse to spend some time alone and gather himself. Edward trotted up the limestone servants' stairs of Thornfield Castle.

Captain, his great wiry wolfhound, spotted him and raced out to meet him, tail wagging. "There's my good boy." Edward gave him a strong pat on the head, feeling a good dose of ease from the dog's presence. Not complete relaxation, but a start.

The dog kept pace with him as they dashed down the narrow back hall. He picked up his stride, determined to avoid being stopped as he headed along the winding route to his private library. It was a sanctuary, his and his alone. He'd created it in such a way that he could collect himself when the presence of others simply became too much, threatening the facade of control he'd kept in place since childhood.

It didn't matter that he was one of the most powerful men in the land; he still internally shook at the necessity of being near or in a crowd, and tonight there was more than a crowd. There was a virtual horde of debutantes his aunt had invited to trot out before him with the intention of marriage.

He'd survive the wildness that so much noise and movement would evoke within him, but first, he would take a moment and sit in the chair he'd had specially designed. It's narrow, winged, high back, facing into a corner, allowed him to close off the rest of the world, the buzzing murmur of it all, because bloody hell, it did buzz when one was a duke.

Edward made the last turn along the dark hallway and flexed and unflexed his hands. His blood pulsed through him like a parade drum beat. Somehow, he needed to tell Aunt Agatha to cease. But she was determined to see him wed for all the usual reasons. An heir, of course. After all, the Dukes of Thornfield had been around for almost a thousand years. But more so, the old gel seemed worried he'd be stuck alone and miserable.

Alone sounded like perfection.

Finally, he reached the small, secret door to his library, pushed it open, and drew in a deep breath as the flames flickering in the fireplace warmed his chilled body.

A long sigh of relief escaped his lips. Captain trotted in behind him, looking for his green cushion near the blazing hearth. Edward pushed the door mostly closed behind him, keeping it open just a crack in case Captain needed to make a quick retreat.

Edward pulled off his drenched and mud-caked coat. He let it thump to the floor, a wet, dirt-encased mass. Methodically, he tugged at his cravat, unwinding it, drawing in the oaky scent of woodsmoke into his lungs. With each step he took into his sacred space, he felt all the tension unwinding.

Yes, this was exactly what he needed.

He opened up the throat of his linen shirt, allowing himself to catch a long breath before he held his hands out to the fire. His body was saturated with the cold of the Yorkshire Moors. He loved his lands, though. They begged for him to go out riding, and if he could, he would have ridden all day, for he preferred to be in action, to be at one with nature and the wild. But when he could not, his library was his other favorite place.

Slowly, trying to calm his racing thoughts, he headed for the grog table, ready to get a snifter of brandy. He picked up the cool decanter, loving the sound of the gentle clink of the crystal and the feel of the engraved pattern beneath his fingers as he poured out the smooth amber liquid.

He lifted it, palmed it, and savored the simple thing he loved. For brandy, unlike people, was not full of ambiguity. Just as he took a sip, the sound of leather creaking punctured his reverie.

He tensed.

He turned.

And eyed his chair.

It couldn't be. It wasn't possible. This room was off limits. *Everyone* knew this. And yet…

He took a step forward. Captain's ears cocked up, sensing something was amiss, and then jumped up and trotted around to the front of the chair. The dog plunked his behind on the floor with a giant *thud* and his tail immediately began wagging.

A shockingly enthusiastic and definite Yorkshire voice said, "Well, hello there, my lovely lad."

Lovely lad?

He thunked his snifter down and strode round to the side of the chair. "Who the blazes are you?" he roared, then stopped short, met with the most shocking pair of blue eyes he'd ever seen.

There was a depth and crystal sharpness to them that nearly stole his breath away. She gazed up at him as if she'd been caught in a trap, but she wasn't the sort of creature to look frightened.

Oh, no, after a moment of assessing, he was certain she was the sort who looked defiant.

Edward was gobsmacked. When given his stare, most became immediately contrite.

"It's none of your business who I am," she replied tartly, and eyed him up and down, her hands clasping one of his favorite books, *Pamela*.

None of his business? "What are you doing in this chair?" he demanded.

"I'm sitting," she said. "Have you no eyes?"

"Indeed, I have eyes," he growled, tempted to pick her up and deposit her somewhere, anywhere, but in his library. "I see you sitting in the chair."

"Well done," she said, with a pert nod. "You are capable of seeing. Now, if you don't mind, I'd like to be left alone. You may go."

He gaped down at her, wondering when the devil someone had ever spoken to him like that before. Never. That was when. "You are extremely impertinent," he ground out.

"No, I am not," she countered, folding the book shut, "but you are very rude."

He drew in a deep breath, ruling out physical measures. He'd never forcibly moved a lady and he wasn't about to start now. He, unlike the impossible woman before him, had standards.

"Get out of the chair," he ordered, then added, "Please."

"Why?" she said. "Do you own it?"

"As a matter of fact, I do."

Her gaze traveled up and down his length, judging every inch of him. "You will never convince me that a man wearing muddy breaches"—she gestured towards his hips—"that clearly do not fit, owns this chair."

Edward grasped for an appropriate reply. He'd never had such a ridiculous conversation in his life. "Never convince you, will I?"

"That's right." She leaned forward and stroked Captain's ears. "I do believe this is your dog, though. What a lovely dog he is. Not at all like you. And he seems to like me quite a lot."

His dog was a complete and total traitor. It was clear Captain thought she was absolutely marvelous, smiling like a dratted, besotted fool and leaning into her touch.

"Captain, kitchen," he said.

At the command, Captain happily bolted up and hurried out into the hallway, eager to find some treat from one of the maids.

"I say," she huffed, shaking her head, "you needn't banish the creature." She glanced at the hearth. "Have you come to add wood to the fire?"

"Wood to the fire?" he repeated, doubting his own ears.

"Indeed." She ventured a smile. "It seems to be growing low. You look as if you're quite capable of carrying a great many logs."

She thought him a servant? He wasn't in his usual attire, true, but surely she would recognize the authority of his demeanor.

Sometimes he struggled to tell what a person was

actually thinking, let alone feeling. So, he forced himself to assess her. Her cheeks were pink. Her eyes sparkled. Her lush, golden hair spilled about her face as if she had given no thought to it, not at all something he was used to in the women who came into his company.

Usually, they had curls that were tight and arranged in artful patterns.

Not this one.

"Miss," he said, "please get up and leave the room."

"No." She snapped the book back open, declaring her determination to stay.

"Why ever not?" he demanded, refusing to beg. Dukes did not beg. But his options were growing rather limited.

"Because I don't like it out there," she replied with unapologetic passion.

"You don't..." He wondered if she might make short work of that newly appointed head of the French army, Napoleon, if given the chance. "You don't like it out there?"

"No, not at all," she said, adamant.

"Well, that's really none of my concern. Though I don't like it out there, either."

"Look," she said, "if you absolutely must have the chair, of course I shall give it to you. I'm not an awful person, but really I was quite enjoying it and I don't wish to go back out there."

"Then don't go back out there," he said. "You can go to the kitchen."

"With your dog?" she asked, her eyes crackling.

He gazed down at her, stunned by the lushness of

her person, the curve of her body, the way her lips parted. She was consumed in the intensity of their discourse, as was he. In his whole life, there'd been no woman who caused him to feel both absolutely infuriated and full of desire at the same time.

She was astounding. He couldn't recall a single person who had ever told him to hie off.

He surprisingly liked it.

Edward stood perplexed, and he knew there was really only one thing to do to make her go. He let a slow smile curve his lips. "If you do not go, then I will kiss you."

Surely, a proper young lady would run at the threat of seduction and potential ruination. And then his chair would be his again. That was what the only thing he longed for, after all. Wasn't it?

She stood still for a moment, as if actually contemplating the bold offer, and then she swallowed hard enough to see her throat work, lifted her chin, and dared him right back. "Well, go on then, if you're so determined."

CHAPTER TWO

Something terrible and incredible had overcome Miss Georgiana Bly.

She stood staring up at this massive man, totally unafraid, absolutely furious, and stunned because there was something about him that made it impossible for her to either give in to his order to leave, or to behave as she normally would.

He had done something to her.

Something had made her feel absolutely compelled to keep her spot in this room and not go back to face the glittering company.

Who did he think he was, ordering her about? She was tired of being told what to do.

From her mother, to her father, to her oldest sister, to her aunts, everyone seemed to think they knew exactly what was best for her. And, truthfully, she felt certain the only person who really did know what was best was herself.

She was willing to listen to others, of course, and she'd often tried to take the advice to be more successful in company. But time and time again, she'd fallen short.

And though the ruggedly beautiful giant of a man was insisting she go back into the elegant masses, she had no place in that ballroom upstairs. Oh, her family had been invited, a rare opportunity for the Blys, who were genteel but only just. No doubt her eldest sister, Elizabeth, was thriving. She was an excellent conversationalist and admired wherever she went, but Georgiana?

Georgiana had a tendency to walk into potted plants or servants bearing wine, and her propensity for saying the wrong thing had become the stuff of legend in her house. She still had not lived down the episode with Lady Farthington and her unfortunate comments about the lady's wig.

She'd learned this the hard way more than once. Despite the fact that she occasionally wished she was a swan sailing gracefully through society's waters, she was, in fact, a practical duck of a person. And she wished her family would come to that same conclusion, so they would stop trying to make her something she could never be.

She wasn't meant for the complicated demands of balls. She was meant for small libraries, such as the one she was standing in now, which was why she was not willing to go.

The ballroom was the worst possible place for someone like her and she was not about to let the threat of a kiss convince her to leave the safety of this nook.

When the beautiful, overbearing man had told her she needed to leave or be kissed, she had chosen to be kissed because he *had* to be bluffing. What sort of man did that, anyway? Stride into a room, bark orders, and then kiss one?

It didn't seem to match anything she'd read in novels or seen in public life. So, even when he wrapped his massive arms about her, she still was not entirely convinced anything more would happen.

The cad was just trying to make her run.

Well, she wouldn't run. She was not that sort of girl. And when she drew in the masculine scent of him, she ignored the thrilling of her body.

All would be fine. She wasn't the slightest bit afraid. It mattered not that he towered over her and his shoulders had the sort of breadth to them that a Corinthian column possessed. He wasn't the least bit frightening. Was he alluring? Yes. In fact, his lips were most interesting and she wondered what effect they might cause upon her own, for she had read of the pleasurable effects of kissing…

No, no, she *truly* didn't desire to be kissed by him. It was all just a tactic on her part to call his jest. Such a girl as herself would never wish such a thing. But as she tilted her head back, gazed up at his remarkably sinewy person and eyes as dark as sin, she found it incredibly difficult to breathe.

Her lips parted and her body was melting in the most delicious and delightful of ways. Botheration, she *wanted* to be in his arms, and she loved how they were as molten as marble.

She was enveloped in pure sensation, a state to which she had never before had opportunity to be in.

Men did not usually go about embracing ducky sort of girls. No, they preferred the swans, as far as she could tell. Remarkably handsome man that he was, he would be no different. She was unaccustomed to being at the attention of such a vital person. And it seemed to leave her slightly off foot.

He certainly took most of the air out of the room, and yet, somehow, she felt empowered in his arms, as if she was just as strong as he.

So, when he cocked his head to the side and his black hair, as jetty as any raven's wings, touched his cheek, she matched the angle of his head, ready to take his kiss, should he so choose to give it.

And give it, he did.

His mouth came down upon hers, devouring with a sort of heady hunger that left her gasping for breath, and yet she did not wish him to stop. *Oh no.* She wished this kiss to never end. His hands stroked her back, guiding her closer to him, arching her into his hard, tempting frame.

Sense abandoned her. She was utterly unprepared for the force and temptation of him. And she did not consider herself an easily led ninny of a person.

As if of their own accord, her hands stole to his biceps. She could feel his perfect skin through the linen of his damp white shirt. Georgiana slid her arms up over his muscled arms to his shoulders, then to the strong curve of his neck, where her fingertips brushed silky strands of his thick hair.

It was heaven.

Glorious, perfect, unbelievable heaven.

And she found she could not put any thoughts together except that she wished to be kissed more.

His tongue gently teased the line of her lips. Startled, she opened to him, and his tongue touched hers. It was like drinking the sweetest, spiciest wine, and she wanted to quaff greater quantities. As he kissed her with a wild hunger, she attempted to kiss him back, still hardly believing this was happening.

With each moment, she kissed him with more confidence and more pleasure, until, breath for breath and kiss for kiss, she knew she was in danger, for his hands began to rove all over her body, moving to the angle of the curve of her hip.

She felt as if they were becoming one, single, delicious body as the heat between them intensified. What would happen next, she could not say; all she knew was she did not want this moment to end, for it was the most alive she had ever felt.

Until, suddenly, a voice chimed from the doorway. "It seems we have found the future Duchess of Thornfield."

What? Who?

Georgiana's blood turned to ice and she froze in his arms. The languid sensation that had made her body feel like warmed honey disappeared in a crush of frigid reality. She didn't need to turn to know they had been well and truly caught.

"Hello, Aunt Agatha," the man ground out.

Georgiana's gaze swung to *Aunt Agatha* and her chest squeezed with horror as she spotted her regal hostess, Lady Strathmore.

The titters of several ladies filled the small room, and all at once, the pieces fit together with a *snap*. The sound of her future shifting course so swiftly it gave her whiplash.

Georgiana took a horrified step back, her fingers trailing down the Duke of Thornfield's arms—she was *touching* the *Duke of Thornfield*—and she gaped up at him. Her mind rioted with unmitigated horror. It couldn't be. Every part of her screamed at the impossibility of this scenario. She had not just kissed the duke!

But she had. She truly had. And dread replaced

the horror rattling through her. If she could have made it do so, the floor would have opened up and swallowed her whole.

His passion vanished as fiercely as it had appeared. Now he gazed down upon her with hard suspicion. The intrigue and hunger that had filled his eyes just a few moments before was gone, replaced by shards of ice.

"Got what you wished, did you?" he drawled before extricating himself from her as if she were a plague victim. He took a rapid step back and strode from the room.

She longed to cry out *no!* But the word choked in her throat.

How could she explain that the life of a duchess was the last thing she'd ever wanted? Because she would utterly fail at it.

• • •

Control.

Edward needed control.

He stormed out of the great house to the back servants' courtyard. The refreshing chill of a Yorkshire night hit his face, and he savored it. Away from the choking air of those judging stares, he tilted his head back and stared up at the flickering silver points in the black sky.

Out here, he could think. It was going to require a good deal of thinking, *deep* thinking, to sort out this mess with any semblance of civility.

He sucked in long breaths of cold air, trying to still the emotions threatening to come undone. He focused on the damp chill filling his lungs and the sharp breeze brushing over his exposed skin.

But then he strode forward and his boots slammed on the cobblestones, shattering the control he'd gathered. Fury pulsed through him. Again and again, he flexed and unflexed his hands, looking for an outlet for the charged feelings thundering inside him.

He'd been caught.

He, the Duke of Thornfield. In a bloody wedding trap.

How in damnation had that happened?

All he'd wished for was a few moments alone. Just a bit of time to collect himself before facing all those marriage-minded fools. He needed that time. Time to make certain he didn't say the factual yet apparently unkind thoughts in his head. That time in his chair meant he could be still, contained, for a few moments and thus survive the hum and overwrought energy of those who wished to be at the perimeters of his power.

Not only had that time been stolen from him, but now his future, too.

All because she'd refused to go.

All because she'd trapped him.

All because he'd had to, for some inexplicable reason, kiss her.

The world spun about him and he sucked in another set of slow breaths. He had to get a hold of himself, and this situation. Allowing himself to come apart would do him no good.

Even as he willed himself to accept that chit had invaded his rooms without invitation, the cobbles seemed to rattle under his feet. The cold air he loved all but shook around him.

A growling curse tore from his lips. "*Bloody poxing hell—*"

"Dear boy, we did not allow you to attend Oxford to espouse such verbiage."

Edward ground his teeth together as he closed his eyes for a moment. "Aunt Agatha, not now."

"On the contrary," the firm, formidable voice announced behind him, "now is the only time we have."

"That is a blatant falsehood," he bit out, refusing to look at her, or else lose his resolve. The gorgon of a woman had been his sole comfort and guide since his parents' unfortunate and untimely death. "Come back in five minutes."

She tutted. "In five minutes the entire house will know your tongue was in that young lady's mouth."

"Aunt Agatha!" He turned to face her, finally, taking in her resplendent and fashionable figure standing upon the limestone step.

Even in his frustration, and despite the fact he'd just insinuated he did not need her, he now found himself relieved that she had followed him. She was, after all, the only person living who remotely understood the challenges he had faced since boyhood.

Her silver hair shone nearly white in the moonlight, curled artfully and without fussiness. She'd eschewed powder some years ago, and her face, though wrinkled, was still beautiful.

The face of a woman who knew her power and how to wield it.

He loved that face.

For though it was stern, it was one of the few he'd

come to understand.

"Don't feign innocence at me, my lad," she declared, driving her silver-headed cane down with a considerable *thump* onto the step. "I know you've put other parts of your anatomy into ladies for some years now." She hesitated, only the rustle of her silvery purple gown filling the silence. At last, she said, "Still, a girl like that? From no family of consequence? She'll be the talk of the *ton* and ruined to boot if you don't do something. Or…*will* you ruin her?"

His chest tightened as he took in her stoic visage. "You know the answer to that."

"Do I?"

"I should hope so," he said with an arch of his brow. The entirety of his life had been spent doing the right thing. The hard thing. Even when it earned him displeasure and censure from the more pleasure-driven parts of the peerage.

In answer, she rolled her eyes. "My dear boy, all I know is that you vacated your room abruptly and said she had gotten what she wanted." She shrugged her bead-trimmed shoulders. "I assume you mean matrimony, but I don't like to assume anything. One never knows the workings of the male mind."

He was certain that she was now being hyperbolic. His aunt knew the workings of the male mind very well. She'd managed enough of them quite effectively over the years. But he also knew he held a special place in her heart to which she might feel blind to his potential faults in such a circumstance as this.

She would love him no matter what, even if he

disappointed her, but he wasn't about to do such a heinous thing.

"You know the sort of man I am," he reminded her.

"Indeed." She gave a slight nod with the barest of relieved smiles. "You've never shirked your duty, Edward. I cannot be quiet and let you start now."

It was true. His father and mother had taken great pains to ensure he was loved, cared for, and taught the importance of respect, even if he struggled to show it in a meaningful way at times. It would be an immense betrayal of them to shirk anything off.

Edward groaned. "This is an utter disaster."

His aunt looked at him without mercy. "Perhaps you should have considered that before you kissed her."

He was not given to having conversations about kissing with his aunt Agatha, though neither of them were prudes. He quite enjoyed carnal activity. He'd garnered a reputation of a rake at Oxford. But kissing a young, innocent lady of Yorkshire was not to his liking.

No, that was a patent falsehood. He'd quite liked kissing her. *Like* was not even the correct word. He'd been completely bowled over. She was the devil, there was no question. That kiss was going to ruin him, not her. Rather, that kiss was going to be the *making* of her.

Neither of their lives would be the same.

"You must find her immediately and remedy this situation, Edward," Agatha pressed. "The entire house will be abuzz with the gossip of that kiss if you do not act quickly."

He hated when his aunt was right and he wrong. After all, he spent a great deal of time ensuring he was always *doing* the right thing. He loathed having to go backward. He loathed making a mistake even more. Over the years, he'd fought so hard to prevent making them.

Making such a large one now galled him.

"I'll announce it, then," he stated.

His aunt blinked. "Announce what?"

"The wedding, of course." He folded his hands behind his back, determined to choose stoicism over drama. Just as Aunt Agatha had done. Just as they would always do.

"Oh dear," she lamented. "I had truly hoped to see you wed this year but I never imagined this is how it would be. And with such a girl."

"That bad, is it?" he asked, dread pooling in his stomach.

Her lips carved into a frown. "Worse, I think."

Well, then, there it was. Nothing could be done now but the only thing he *would* do…which of course, was the right thing.

But first, he'd charge up the stairs and put on a pair of his own damned breeches.

CHAPTER THREE

"Mama, we must leave immediately," Georgiana said, her heart racing.

Panic laced through her gut as she held herself back from grabbing her mother's gloved hand to make a dash for the coach. Like her mother, she was made of strong stuff. She wouldn't go to pieces. But it was difficult knowing a wave of gossip that would ruin her entire family was about to be unleashed.

How could she have been such a fool?

Her mother turned to her, the simple but well made frock of deepest rose skimming her lovely frame. Slowly, she waved her ivory painted fan, smiling strangely at her daughter's abrupt proclamation. "Whatever can you mean, Georgiana? Don't be absurd. Your sister is dancing with the Earl of Deptford."

"Mama!" Georgiana exclaimed, before she gulped back a storm of words. She forced herself to mirror her mother's composure. Everyone would be staring soon enough; she needn't cause a scene now. "You don't understand. We must leave immediately. I cannot tell you what catastrophe is about to unfold."

Her mother snapped her fan shut and turned to her with fresh concern. "Catastrophe?" she echoed with veiled alarm. "I do not comprehend, what are you saying? Explain at once, Georgiana."

"Mama, I may be ruined," Georgiana whispered,

her eyes burning as her throat tightened. Dear God, the shame of it! With one exceptionally poor, though pleasurable, decision, she had placed her mother, father, and sisters on an unalterable course.

Oh why the blazes hadn't she just endured the ballroom? No social awkwardness she'd have encountered could compare to this irreversible mess.

"Ruined?" her mother said, her face paling with horror. "Come immediately and tell me what this is about."

Her mother pulled her deftly but gently through the crush of people. There was a titter of gossip beginning at one end of the room, and Georgiana could barely breathe. That gossip was about her. It had to be, what else could it be?

Her mother whisked her behind a particularly tall potted tree and faced her with kind, loving eyes that had never once been filled with recrimination. Even now, they were worried, not full of anger.

That kind look nearly undid Georgiana, but there was no escaping the truth.

"Mama"—Georgiana swallowed—"I've done something truly terrible."

And she hated to say it *was* terrible, for she had enjoyed it so much. But now it felt as if it had been an utter debacle. For what? To keep a chair? To be defiant? To tangle with an intriguing man?

That moment of boldness was going to cost her everything. More to the point, it would cost her family everything if the duke chose.

"What have you done?" her mother prompted firmly but without censure.

Georgiana licked her lips and gathered her

courage. "The Duke of Thornfield and I...kissed."

Her mother blinked. "I beg your pardon?"

"I kissed the Duke of—"

"No, no, I heard you," she said over her, "but how is that even possible, Georgiana? You have not had chance to meet him yet."

She grimaced. "If you must know, I was in his private library. Alone."

Her mother's face turned deathly white. "Tell me you were not."

This was far more painful than the judgment of any stranger.

"I know you've warned me about wandering off, but I couldn't bear to be in this ballroom any longer."

"And now you might be ruined," her mother surmised quietly. Her brow furrowed and suddenly she rasped, "My God, your sisters. Whatever will we do?"

"I don't know, Mama," she replied honestly. She darted a look to the crowd that was beginning to whisper rather loudly. Georgiana's stomach twisted; her escapades were about to be the choice gossip of the evening. She placed a hand to her forehead. Actually, she'd likely be gossip of the *year* and a warning to other young ladies for a decade. Gerogiana squeezed her mother's hand. "We must leave."

She nodded, but as she cast her gaze about, she looked at a loss. "Your father is in the next room, and your sisters are all dancing. However shall we get them off the floor before—"

"Miss Georgiana *Bly*?" a shrill voice cried out.

"You cannot possibly be serious. She is as plain as they come."

Georgiana cringed and closed her eyes for a brief moment, as if she could block out the nightmare of it all.

They would not be able to escape so easily. It was done unless the duke rescued her. Now she and her family would be shamed for her behavior. In that instant, she realized what it meant to be at the mercy of a man's whim. And oh how she hated it. But she couldn't blame him. Not entirely. She had chosen that kiss just as much as he had.

The voices continued from the other side of the plant.

"Oh, yes," another lady said. "It is quite true. The Duke of Thornfield had his hands upon her back. His mouth upon her lips. It is going to be the scandal of the season. The girl must be an absolute trollop."

A trollop.

Her mother clutched Georgiana's hand tighter, her eyes widening with shock. "My God, that I should see the day when one of my daughters would be labeled thus. And it is not true. He must've taken advantage of you."

She sighed. She wouldn't lie. "He did not. I was quite a willing participant."

"Well, I am glad he did not harm you," her mother said firmly. "You have always been the adventurous type, and I have liked you for it, but I worry this is going to prove an adventure too far."

Georgiana bit the inside of her cheek, unable to reply. She knew it to be true, but there was nothing she could do about it now. She only wished…

She only wished she was not dragging her family down into the mire with her.

"Please," Georgiana urged, "let us gather everyone and go."

The beautiful string orchestra came to a stop.

"Now is our chance," she hissed.

But instead of the room filling the silence with more conversation, a hushed murmur fell over the crowd, and then a voice she had only just come to know boomed out. "Ladies and gentlemen," said the duke, "I have an announcement to make. Please lift your champagne glasses."

Servants were making their way in an artful pattern all about the room, passing out flutes of champagne with a grace and speed that would have outdone the finest dancers at the Royal Opera, something she had only seen once as a little girl.

What could the duke possibly be celebrating after such a horrid interchange?

Her mother locked hands with her, their eyes meeting.

"You must be strong, Georgiana," she said. "Whatever is about to happen, you must be strong. It is the only way we shall survive this."

Georgiana gave a tight but terrified nod. Her mother was no fool and never had been. Somehow, she had survived the various machinations of their father and silliness of him over the years. Her mother had been her rock.

So now she must be just like her. A rock, unbroken in a tumultuous stream.

"Miss Georgiana Bly?" the duke called out, his voice rich and deep as it cut through the room. "My darling, please come."

My darling?

The whole evening had taken on a tinge of madness. Surely, it was all some impossible dream? This couldn't be happening to her, Miss Georgiana Bly from Green Crossing, who had spent her entire life in the small society of a town on the edge of a Yorkshire Dale?

The world spun into absolute stillness, as the entire company seemed to take a collective breath, waiting for her to appear.

Even though logically she knew this was no dream, no nightmare, she couldn't countenance that what was about to take place was real. Her body hummed in the silence that stretched over the ballroom, a ballroom packed with Yorkshire's finest society and the elites of the English peerage.

Her mother gave her a little nudge. "Go," she mouthed.

Georgiana nearly jumped, and then she was walking out from behind the plant. The crowd parted like the Red Sea, and she found herself moving straight toward the towering Duke of Thornfield.

Good God, he was handsome...but austere. His eyes cut through the crowd like blades. Dark hair fell over his sharp features, a gesture that should have been boyish but made him appear rugged.

There was nothing particularly inviting about him now, but somehow she still felt drawn to him, as if being pulled by an invisible rope. He was as cold as granite, cool as steel. And he looked completely implacable. How was she not a trembling leaf of fear?

Instead she faced the danger of him head on. Once again, his mere presence turned her into someone she hardly recognized. Someone bold and daring and *alive*.

He held out his broad hand to her, his emerald crest ring winking in the candle light.

She forced herself to take that hand. She slid her fingers along his warm palm. He was offering her his gloved hand, which meant...

He peered down his rather striking nose at her, and whispered, "Turn and face them, if you dare."

And she did dare.

For what else could she do?

She turned to face the staring crowd of aristocrats and wealthy county people as he held her hand.

"I would like to announce to all of you my engagement to Miss Georgiana Bly," he declared firmly and without a hint of irony. "I find myself to be the luckiest of fellows. Miss Georgiana is a treasure."

There was another long silence as everyone took in this news. Blank faces and disbelief so palpable she could have cut it with a knife met his words.

His aunt began applauding first, and soon everyone else had taken up the celebration.

The duke lifted his crystal champagne glass. "Three cheers for Miss Georgiana Bly."

Everyone did as he did.

Exactly as they were told.

Simply because he had said so.

The room lifted their chargers toward her, and in unison they cried out, "Hip hip hurrah!"

Georgiana was forced to recall the importance of breathing as she took in the daunting announcement. He had not even asked her if she would marry him. He had decided it for both of them. She knew she should be deeply grateful, because, after all, if he had not done so her entire family would be destroyed by the gossip.

But marriage to the Duke of Thornfield? Her?

It was such an upsetting proposition that she couldn't feel her feet and was certain she'd do something as inelegant as trip upon him any moment.

She forced a smile and inclined her head toward him.

"Pray, do forgive me," she whispered, trying to imbue the words with the sincere regret she felt.

His eyes narrowed as he replied just under his breath, "Don't bother. I know this was your plan."

"It wasn't," she hissed with more force than she'd meant, her good will fading.

Dear God, *trapped*. He thought this her *plan*? The very idea that she'd attempt to trap any peer, let alone a duke, was laughable! Or at least, it should have been. She was a *spinster*.

How could she convince him she'd rather join a convent than marry a man of his importance? As long as the convent had a suitable library, of course.

"Please, I don't like liars," he warned softly. "I will take you as my wife because I'm not a cad. But your adventures in other people's libraries will end now, do you understand?"

She gave a tight nod, but she knew she'd have to explain to him soon that she was not a liar, even if events suggested otherwise. Obviously, he had yet to discern her horror at their mutual doom.

"At some point, I shall have to meet your parents," he stated, as though the very idea was as appealing as catching the plague.

He indicated for the music to begin again, and the orchestra immediately started with a sprightly waltz.

"Come, then, my *dear*," he drawled. "I suppose we must show them we are of an accord."

Without another word, he led her out onto the gleaming, polished floor. His guests stared at them even as they gossiped behind waving fans and gloved hands.

Georgiana had thought the evening couldn't possibly get any worse, but she was vastly mistaken. For certain, the quickest path to disaster would be a dance. She'd been engaged to a duke for only minutes, and already she was about to make the newssheets for all the wrong reasons.

CHAPTER FOUR

"I don't like to dance," Georgiana said, eyeing the empty floor as if it might suddenly swallow her up. "I told you this."

"No, you said you don't like people. There's a vast difference," he insisted.

"I'm not particularly good at dancing, though." She was tempted to plant her feet and hold back, lest she make a public fool of herself in an already awful situation.

"Neither am I," he said with a dry, matter-of-fact tone, "so I suppose we shall have to hobble along together."

She swallowed the growing lump in her suddenly parched throat. "I shall try not to tread on you."

"Most appreciated," he said coolly. "I shall endeavor to do the same."

Once they reached the center of the room, the duke placed his hand on her back, just beneath her shoulder blade, and took up her other hand in his free one.

Their gloves rubbed ever so slightly against each other, a subtle friction. The duke did not look down at her, though. He stared over her head as if she did not exist at all, his face stern.

An acrid taste filled her mouth.

It was a terrible feeling to not exist.

The temptation to stomp on his shining shoe flitted through her. She refrained, of course. But only just. The Duke of Thornfield was such a remarkable human from the hallowed realms of society, and just a few minutes before they had been in the most passionate of embraces.

To have this sort of emptiness between them was bizarre. But then he swayed back and forth in time to the lilting music, and the next thing she knew, they were off around the room.

Quickly, the floor filled with other couples, and the duke led her seamlessly around them with incredible grace and ease.

Georgiana narrowed her eyes up at him, though he didn't see it.

He was distinctly *not* a terrible dancer.

He had lied to her on that score, the scoundrel.

Thornfield was most definitely a *capable* dancer. No, not capable. Powerful. Oh, he might be more efficient than graceful, but he swept her around in huge arcs, his long legs eating up the great distance of the waxed wood floor.

And it was all she could do to catch up with him.

He did not seem to mind or to bother with the fact she was all but scampering along.

No, he simply swept her about in circling patterns, her pale skirts encompassing both their legs. "I do beg your pardon, Your Grace," she managed as she strained on tiptoe, "but my legs are not as long as yours."

He did not reply.

And then to her amazement, he lifted her slightly off the ground and took another large step. For one shocking moment her breasts skimmed his hard chest, and once again, that kiss came forefront to her memory.

He was in complete control of her movement.

While it was rather fascinating, the feel of his body and his strength, it was also absolutely irritating. Was this to be her life, then? A rag doll directed by another person?

She did not think so. She, for one, would not be having it, and she immediately knew she had better start as she meant to go.

"Your Grace," she said firmly, determined to be heard, "you are being most rude."

"*I* am being rude?" he queried, his voice low.

"Yes, you." She cocked her head back so she might see more than his cravat. "Could you be so kind as to measure your steps so I am not being whipped about?"

He snapped his crackling gaze down toward hers. Those dark eyes of his were unyielding in their assessment "Whipped about, you say? You mean like me, from bachelorhood to marriage in one moment?"

"If it's such a hardship, you don't have to marry me," she replied.

After all, *he* had kissed her!

"Don't I?" he returned, imperious. "If I don't, your entire family will be ruined. And I will be named a cad. I don't debauch innocents, you know."

"Just wives," she blurted, and then wanted to kick herself. If she weren't being flung around a ballroom, she might have tried.

He gaped down at her, narrowly avoiding another couple. "I beg your pardon?"

"You debauch wives, but not young ladies," she

clarified. She had no idea why she was being as blunt with him as she was with others. He was not others. He was a duke, but it seemed she was incapable of deference. At least with him, for she could not shake the image of him, muddy breeches, wild hair, and his kiss from her mind.

He arched a dark brow. "Wives cannot be debauched. They choose their own paths."

"So do young ladies," she said. "But it was never my intention to let you debauch me. Or do you not recall it was you who offered to kiss me in the first place?"

"Yes, because you would not leave my room," he ground out. He arced them in great sweeping motions down the length of the floor.

Frustration rattled through her. She would not take the blame in this, not solely. And if he thought she would, he was vastly mistaken. But how could she make herself plain? "I didn't realize it was *your* room."

"How could you not?" he scoffed. "Did you truly think I was a servant? If you did, you must be rather dim."

The heat of debate flared in her chest. She had to stand up for herself, even to a formidable duke; if she didn't, then who would? "I am not dim at all. I am just inexperienced with society. I try to avoid it as much as possible."

"Yet you are to be a duchess now. It is a catastrophe. *You*," he emphasized, though his tone wasn't irate. It seemed more like he was schooling her. "A duchess. A miss of little importance from some country town."

"Now," she huffed, "that is going too far, Your Grace. I may be a miss and I may be from a country town, but I am neither dim nor an incapable person."

His words were pointed, direct, and rather off-putting. Was he usually so rude? She granted this was a unique event and hoped that explained his terse nature and willingness to look down upon her with so much superiority, duke or not.

"Incapable of being a duchess," he corrected, his voice a shockingly deep rumble. "But worry not. I'll have you trained up, and all will be well."

"Trained up?" she echoed, nearly choking on her words. Georgiana gave him a withering stare and countered, "I am not a dog, Your Grace."

"My dog is obedient and causes me a great deal of happiness. So we can agree on that point. You, Miss Bly, are not a dog."

She gasped. It was all she could do not to yank her hands from his, turn and leave him standing alone on the dance floor. Perhaps it was what she should have done. The only thing that kept her from storming off in high dudgeon was the thought of her family, and especially her sister Elizabeth's prospects.

"You are an utter boor," she hissed.

"And you have ruined my life," he returned, with a mocking inclination of his head.

"I am sorry," she said, her heart thudding wildly in her chest. This moment warranted apology, but she bloody well needed him to understand the stakes of all this was not just about him.

"I beg your pardon?" He stared down at her, agog.

Quickly, he arced her under his arms, guiding her in a circling motion, and then back again.

"I am sorry for ruining your life," she repeated, trying not to trip over her own slippered toes as she turned. "But I'll have you know, mine has been ruined as well. I have no desire to be a duchess. It seems like a terrible life."

"You don't wish to be a duchess?" he challenged. "And yet you waited alone in my room and had the audacity to allow me to kiss you."

"You admit that you kissed me," she rushed, wishing she could throw her hands up in frustration. Alas, whilst engaged in the dance that never seemed to end, she could not. "And I truly didn't know it was your room. I haven't a mercenary bone in my body. So the only question that remains is why did you do it?"

He looked away.

"Your Grace?" she prompted, surprised by his response. She had expected more anger, more mockery. Not this moment's retreat.

"There was something terribly inviting about your person," he snapped, as if annoyed by his answer.

The words tumbled over her, surprising her as much as his kiss had. He'd *desired* her? She was not usually men's focus. And she did not mind, but he... He'd brought something to life within her she'd scarce known existed.

She'd quite liked it, until it had all gone terribly wrong

"It wasn't only about shunting me out of your room?" she asked.

"It was both," he admitted, looking and sounding perplexed. "I wanted you to leave and I wanted you to stay."

"A contradiction," she said.

A look of surprise crossed his handsome face as he turned them slowly, arranging their hands so that they gently clasped above her head, which only emphasized the difference in their height.

"I'm not limited to ribbons and lace," she replied tartly. Why did so many men seem shocked by her vocabulary?

The look that crossed his face was not dismay but intrigue. Then it vanished as quickly as it had arrived.

"Well, that's heartening," he drawled. "At least you shall be interested in the educations of our children."

Oh my… The mere idea of their children and the getting of said children had her gobsmacked. "Your Grace, are you usually so glib?"

He looked at her as if she'd gone absolutely mad as he lowered their hands and placed his palm to her upper back. "No one has ever asked such a thing of me before."

"Well, it was about time. As I'm not one of the ladies you seem so terribly accustomed to, I suppose I shall say things which surprise you often."

"Well," he all but growled. "At least you won't bore me to death. Not that we need to speak often."

"No?" What the botheration was he on about now?

"Married couples don't need to speak at all." His brow furrowed as he studied her face. "All that married couples need do is produce an heir."

She stumbled against him at the actual mention of the *creation* of an heir, and the idea that they might never speak. Not even when they were—

As he hauled her back up, she sucked in a steadying breath. "But don't you think that producing an heir might be made easier with some conversation?"

"No," he countered, his hands more firm now, guiding her about the room. "Talking might make things worse."

She blinked, completely at a loss. For what did she know about it, anyway? She'd never been with a man before, and now, with him holding her so close, she wondered what it would be like, and what it would be like with *him*. "Indeed," she said absently, her mind awhirl.

"I find young ladies and talking do not go well together," he said.

That snapped her back to her senses. The statement was so simple and so declarative she was tempted to brain him, even if he was a duke.

"My goodness, you really are pompous, aren't you? But you kiss rather well," she said, determined to find something good about her future husband. She was in a sea of potential despair; she had to find one thing to keep her afloat. It seemed it was their kiss.

Something changed in his gaze then, as if he was thinking of their kiss and the kisses they would share when married. The coldness seemed to slip from him and his eyes sparked with flame.

"You're very strange, Miss Bly," he said softly.

"No stranger than you are." A rueful smile pulled

at her lips.

"I doubt that very much. I'm far stranger."

"Are you?" she asked, astonished he'd make such an admission.

"Oh yes. I've grown accustomed to it, you see. The world has grown accustomed to it, too. And no doubt, as my intended, you shall hear all about it soon."

"Oh," she said. "I'd already heard that you were a bit cold. Your reputation precedes you, you know, but you weren't cold at all. There was nothing about you that was cold." At the memory of his kiss, her lips parted. "You were actually quite fiery."

He gaped at her. "Fiery?"

"Yes," she whispered, rather happy she could cause such consternation in him. "As in passionate."

"I understood, thank you very much." He cleared his throat. "I'm not fiery at all, though. I must maintain distance."

"Why?"

"Because it's what I do."

"That sounds very hard." She might not be particularly adept in society, but she wasn't distant from people, especially her family. She couldn't imagine the loneliness of it.

"It serves me well," he said tightly.

"Why?" she asked, genuinely curious.

"Because people always wish something from a duke…just like you."

"I did not wish anything," she exclaimed before she realized she'd very nearly shouted. She forced herself to continue quietly. "You were the one who—"

"Yes, yes, we've already crossed this ground. But

you never should have been in my library in the first place."

She scowled. "You did not have a sign upon it that said it was your private library. Enter at your own risk. Trespassers shall be kissed on sight."

He groaned. "Is this to be the same as the debate about the chair?"

"The chair did not have your name upon it," she said, realizing she was growing heated. "The library did not have your name upon it."

"The *house* has my name upon it. This is my house in its *entirety*."

"And," she pointed out, refusing to be daunted, "there are people all over it and only one duke. You didn't think it possible someone might mistake your identity, dressed as you were? What kind of duke wears muddy, worn breeches and expects one to know he's lord of the castle?"

He blew out a weary breath. "You are going to be a great deal of trouble."

"It's not my intention," she said but did not bother to correct him. Many people found her difficult. It was not her fault she was born to be so ill-fitted for the confines of society. "I shall just find a little nook in your library once we are wed, and you'll never know I'm here."

"That's not possible for a duchess, Miss Bly. Duchesses don't hide in quiet corners," he said so softly his voice sounded like hot whiskey on a winter's eve. "They rule the room."

She swallowed at the horrifying thought.

Rule the room? She was used to being a wallflower.

The music came to a stop. He pulled her close as he ceased his masterful circling. The room seemed to continue to spin as conversation buzzed about them combined with the excited applause of the dancers.

The duke—her future husband—glared down at her and shook his head. "This marriage is going to be a disaster."

"Yes," she agreed without hesitation. "It is."

CHAPTER FIVE

"Your Grace, Your Grace," a deep Yorkshire voice that sounded like it might belong to a rather jolly St. Nicholas filled Edward's ear and half the refreshment room. "What a pleasure it is to meet you."

Miss Bly, who had had the bravery to introduce him to her family after their dance, nervously darted glances at her father and then to Edward...then back to her father. Mr. Bly was apparently unaware of his daughter's concern.

Edward winced inwardly and did his best to keep his face implacable.

Oh dear God, was this to be his father-in-law?

Mr. Bly all but bounced on his heels as he vigorously pumped Edward's arm up and down. "A pleasure to meet you, Your Grace," he repeated, "a pleasure indeed."

Edward did not reply that he wished he could say the same.

It was perhaps a bridge too far to state he had to resist the urge to recoil at Mr. Bly's enthusiasm. One likely shouldn't show such feelings to their future father-in-law.

But the man all but bubbled.

Mr. Bly was an overenthusiastic spaniel of a person.

Edward did not generally endure spaniel-type people. No, he preferred quiet, stoic individuals. But he would somehow have to persevere. At least he would not have to invite the man to his house often, surely. Perhaps he would be very lucky in that Georgiana did not feel a particular closeness to her family. Perhaps she'd be relieved to not be too close to them.

His favorite house was fifty miles from the ducal estate. He and Georgiana could live there, if necessary. Then he would only have to bear her family upon occasion.

When they did come to stay, because unwanted family always did, he could put them in rooms in the opposite wing from his own.

Several of Edward's guests stared as they collected glasses of wine. Oh, they tried to appear nonchalant, but the sheer absurdity of the evening was leading to blatant eavesdropping. Edward ignored them all.

"Your daughter is most…unique," Edward said.

Because he had to say something about her, after all.

And if he was going to paint a picture that their marriage was not entirely the result of a disastrous encounter in his library, he had to make it seem as if he esteemed Georgiana to some degree.

He'd already surmised she was an absolute bluestocking terror, which on its own was no ill thing. But her lack of understanding of how society worked? That was the last thing he'd wished for in a duchess. If and when he'd married, he'd planned on choosing someone he had to give little assistance or notice to.

But it was too late to go back now, and he would never be a cad or a bounder. Edward could not face himself in the proverbial mirror or endure his own self-recriminations if he abandoned her.

But alliance with the Blys would prove a challenge.

"This is my wife, Mrs. Bly," Mr. Bly enthused, gesturing with a flourish of his wrist to the rather dignified and handsome woman standing beside him.

Heretofore, she had been silent.

Edward turned to his future mother-in-law, curious and wary. Dressed simply in a rose-hued frock, her silver-tinged dark hair coiled atop her head, Mrs. Bly took him in. Her sparkling blue eyes swept quickly from the top of his head to his polished dancing shoes.

She was entirely different from her husband. She did not bounce.

No, there was a calmness to her, a steel like the finest forged Spanish blade. This was the temperament that had shaped Georgiana's formidable spine. He knew that immediately.

She held out her hand. "How do you do, Your Grace?"

"I do as well as one can in such a circumstance," he said.

He could feel the eyes of the multitudes staring at them. He ground his teeth together at the discomfort it always caused him to be firmly at the center of attention.

"You do not care for company?" Mrs. Bly offered, rather optimistically considering her daughter had trapped him into matrimony.

"No," he said, "I do not care for company. But

I'm sure my reputation precedes me."

"Oh, indeed, it does, Your Grace. It is well renowned, the fact that you are not overly zealous about these affairs." Mrs. Bly cocked her head to the side, considering him, as her husband's brow furrowed, swinging his gaze back and forth like an eager audience member at a cricket match.

"And yet you must hold them," Mrs. Bly concluded.

"Indeed, I must." Edward smiled tightly, unable to relax, though he found himself at least not appalled by his future mother-in-law. "And now your daughter will be so lucky as to hold them and proceed over them. No doubt, such a thing has been at the forefront of her desires."

At that, Mrs. Bly's smile seemed to wane into worry. "Georgiana has never esteemed such events. Nor has she been led to expect she would one day oversee them. I do hope you shall be a kind guide to her so that she may learn how to be a suitable hostess."

Was this the truth, then? Georgiana was not feigning her lack of ability in polite society?

She had been such a remarkable firebrand in his library that he assumed she was liked wherever she went, but it seemed it was not true. Her protestations of awkwardness in company seemed supported by her mother—a mother who did not seem prone to exaggeration.

And as he studied Miss Bly now, he realized she did seem quite uncomfortable standing by her mother as the entire room watched them. He had attributed her ill ease to the fact that she had nearly been ruined, but now he wondered if perhaps she truly did loathe polite company as he did.

It was something which piqued his interest, and something he would have to pursue.

But right now, he could think only that this was a family he was going to be latched to for the rest of his life. Though the mother was not a lost cause, the father...

He dared not think of it too long. What were the other daughters like? They certainly had little standing from the state of their dress.

He had nothing against tradespeople, but they generally did not marry into his class.

It was all he could do not to groan.

As Edward contemplated Mr. Bly, Mrs. Bly, and Georgiana, their clothes, their speech, and her father's quite questionable manners, it felt as if he had been thrust into a horrific novel, where his life and everything he'd so painfully worked for was about to come undone.

CHAPTER SIX

A summons had come from the duke and Georgiana had answered.

It mattered not that perhaps only twelve hours had passed since the announcement of their marriage, her lessons were to begin without delay.

And as she looked anew upon his home, she understood why he wished to begin at once. In the light of day, Thornfield Castle only impressed Georgiana more than it had by torchlight the night before. It sprawled like a mammoth beast across the wild hillside. The towering limestone was most impressive.

It was truly a castle in every sense of the word. There was no question. It was not like the great houses that so many had seen built since the time of Queen Elizabeth I, houses meant to impress for the sake of impressing.

No, this house had been meant to show might and power, to defend against invaders, and secure the landscape. It was not even a house, per se. To call it such was an insult to the place.

It was a fortress. A magnificent dwelling!

Georgiana was positively thrilled. For it was clear that vast amounts of history had occurred in this place. Hundreds and hundreds of years of it.

She gazed in wonder.

And she was going to be mistress here.

It was a remarkable thought, almost impossible

to take in, but that was the truth. She was going to be mistress of all of this in the very near future.

A castle!

A castle that had sat upon the wild Yorkshire dales for centuries and seen the turning tides of armies and kings. Could she do it? She had no choice, did she?

She was going to be the Duchess of Thornfield, and there it was.

It was as terrifying as it was thrilling.

The idea of having to host people in this place was overwhelming, but simultaneously, the idea of exploring its meandering and wandering halls, seeing every tapestry, reading every book…That? That was magical.

She could not wait to be cast under its spell.

As she took the stairs that led up to an ancient archway, the double doors swung open before she could touch the great iron knocker. A butler in a starched livery peered at her as if she'd crawled up from the bottom of the lake across the long acre of groomed grass before the place.

It was not something she appreciated, but she understood. She was not the sort of person the duke was accustomed to entertaining, let alone marrying. And she was not renowned for any particular thing.

No doubt, the swiftness of her engagement, and her family's lack of pedigree, had been discussed in the servants' hall. Still, the butler stepped back, lifted a gloved hand to his mouth, cleared his throat, and said, "Miss Bly, I presume?"

For one rather weak moment, Georgiana wished she could shrink up into a little ball and roll away.

The butler peered at her with neither pleasure nor particular welcome. She was not surprised, for she had neither looks to recommend her nor grandeur.

Her clothes were that of a barely acceptable miss. Her face, she knew, was plain.

What about her could possibly inspire the Duke of Thornfield to ask for her hand?

Any person with any sense would know it was something nefarious. So she lifted her chin, determined not to seem meek. One had to go at this with a sense of unflappable determination.

If she were the slightest bit timid, everyone would sense her weakness. And one thing she had learned about society was when one displayed weakness, one would be devoured.

She gave the butler a slight smile, but before she could say anything, a voice bellowed from the top of the steps. "Miss Bly, you are late. Lateness is not a tolerable quality."

Her eyes snapped up and locked on the Duke of Thornfield. He stood at the top of the stairs, peering down at them like some great god.

Zeus came to mind.

No, not Zeus. Zeus was too gregarious.

Thornfield, with his chiseled features, dark eyes, and imperious nature, was rather cold and distant.

Hades.

Yes, Hades made far more sense. A god, but a god of a much darker world.

As Thornfield took one step down at a time, light cast into his dark hair, leaving it a strange blue-tinged mass of thick waves.

Unlike so many gentlemen, it was clear he did

not spend hours at his toilet perfecting curls or pomading until his hair would not move an inch.

Oh no.

His hair was a bit wild, which seemed odd because he was such an ordered person. The soft, waving curl did not give him a relaxed air, as one might expect.

No, it only served to amplify his intensity, to sharpen the hardness of his face.

When he reached the bottom of the stairs, she curtsied. "Forgive me, Your Grace. I came as fast as my limbs would carry me."

He stared at her, uncomprehending, before he swung his gaze to the door then back to her. "You walked?"

"Indeed. It is not such a distance," she replied simply, preferring not to explain that the coaching horses were being used for other purposes.

Thornfield's face was unreadable. "It is good to know your health is not delicate."

Delicate? Of course it wasn't. But the slight arch of his brow did seem to indicate he might think her health was on the same sort of strata as a milk maid rather than a lady. "You requested my presence," she said tightly. She'd only just arrived and already he was provoking her irritation.

He did not bother to offer his hand to her in greeting before he said tersely, "You've come alone? You have no chaperone?"

"Do I need one?" The last thing she wished was to be accompanied by her fluttering younger sisters, and Elizabeth and her mother were far too busy taking care of the kitchen garden. Her father... No doubt, he'd have been delighted to come, but she did not wish to have to constantly be shushing her own papa.

He gave her the oddest look. "Unmarried ladies usually have them."

"Oh." She cleared her throat. "Are you planning to ruin me? Again."

The duke narrowed his eyes. "Your sense of humor is questionable."

"But you acknowledge that I have one," she said as cheerfully as she could under the rather gloomy circumstances. And she found herself wondering if her future husband had a sense of humor at all.

If he did not, that boded most ill.

"Come," he all but barked, his voice filling the cavern-like foyer. The tones seemed to boom off the marble floor and ricochet off the muraled ceiling. "We shall begin at once. And the first thing you must do is have an audience with my aunt. She will determine just how…lacking you are."

He turned and started down the hall, clearly expecting her to obediently follow.

It was tempting to let some tart reprimand out. It was equally tempting to pop him in the nose. She did not; she wasn't a child. But oh how he tested her.

Lacking, indeed.

She understood the disdain he felt for her given the greatness of his position was the way of things, but it felt… *Botheration*. She wasn't something questionable to be scraped off one's shoe. And she wasn't going to allow him to treat her thus.

"You are being rude again, Your Grace," she called to his back.

The Duke of Thornfield hesitated halfway down the hall, and Georgiana was certain he had heard her. There was a slight bunching of his shoulders, an angle to his head as he hesitated for one single moment.

Would he apologize?

"I am not rude," he said. "I am a duke. And you're taking up a good portion of my morning with unexpected necessities. I was supposed to be inspecting plans for drainage in my southern fields."

Had she just been called slightly more important than a drainage plan? Or had he suggested that the drainage plan was preferable to time spent with her?

She had a feeling with Thornfield it was going to be difficult to discern. But one thing was already crystal clear—he was incapable of apologizing.

He resumed his purposeful stride down the hall. Georgiana all but scurried after his rapidly disappearing form. He was so icy, she wondered if it was possible for him to freeze someone to death with a well-aimed glance. There was really only one thing to do. She'd ignore his strange attitudes.

Swallowing her unease, she took in the magnificence of the castle. She refused to be intimidated by him, duke or no. But that did not mean she could not be in awe of the beauty of her surroundings.

The carpet that they walked along was a beautiful, green-and-gold woven runner.

No doubt from Persia.

Paintings of vast sizes hung upon the burgundy silk-covered walls, depicting various battles from different time periods. She spotted one from the time of Charles I, another from the time of Queen

Anne. And at last, one from the recent wars in Scotland.

This family had survived many a royal upheaval, and she was amazed to be part of it. It would make this bearable, the glorious history of the place. So when she followed him into the parlor done in the French style, she tried not to gape at the surroundings.

All her life she'd grown up in genteel but rather plain circumstances. They lived within their means, having to be rather careful with their pennies. This, to her, was splendor beyond anyone's wildest imagination. Though it was a castle, the interior clearly had been updated in the last fifty years. The pale blue watered silk walls were accented with gold filigree and superb plasterwork.

An exquisite mural dominated the ceiling, depicting a group of Greek Gods frolicking around a pond, admiring themselves and each other in brightly hued garments.

She tried not to cock her head up to take it all in. Such a thing of course was not done, but it was so magnificent it was difficult not to.

A rather interesting and gruff female voice said from the end of the long parlor, "Do you like it, Miss Bly? It is exquisite, is it not?"

Georgiana knew she should, but she couldn't quite look away from the sprawling painting that danced with such life.

"It is," she agreed happily. "I find it to be most beautiful."

The duke's aunt, Lady Strathmore, nodded from her perch upon the blue watered silk settee. "The

Italian man stayed in the house for over a year when I was a child. We got quite used to him, you know, and he painted most of the ceilings in the house. Quite good, he was. Poor fellow was always having a crick in his neck from looking up. Now, you must not develop such a thing, my dear."

Georgiana wrenched her gaze down, and as she did her toe caught upon the edge of the woven Axminster rug. Just before she was about to make rather intimate acquaintance with said rug, Thornfield caught hold of her arm and righted her.

The touch of his hand upon her was firm, warm… charged with energy. She snapped her gaze to his, her breath catching in her throat.

"Thank you," she managed as her cheeks flushed with embarrassment. Why the blazes did she have to go and almost trip?

He let go of her quickly and looked away. "Not at all," he replied. "We shall add walking to your list of tutorials."

She scowled at him, ready to castigate him for such a remark, but then a smile tilted his lips into a devilish grin.

"At least you have an appreciation for art," he said, his voice a low rumble. "Most people never bother to look up, let alone allow it to captivate them."

The elder lady laughed delightedly at her nephew's summation then gestured with a wrinkled, beringed hand to the delicate seats about her. "How true. Boring fools, the lot of them. Now, come along, come along. There'll be plenty of time to examine the ceilings. After all, you will be mistress here soon."

Georgiana swallowed, surprised how they had both seemed to compliment her love for the castle to overcome her clumsiness. Carefully, she took in the woman who was to be her family.

Silvery locks were arranged in a waving coiffure about her strong face. She looked a good deal like her nephew, but Lady Strathmore had a sort of sparkle to her eyes that suggested she was ready to make merry at any particular moment. Yet it was also clear she was steely. Her shoulders were back. Her spine was straight. And her gown of the deepest emerald green was the height of fashion.

No clinging to the previous decades, this lady.

"Do make yourself comfortable," Lady Strathmore all but ordered.

Georgiana sat down with a growing determination not to appear ill at ease. In that moment, she drew upon her mother's self-possession.

And for once she was most glad her mother had been the daughter of an earl. It had always seemed rather against her views and the joys she had in reading books from France. She quite admired the Liberté, Egalité, Fraternité proclamation, though she secretly whispered Sororité to herself whenever she read the credo.

At least her mother was not a complete stranger to the highest echelons of society and she had passed some of that education on to Georgiana, even if she was ill-suited to company.

Lady Strathmore reached for the elegantly made silver tea service beside her. "Will you take tea?"

She nodded, though she wondered if the duke would be taking notes on her consumption of the beverage, deciding how to improve her sipping.

Lady Strathmore seemed completely unperturbed by the turn of events. "There is much to be arranged. Now, you seem a most sensible girl."

Georgiana wound her gloved fingers together, glancing from Lady Strathmore to her future husband. "I've always tried to be a reasoned person."

"Of course, my dear, but one does wonder if a reasoned girl from Yorkshire from such a—forgive me—humble position will be up to the task of being the Duchess of Thornfield."

Georgiana swallowed. Clearly, the duke and his aunt were in agreement about her suitability, or more correctly, her lack thereof.

Utterly mortifying, but it was an unavoidable topic.

She cleared her throat, feeling as though she'd been thrown into the lion's den. And yet, she wasn't afraid, only nervous. "There is no going back now," she said evenly. "I am a quick study and I will do my very best."

Lady Strathmore gave a grim nod, indicating her doubts. "Indeed, no going back. And we shall have to do everything in our power to ensure you do not drown in the waters of the *ton*. You have had a season and been presented, of course?"

And of course…Lady Strathmore must've known that she had not.

Georgiana's insides tightened. "I have only been to London once. When I was a small girl."

The duke let out a derisive sound.

Lady Strathmore attempted a smile and said, "London is the center of the world, Miss Bly. As

Samuel Johnson said, 'When one is tired of London, one is tired of life.'"

"I find I cannot agree."

She whipped her sharp gaze to her. "I beg your pardon?"

Georgiana did not back down, but rather leaned forward. "How can one say such a thing? For the wild moors of Yorkshire are the most glorious to behold. The countryside is absolutely breathtaking. Surely, if one was to spend their entire life in London and to never venture out, they would not see such beautiful places. And I assume that all those gentlemen who go out on tours to Europe, they must tire a little bit of London, or else they should never wish to leave."

"Hmmph." Lady Strathmore plunked a lump of sugar in a cup of tea and thrust it at Georgiana. "You have very strong opinions for one so young."

"I confess, I do," Georgiana said without apology. She took the cup and happily drank the exquisitely steeped beverage.

Much to her surprise, Thornfield was staring at her anew, but it was impossible to identify whatever thoughts were taking place within his enigmatic brain.

Lady Strathmore pursed her lips, looking like a gorgon preparing to attack. But then she arched an eyebrow and said, "I'm glad to hear it, my dear. A duchess needs strong opinions. And if you're going to survive this *ton*, you'll need to not only have them but also wear them well."

Georgiana blinked, stunned by Lady Strathmore's approval. "You don't mind if I have strong opinions?"

"Not at all, my gel." Lady Strathmore took a fortifying sip of tea. "You are the better for it." She handed her nephew a cup of tea then stirred her own with a delicate silver spoon. "You know they're all going to look down upon you, don't you?"

The blunt truth was hard to take, but Georgiana nodded. "I do."

"Let's all be honest here." Lady Strathmore drew in a long breath, which sent the lace on her fichu aflutter. "You are no one from nowhere. Your family is questionable. Your father's behavior is most odd. And your sisters, well, there are a great many of them, are there not? Your financial situation is rather precarious, from the accounts we have heard."

She couldn't argue any of it.

Lady Strathmore removed her spoon, placed in on her saucer, and peered at her assessingly. "And yet you're going to be the Duchess of Thornfield. Everyone will assume you have manipulated my nephew into marriage. Some will admire you for it. Others? They'll try to cut you to ribbons."

"And you?" Georgiana asked. She wouldn't be shamed into a shrinking violet. "Do you think that?"

"I?" Lady Strathmore dramatically placed a hand to her bosom before she looked to Thornfield, then frowned. "No, my dear, no. My nephew is not easily manipulated. He sees those games a million miles away. Yesterday he might've declared you had gotten what you desired, but sitting here, speaking with you now, I think marrying my nephew is the last thing that you desired. Am I mistaken?"

She studied her betrothed, praying he would

agree with his aunt. But he said nothing. In fact, his jaw was tight as if the whole conversation was absolutely insupportable.

Georgiana blinked, grateful at least she would not have to contend with family who thought her to be a manipulative, scheming minx. "You are not mistaken."

"Which makes this all the worse." Lady Strathmore gave a sad shake of her head.

"Why?"

"Because," Thornfield growled suddenly, "if this isn't what you desired, and I'm not entirely convinced… Well, that shall make it far more difficult for you to negotiate. This shall be wonderful for your father, your mother, and your sisters. However, it will be a daily challenge for *you*."

Those words hung in the air, threatening to crush her, but she drew in a deep breath.

Going to pieces over his honesty would do no good.

After a long pause, Lady Strathmore said with some delicacy, "We shall be holding a great many balls, Miss Bly. You have many sisters in need of marriage, have you not?"

"Shall we?" Georgiana asked, fighting off a groan of dismay "Be holding many balls?"

"It is what a duchess does," drawled her future husband. "You will hold parties, teas, hunts, literary salons."

"Literary salons?" Georgiana repeated, sparking up.

"Why, yes," informed Lady Strathmore as if it were the most obvious thing in the world. "We do support a great many artists."

At that, Georgiana could barely contain her enthusiasm. Her insides positively fluttered. "That is something I think I should like a great deal."

"Good." Lady Strathmore smiled.

The Duke of Thornfield blew out a sigh then stalked toward the tall windows at the far end of the room. It appeared the conversation was simply too much for him to bear. He stared out the polished panes, his remarkable physique silhouetted by the sun pouring in through the glass.

A genuine smile tilted Lady Strathmore's lips and it did the most remarkable thing to her stern face. It made her...welcoming. Almost motherly.

Her eyes sparked with a decided calculation, and she leaned forward and whispered, "Let me tell you a secret, dear gel. I'm rather glad this happened."

"Are you?" Georgiana breathed.

A snort of disdain filled the room as Lady Strathmore rolled her eyes. "If not for you, I think Thornfield would have married some titled milk sop. Suitable to be sure. But a chit like that would drive him mad. You, on the other hand? You're not some sparkling fool; you simply require a bit of polish. And once we've polished you, you should make an excellent duchess. Let me take you in hand and all shall be well."

"I know you're discussing me over there," the duke called over his shoulder.

"Then don't go wandering off, my boy," his aunt replied.

Georgiana felt slightly dazed. She didn't feel that all should be well, at all.

As a matter of fact, she felt dread pooling in her belly, but as she herself had so boldly declared, there was no going back.

Only forward for her now, into the unknown.

CHAPTER SEVEN

The first few days of lessons were nothing but learning names, the names of every servant, their purpose, what they did in the house, and the title they held.

Georgiana was positively in awe of it all. She spent every spare moment that she had studying the lists of names and how she would one day instruct the owners of them.

Once she had finished that, she was shocked to find the duke had a whole room waiting for her. Or so he claimed.

Thornfield stood at the doorway and said, "Enter your schoolroom."

It was an odd thing to say. She had been out of the schoolroom for years. Well, if she was honest, she had never been in one. They had not had a governess. She had simply been lucky in the fact that her mother was very educated and had spent a great deal of time teaching her daughters.

Georgiana had also had the opportunity to read a great deal of literature.

She crossed through the door and gasped.

The vast library was full of books. Shelf after shelf stretched out before her, baring hundreds upon hundreds of leather-bound books. The beautiful ceiling was painted with gold filigree. Mirrors hung from every free surface, reflecting the sun so that one might be able to read by natural light.

It did not look like a mere schoolroom.

It looked like heaven.

The duke strode into the room and immediately went to a series of long tables in the center of the space. Stacks of books, cards, a wooden box, and sheets of paper awaited.

"Come," he urged. "I wish to show you these."

She could not tear her gaze away from the books, the ceiling…all of it. Lead-pane windows overlooked vast gardens that were as beautiful as any wild moor.

She'd grown up admiring wild things, for Yorkshire was a place of great beauty. But she admitted that the sculpted gardens of the duke's castle were remarkable.

"Miss Bly," he called, slightly more insistent this time.

She turned away from the windows at last and crossed to the table.

"These," he said, "are the great families of England." He pushed a stack of cards to her. "You will learn their titles and their histories so you might understand how they essentially rule England."

Then he took a large stack of books and pushed them forward. "One of these is my family history. The others are books of etiquette and precedence. They will tell you whom you are to curtsy to and whom you are not to curtsy to. There are a vast many rules as to where people sit at dinner, whom one speaks to, and the like. You will learn it all."

She nodded, determined not to be overwhelmed.

Georgiana knew about rules of precedence, but as a minor person of a barely genteel family, she'd never had to give much attention to rules before. For the highest person of rank she had ever met until Thornfield's ball had been a mere knight.

Before she could reply, he unfurled a series of drawings. Pointing to the one at the top, he said, "This is the castle. You will learn every room in it and identify where the servants go and what their work is just as you memorized their names." He set that piece of paper aside and focused on the next. "This is our London town house. Get acquainted with it so that when you arrive there, you will manage it adeptly."

She smiled tightly at him, tempted to scowl. *Botheration.* Could he not see how terse he was being, how manufactured all of this was? How was she to bear a lifetime of this?

His reputation was not false but accurate. He was so chilly she nearly shuddered.

Georgiana swallowed, willing him to show a bit of the passion she'd seen at the ball. He seemed to not care about her as a person. He was treating her as if she was someone who had little feeling at all and certainly not someone that he was going to marry. Had he forgotten that they had kissed? Had he forgotten their fiery conversation upon the dance floor?

It seemed so.

Perhaps it was too much to ask for a bit of encouragement and support, given the fact that he had not wished for this marriage.

"This…" he said, picking up and extending a small notebook. He gave her a pointed look, as if this was particularly significant. "…is a list of phrases you can use. They're all rather boring and pedantic, but you will often have to stand with me, greeting guests for a very long time. Sometimes we have hundreds, and you must not say the exact same thing to every single one of them. You must have a variety of things to say."

The image of hundreds of aristocrats parading before her flashed through her head.

She gaped at him. "I beg your pardon?"

The duke sighed. "You did not know?"

"I never really thought about it before," she confessed, feeling completely off foot. "I never realized I would need to rehearse my conversations."

He stared at her as if she had not a sensible bone in her body.

The Duke of Thornfield cocked his beautiful head to the side and folded his strong hands, apparently about to give a lecture. "Miss Bly, hundreds will come into the house and you will shake their hand or allow them to curtsy to you. You must say something and you're not going to say 'good evening' to every single one of them and nothing else. You must recognize them and ask them about their families. Or you must ask them about their racehorse or their house, or say how glad you are of their company or that they are most welcome. It is a great deal to remember, but you must."

The sheer volume of it all made her light-headed.

He narrowed his gaze. "Breathe, Miss Bly."

At his words, she realized she had not taken breath for several moments and her entire body was as tense as a chord within a pianoforte. She gasped.

Something shifted in his gaze, then, and his voice

softened. "Don't overly concern yourself. We will give you time to memorize it all."

She nodded and let out a breathy laugh.

"What is amusing?"

"I always told Mama that memorizing all of Mr. Shakespeare's sonnets was not necessary." Georgiana shrugged. "Mama insisted. It turns out she had incredible foresight teaching me such a vital skill."

His brow furrowed. "All of them?"

"All."

"Sonnet 18?"

She laughed again. "Far too easy. Are you mocking me?"

"Indulge me."

Indulge him? He did not seem to enjoy indulgence of any kind.

At her pause, he said, "You don't know it, then."

"Shall I compare thee to a summer's day? Thou are more lovely and more temperate…" She frowned. "I say, why that one? It's rather overdone."

"For a reason." He unfolded his hands, his gaze studying her face. "You don't care for it?"

"It's an ode to beauty and good-tempered people," she replied factually. "I am neither beautiful nor placid."

A booming laugh rolled from him. It filled the library, reverberating off the ceiling and surrounding her like a rich embrace. But then his gaze locked with hers and something positively electric shone in them. "What you have is better than beauty, Miss Bly."

"And what is that?" she asked, folding her arms just beneath her breasts.

His gaze was drawn to the small movement, but then he immediately returned his attention to her face. Slowly, his voice a rough growl of a sound, he began, "In faith, I do not love thee with mine eyes, For they in thee a thousand errors note; But 'tis my heart that loves what they despise."

"Are you saying you love me?" she asked, astonished.

"I barely know you," he stated without sentimentality. "But what I do know? For all the errors I see, my instincts know you are strong, determined, and not to be intimidated. Beauty has nothing on those three things, Miss Bly."

The room hummed with his summation of her character. She fairly glowed with it. Just as she was about to reply, he yanked his gaze away from hers and strode toward her.

"Now," he stated, as if he had not just spun magic with his words. "We must do something about your posture."

Her shoulders jerked. "What's wrong with my posture?"

"Quite a good deal," he replied evenly, stopping but a few inches before her.

He was so dratted tall she had to tilt her head back to look upon his face. "I quite like the way I stand," she said.

"Do you?"

"Of course I do," she said, suddenly feeling a bit warm. He was rather near, after all, even if he was being his rude self again. Whilst she couldn't agree that he was superior to her, as he seemed to think, she couldn't deny he was a physical specimen which inspired a good deal of admiration.

"You shouldn't."

"I beg your pardon?" she returned, her voice much higher than she'd intended.

"You don't have the bearing of a duchess."

She was tempted to do something that might affect *his* presently perfect posture. But she wasn't about to let him get the better of her.

"I wasn't born to be a duchess," she said through gritted teeth. "Why on earth would I have the bearing of one?"

"Because you are actually quite a confident young woman."

Oh… Did he truly think so? "How can you say such a thing when I was hiding away in your library?"

He inclined his head ever so slightly. "The way you spoke to me was quite self-possessed."

She cleared her throat, recalling her behavior. "That's only because I didn't know who you were."

He was silent for a moment, then took her chin gently with thumb and forefinger. It was the softest, most caring touch. "You're telling me you would have been quite shy and reticent if you had known I was a duke?"

She considered him for a moment. "No, I suppose I wouldn't. I am rather forceful."

"Yes," he agreed. "I think that's what has given you trouble over the years. Being blunt. When you are a miss from nowhere, you cannot be blunt."

Thornfield tilted her head back ever so slightly as he let his gaze wander over her face. "But Miss Bly," he continued in that intoxicating voice. "This may run in your favor. A duchess can be as blunt as she chooses. It will be more difficult for you because you're not from a great family, of course, but no one will be able to gain say you."

The promise of that was strangely heartening. It was the first piece of good news that she'd heard.

"Now, draw your shoulders back," he instructed.

She did.

"No, no, not like that."

"How on earth is one supposed to draw their shoulders back?" she exclaimed, feeling most confused by him. Was he always so mercurial?

He shook his head, his dark hair brushing his cheekbones. "You're tense. Thus your shoulders are halfway up to your ears. Now draw in a deep breath through your nose and then release the air slowly out your mouth. Allow your shoulders to fall in place. Allow your ribs to float above your hips."

"I beg your pardon?" she said, a phrase she was using far too often with him. But he did seem to provoke confusion. Her surprise was natural. After all, she'd never heard the word "hips" from a man before.

"You must allow your ribs to float pleasantly above your hips," he explained, his comments seemingly obvious to him. "It will give you an immense air of confidence."

Though she felt foolish, she did as he asked. And as her breath easily flowed past her lips and her shoulders eased, she beamed.

"How does that feel?" he asked.

"Wonderful."

He gave her a single, slow smile. A smile which did the most shockingly inviting thing to his handsome face.

For the briefest instant, that look transformed him.

But then, he cleared his throat. "Well, then it's a beginning. I shall leave you to get started studying."

"You're going?" she asked, feeling rather like the victim of unpredictable weather.

"I must," he told her. "I have a great deal to do, but don't worry, I shall check on you in an hour to see what you've learned. And if you need anything, ring the bell by the fire."

He strode to the door then stopped. Over his shoulder, he said, "Miss Bly, the box is for you. Feel free to open it."

With that he left the room. She remained unmoving for several moments. Still reeling from their lesson, she eyed the box. What lesson waited for her? Some treatise on the behavior of a superior duchess? A device to ensure she did not trip?

Georgiana crossed the room and reached out to the walnut box. Her fingers lingered over the surface. *Goodness*. It wasn't going to bite her. Girding her proverbial loins, she whipped the lid open.

A coronet of diamonds rested upon a blue velvet panel. Her mouth fell open in the most cliché of fashion. It was a *crown*. And it was hers.

She swung her gaze from the glittering jewels to the door. He'd wanted her to have it. She trembled as she took the shockingly heavy piece into her hands.

It should have felt wrong. It did not. And then, oh so slowly, Georgiana lifted it and placed it atop her head. Despite its weight, she suddenly felt the excitement of possibility.

Perhaps she could do this, after all.

CHAPTER EIGHT

Georgiana sat in blessed silence, tucked into the window seat that overlooked the elaborately landscaped garden. There were sprawling trees of many varieties and steps of artfully displayed stones, which led down a tiered embankment to a small lake. Fountains of water sprayed up into the air from Trident's fork, pouring over his stallions that seemed to be pawing at the surface.

This small nook in the library, larger than most people's entire homes, was a place she could get away from her blasted lessons and her dos and don'ts of being a duchess.

She'd found the nook after a particularly long session with Thornfield's graphs. Graphs which explained important subjects from political commentary to the right phrases to use when a fight appeared imminent between guests.

Her current lesson, a stack of the most prestigious peers in the land, awaited her on the long mahogany table in the center of the library. She would resume their study soon, but even Thornfield had accepted she needed to have a few moments' rest.

Or more likely, she had these few minutes after Lady Strathmore's daily deportment lesson, because Thornfield had gone out to inspect his drainage works before Georgiana had even arrived for the day's tutorials.

With a leather-bound volume of Shakespeare's comedies, she did her best to not think of the myriad facts and rules she'd been cramming into her head for several days now. Opportunities to be alone were rare and few.

Georgiana tucked her skirts about her, allowing the soft light of a northern summer to beam through the paned glass and fall upon her. Happily, she turned the pages, covered from top to bottom in inky black typeface.

She easily read through the dialogue of act one of *Much Ado About Nothing*. She adored Benedick and Beatrice, their merciless witticisms, and clear love for each other. She was glad a couple who was clearly so deeply in love with each other found true love in the end, even if there were some truly harrowing moments along the way.

She tried not to think about the fact that it would not come to pass for her. She told herself true love was something found only in novels and plays.

Her life was not a play. Her life was, well, rather mundane.

So, she was most aware that she would have to find contentment within the pages of her books if she longed for love. After all, it would be deeply disingenuous to not realize the extent of her good fortune compared to so many.

Even so, she continued to stare at the first few pages, which took place in Spain. She could only imagine Spain from the history, geography, and travel memoir books she had all but devoured over the years. And thank goodness for Mr. Shakespeare, who could take her there on a rather chilly afternoon in the North of Yorkshire.

Soon, she would leave for London, where her wedding was to take place. She winced at her wandering thoughts. Mr. Shakespeare was such a dear friend to her that it was a shocking thing she was having such trouble giving him the attention he was due.

But there it was.

Footsteps echoed on the opposite side of the library. *His* footsteps. She could tell by their confident, familiar rhythm. Her entire body seemed to reverberate at the promise of his presence. How the blazes did he do that to her?

Clearing her throat, Georgiana pored over the familiar pages with zeal, even though every bit of her felt completely alert to the fact that she was going to be alone with him. Her future husband.

Bootsteps echoed down the library, solid, strong steps. They stopped on the carpet several feet before her, at the other side of table between them.

She did not look up. She wanted to make him wait just a little. She wanted him to understand she did not feel completely deferential to him. She was not going to bow and scrape, even if that was what he was accustomed to, or what he expected of a wife.

Had he no idea of equality or brotherhood? If not, she was going to have to teach him. Ever so slowly, she lifted her gaze. "*Oh*," she exclaimed lightly. "Do forgive me. I did not hear you enter."

He arched a dark brow. "Your book is so very enthralling?"

"Indeed it is," she said. "I was most immersed."

"May one inquire as to what you are reading?"

he asked coolly, his hands folded behind his immaculately tailored blue morning coat.

"You may," she said. "I am reading *Much Ado About Nothing*."

"Aha. Shakespeare again."

"Yes," she said dryly. "Are you aware he wrote plays as well as poetry?"

He rolled his eyes. "Someone of my standing is well versed in *all* the works of Mr. Shakespeare. I also know the writings of Mr. Jonson, Mr. Marlowe, and Ms. Behn. Do you?"

"I do." She cocked her head to the side, stunned he would mention a female writer. "I don't find Mr. Jonson's voice particularly good, if you must know. I also like Congreve and Wycherley, though they are significantly later in period."

"They are," he said, tense, as if the room was entirely too small for him. "I hope you don't plan on behaving like the female characters in those plays."

She frowned, taking his meaning. "I won't behave thus if you won't. I've heard you're a bit of a rake."

He wound his way around the table piled high with books and stopped right before her. "Where have you heard such rumors?"

"Do you suggest that they're not true?" she asked, resting her book upon her knees.

"I suggest no such thing," he countered with the sort of tone one might expect when discussing which jam one preferred on their toast. "I merely ask where you gather your information from."

She sighed then admitted, "My sister."

His lips twitched, though he didn't appear amused. He was, once again, a contradiction. "And your sister has a great deal of information of the *ton*, does she?"

That put her on the defensive. "You will find the sisters in my family are well-read, even if some of them are interested in trifles. We do like the news-sheets."

"If you read of me being a rake, you are not reading newssheets. You are reading gossip rags."

Georgiana swung her legs from the window seat and rested her slippered feet upon the floor. "For me, even newssheets have a tendency to be full of addlepated gossip."

His brow furrowed, apparently confused by her commentary. "Why ever do you think so?"

She gestured with her hand, twirling it as she sought a way to describe her frustration. "Do you not find that all such articles are given to the leaning of one particular point of view?" she asked. "Is that not itself a bit of gossip? The political leanings of Mr. Fox or the Tories?"

He stared at her as if she had grown another head. "You know about Mr. Fox verses the political leanings of the Tories?"

"What person does not?" she scoffed.

"A great many persons," he said, as he took up a rather large volume of *The Aeneid*. "I have a whole lesson planned out for you regarding them. Put this on your head." He held out the volume to her. "You must practice while we hold debate. It will be good for you. To maintain your composure."

She fought a scowl, tempted to tell him exactly what he could do with his suggestions for composure and debate.

"And may I ask?" she said, taking the book without bothering to argue, as he no doubt expected she might. She wished to improve in the privacy of his home. Public failure did not appeal to her. So, she did as bid, carefully resting the book atop her simple coif. "What do you think of the affairs in France?"

He gestured for her to begin walking. "Does my opinion make such a difference?"

"Well," she began softly as she strode forward with the book balanced precariously. "It wouldn't make a difference in the fact that I'm going to marry you, but it might make a difference in my estimation of you."

He frowned. "Your estimation?"

The words came out of his mouth in such a terse way that she could only imagine he gave little consideration to her opinion of him.

The realization sent a flood of fury through her. The book wobbled. She drew in a deep breath, as he had taught her, and surpassed her own annoyance. Keeping her shoulders back and her chin parallel to the floor, she continued walking.

"Are you one of those stodgy old lords trapped in a bygone era who believe that only titled men should make change in our land?" she asked calmly as she faced him.

"No, I don't believe that at all. If we continue in the rigidity of old, we shall soon find ourselves to be in the same shoes as the fellows over in France."

She gaped at him, then, hiding her surprise, walked about the long mahogany table which bore the ledgers, cards, and graphs he used to teach her.

"Do you truly believe that?"

"Yes," he said.

"Then you must believe in the basic tenets of the American Revolution and—"

"Good God, woman, I am an Englishman through and through. Am I marrying a revolutionary?"

"Not exactly," she admitted, smiling. She pivoted and turned in the opposite direction, quite pleased she could walk so smoothly and engage in a discourse at the same time… All while balancing an ancient Greek story atop her head. "I did find a great deal to be admired in the Jacobin cause, but they seem to have gone completely wrong."

He blew out a derisive breath. "If one can say blood in the streets and heads being lopped off right, left, and center is going wrong, then yes, the Jacobin cause has indeed."

"A few people have truly ruined it," she said with a sigh. Or at least so the reports in the newssheets made plain.

He studied her for a long moment. "You do seem to have an understanding of the world."

"I cannot help my penchant for it." She shrugged, with the book still balanced, and she beamed. Practice really did make progress! Soon, she'd be perfect if she kept this up. And she felt oddly confident with her new posture, as if she could take on the world. "It is far more interesting than lace and fans."

"Young ladies are generally supposed to limit themselves to languages, music, and design."

"Young ladies are meant to limit themselves to

very boring things indeed, though language is not so very boring, for if one can speak French, they can read French in the original."

"Dear God," he groaned, but then his face began to transform into one of calculation and he raked his gaze up and down her body in a slow sweep. "You read French in the original?"

"I do," she said proudly. "I quite like it. The writings of Olympe de Gouge are my favorite."

He blinked at her, unreadable, though his stance had changed ever so slightly from the rigidity of a statue to that of one who was intrigued by an animal on display.

"Olympe de Gouge," she repeated slowly.

"You know who she is?" he asked, apparently stunned. "Speaking French is common enough in the ladies of the peerage. But familiarity with Madame de Gouge?"

"I have read her treatise more than a dozen times," she said, and then it hit her quite firmly. A man of his power and position? His travel? The people he had met was awe inducing. "Do you *know* her? Have you met her?"

"I had the good fortune to meet her in Paris." His face grew drawn. "Yes. Before things went—"

"How remarkable," Georgiana breathed, unable to stop herself.

"This is the strangest conversation I have ever had."

Georgiana paid no attention to the remark, nearly skipping at the proximity to Madame de Gouge, though she had been cruelly martyred. "She proclaimed the rights of women, you know."

"Yes. I know," he said with little patience. "I met her and Mary Wollstonecraft at the same party. Now, one is dead. And the other, well, most disappointed."

"That's because the reformation of women's issues is so completely ignored in this country," Georgiana said, lamenting for both women writers.

"You know about the women's issues in this country, as well?" he asked, eyeing her carefully again.

Oddly, he did not seem…disappointed.

"I do," she said, proud of her own education, as she stepped before him. She took a single moment to prepare then executed a perfect curtsy. One that was not too deep, given her future station. When she was presented eventually to the queen, as she must be… Well, she'd have to sink much lower and without a single bobble.

Slowly, she put her hands to the book atop her head and took it down. "I may live in Yorkshire, but that does not limit me to the fact that I am absolutely affected by the rules of our society. Now, if you think about the fact that women are half the population and yet we haven't a single vote in Parliament—"

"I am beginning to believe I was vastly mistaken in my estimation of your ability to be duchess, Georgiana. I do not need to school you in politics, apparently. You could school half the *ton* due to your voracious curiosity and passion. You shall do quite well at the political dinners I hold every week."

"Thank you," she replied, both shocked and warmed by the compliment. He seemed little given to praise, and that particular praise was great indeed. It left a heady feeling humming within her. "I am glad we shall at least have such discourse. I doubt you and I shall ever bare our souls to each other. You've made your opinion of me very clear."

"Bare our souls," he repeated, his brow furrowing as if the very idea was positively mad.

"Yes." With patience, she explained, "One discusses the inner workings of one's heart—"

"Please," he cut in, grabbing up a stack of ledgers from the table and holding it before his heart, a veritable shield of facts. "I did not imagine you were a complete and total romantic fool."

"Why would you not think such a thing?"

For evidence, she retrieved her volume of Shakespeare. "I'm sitting here reading about romance. The fateful night we met, I was reading *Pamela* in your study. Why should I not be a *romantic fool*?"

"Fair point." He looked away for a long moment then gestured at one of the shelves laden with the latest novels of the day. "But be careful. Heroines like Pamela, interesting creatures that they are, seldom make good duchesses in real life."

"I cannot believe that to be true."

"Why?"

She licked her lips, preparing to make her defense, but then she stopped and picked up a slender volume from the long table. The volume containing the history of his family. "Well, when thinking of history, the most powerful women in the country have a tendency to be interesting, do they not?"

His gaze flicked to her mouth, drawn by the touch of her tongue, and then, his gaze lifted to hers.

There was a fiery intensity in them that nearly stole her breath away.

"Many of the women of your family, including your aunt Agatha, have been powerful creatures indeed."

"You must be careful, Georgiana," he warned. "Much of society will not be forgiving. You aren't from a powerful family. They will not like that you've upended the rules."

"I don't mind if I'm not liked," she said, though a wave of trepidation slid through her. She held her own volume of rebellious women in her hands, the women of his family, and felt a strange sense of liberation.

"I find, Your Grace, that I am beginning to like the idea of having power, for in power is the ability to make change for my sex." She swallowed back a wave of anxiety. "But I confess, the large crowds I must face give me pause."

He cocked his head to the side, and his dark, waving hair, hair untouched by the artificial curls of the day, fell over his brow. "Georgiana," he said with a shocking gentleness, "I do not particularly like large crowds myself."

"But you are a duke."

"I *am* a duke, which makes it very inconvenient to struggle in the company of those beneath me."

She peered at him, trying to make sense of the man who was to be her husband, of his arrogance, and his discomfort. Was that why he was so distant? Because he so disliked to be in company?

The volume in her hands bore the generations of his ancestors who, since Norman times, had ruled this country. She'd read the battle they'd fought, the laws enacted, the positions they'd held. She drew in a slow breath, then rushed before she could stop herself. "Do you truly think yourself so superior to others?"

"I am superior," he said without the slightest hint of remorse. "There's no question. You see"—he gestured to his family history pressed to her chest—"one cannot escape the fact that my family has been in power since William the Conqueror."

"But surely that does not make you superior."

"I think it does. My family has not fallen to the wayside as many families have. What else does that not say, except the fact we are superior? We never give in. We endure."

The brief pleasure she'd experienced in their discussion faded entirely. She quite disliked him. There was no getting around it. And he clearly did not like her, either, even if he found her a bit more acceptable now.

"What can you say of your family?" he continued, apparently oblivious to the offense he was causing. "Where have you come from? Are you not merely descended from Yorkshire sheepherders? There's nothing wrong with being a Yorkshire sheepherder," he added quickly. "But Yorkshire sheepherders do not control the country. My family does."

With each word that he proclaimed, fury bubbled through her until she boiled over. She tried to draw in calming breaths, but they did nothing to dissipate her anger. Was this truly how he saw the world? Did he wish her to see it thus as well, simply because she was to be his wife? If he did, he would be sorely disappointed.

Dear God, his arrogance was just absolutely astounding. Could he not hear himself speak? Did he not realize how horrid he sounded?

She leveled him with a hard stare. "You are suggesting that your life is more valuable than mine, *Your Grace*?"

He blinked. "Well… Yes. I suppose I am. Except for now that you're going to be a duchess, of course, your life has increased in its worth estimably."

"You, sir, are despicable," she bit out, any good feeling she'd had toward him all but vanished.

"Many people seem to think so," he agreed, though the opinions of others seemed not to affect him.

"They are absolutely *correct*." She slammed her book down on the table. "I think you should go. I cannot imagine our lessons continuing at present."

"First," he said, with a shocking level of calm for the situation, "you have an excellent imagination, so I doubt you cannot imagine it. Second, I think I should stay."

"Whatever for?" To continue torturing her, no doubt.

"Since we're to be wed, we should become accustomed to disagreement. As I understand, disagreement is quite normal in marriage."

She threw her hands up. "Do you know anything at all of a *happy* marriage?"

He was silent for a long time, then said, "My parents were quite happy, from what I recall as a boy."

The mention of his parents gave her temporary

pause, for she found herself curious. "Were they?"

He nodded, wordless. Some strange emotion danced over his face and he quickly looked to the windows, squinting, as if the sun was far too bright. But he didn't turn away from it.

"I'm very sorry they died when you were so young," she said, though she was still furious with him.

"Thank you. Your sympathy is noted."

"I truly mean what I say, Thornfield," she whispered, relenting a bit as she imagined him as a child, left entirely alone.

Blast, she did have a good imagination. Her heart ached for the small boy, adrift and isolated.

"I'm sure you do." He clasped his hands behind his back, drawing his gaze back to her. "You seem to be a woman of soft heart."

The comment was not a compliment. She knew it in her bones. To someone like him, to have a soft heart was to have a soft head.

"Do you think your parents would admire your coldness?" she asked. "Were they cold in their happiness?"

A look of sheer ice shuttered his already implacable features. "Forgive me, you are indeed correct. We shall not continue your lessons today."

He bowed, ready to take his leave.

But she took a quick step forward, hand held out. "I don't wish to upset you in regards to your parents. I only wish to understand. My parents are no doubt very different than yours were."

"They are," he agreed, with no attempt to ease the tension between them. But then he allowed,

"Your mother seems to have some sense, however."

Georgiana ignored the fact that he was definitely insinuating that her father was a fool. She couldn't particularly argue with him. There were many times that she felt the same. Still, it was upsetting that he looked so firmly down upon them.

Georgiana drew her shoulders back, lifted her chin, and locked gazes with him. "Your Grace, I'm sure it's going to be difficult for you to bring yourself into the mire of my family. Somehow, you'll have to slog your way through it, to take on the mud of such mediocrity upon your boots. But I am sure a gentleman of your perseverance shall somehow survive it."

He stared at her. "You're mocking me."

"Am I?" she queried dryly. She would have laughed if it wasn't necessary for her to wed him.

His mouth tightened with displeasure. "I do not always follow such things, for I do not find emotional nuance easy to understand, Miss Bly. But you most definitely are."

She laughed, a full-throated sound, determined not to be brought down by his impossible arrogance. If she did not laugh, she would cry. Besides, she had to point all of this out to him. She had to teach him to be a decent fellow, or during one of his arrogant orations, she was going to murder him one day.

"Yes, Your Grace," she replied. "I am mocking you, for you make it so easy. You are so very *superior*. I cannot help but find that the only way I have to deal with it is to tease you. Do you find it upsetting to be teased?"

"Not upsetting," he ground out. "Unfamiliar. I'm unaccustomed to being teased."

"Teasing would do you a world of good."

Thornfield shook his head. "Teasing will not do me a world of good, for I can scarcely tell when it is happening. I must warn you that if you continue to tease me, it might not go in your favor."

"And how might it not?" she said. "For teasing you unduly?"

He took a step forward, gazing down upon her with a spark of something she could not name.

"I think I would have to find a way to stop your mouth," he said.

"Stop my mouth?" She folded her arms tight beneath her breasts, unsure where this was headed. Had she pushed him too far? "However will you do that? A scold's bridal?"

"Oh, no," he said softly, his gaze falling to her breasts now that she had unwittingly drawn attention to them. "That is something of the past, something barbaric. I'm not barbaric, Georgiana. I'm a man of progress. A man of the future, a man who recognizes that women have their needs, too. There are far more pleasurable ways to stop a woman's tongue."

Then... *Oh then*, his lips turned upward in a burning smile, a smile meant to torture a lady with a promise she did not quite understand.

He looked to her book then back to her mouth. "Mr. Shakespeare clearly knew of them. I would most definitely undertake one of those."

"And what, pray tell, are they?"

"To begin with?" He took another step toward her, so close now that his boots were skimming the hem of her gown. "A kiss, Georgiana."

"You want to kiss me?"

"Unless you are still so inclined to end today's lesson, in which case I will take my leave and you may continue using your mouth in any way you desire, alone."

She stared up at him, her heart thundering. And made her choice.

CHAPTER NINE

Georgiana gave no protest, and Edward pulled her into his arms, taking her mouth in a ravenous kiss. He meant it when he said he wished to stop her mouth, but it wasn't because he disliked what he heard. It was because it was a revelation. Both upsetting and remarkable.

Every word that came out of her mouth was utterly strange and foreign to him. No one spoke to him like this, and though he gave evidence to the contrary, he liked it far too well.

Georgiana Bly was going to be a great deal of trouble. She was not at all the sort of woman that a duchess should be. No, no, no, *no*, for she entertained ideas that were extremely dangerous to his entire way of life and thinking. But oh how passionately she proclaimed them. He could not help but admire her to some degree, even if she drove him mad.

And if he was honest…she made him consider his own position. Was she correct? Was he too cold? Would his parents be ashamed? That had been a particularly galling moment.

He shook that thought from his head for now, knowing he would take it out in the dark of night and examine every aspect of such an accusation.

Edward traced his hands along the simple cotton gown covering her back. The feel of her beneath his palms, incomparable to any desire he'd ever known. Needing more of her, all of her, the promise of the passion between them, he slipped one hand up to the nape of her neck, angling it back, and he deepened their kiss.

This.

This was what would bring them together, even when everything else was tearing them apart. Of that he was certain.

Her lips parted as she gasped against him. Then her own hands were upon his shoulders, holding on tightly as he kissed her again and again. She took those kisses hungrily until at last she was kissing him back with a wild abandon.

Georgiana Bly was not the sort of woman he would have thought at all to wish for. But there was no question, wish for her he did. Every day in her frustrating, fascinating company only solidified that for him.

She was a conundrum, ready to be kissed, and completely unadapted to his society. She was learning, true, but she was also shaking his very foundations, asking him to let go of the walls that had made his life bearable.

What the devil was he going to do?

The only thing it seemed to him was to make love to her. And so he held her tightly, until suddenly she shoved against him, her face twisting as if she'd had the most horrific thought.

"I beg your pardon!" she exclaimed.

In the depth of need for her, his body protested at the abrupt ceasing of their kiss. Every instinct told him to pull her back, to tempt her with more passion.

"What is the matter?" he asked, his breath ragged. Good God, what had she done to him?

He wished to devour her whole, to lay her back against the window seat or the mahogany table and to take her right here. Of course, he wouldn't. Such a thing would be completely ill-advised, even if she was to be his wife. Anyone could come in at any moment. And while he was used to sating his passions as all dukes did, he was not about to take an inexperienced young lady's virtue in his library. That was something beyond the pale even for him.

"Let a kiss be a kiss, not a means to an end." Her dark blue eyes flashed. "I find it incredibly patronizing that you so undervalue my intelligence as to believe I could be dissuaded thus."

"Undervalue?" he asked, surveying her pink-cheeked face. She looked as if she could scarce draw breath. "Your intelligence is superior to most men of my acquaintance. But a kiss can distract even the greatest intellect, Georgiana, *because* it is a kiss being a kiss."

The pink of her cheeks only deepened. She smoothed her hands over her gown, assuring it was put to rights, for the skirts had gone quite askew. In fact, she was delightfully mussed. Her unruly, curly hair all but bounced around her face.

He, too, adjusted his cravat and waistcoat, lest someone come in and deduce what they'd been about—and presume even more.

A perplexed frown crossed her features. "Oh bother. What was it that I wished to say to you? Oh yes." She cleared her throat, folded her hands before her, and gave him a deadly stare. "I think your behavior is quite appalling, sir, and if this is how you intend to act whilst we are wed, we shall have to have several discussions about the proper behavior of intelligent men with intelligent women."

"Shall we?" he said, oddly amused and intrigued. She was passionate and fiery beyond recognition at this moment. Did she even know her determination? He doubted it. "I don't think that's necessary. I am to be your husband, after all, therefore you shall give deference where due."

"Shall I?"

"Indeed. Besides, not only am I to be your husband, but I'm also a duke. *Everyone* who is beneath me does as they are told." He stated it all as fact, because that's exactly what it was. These were simply the rules they all lived by.

Her mouth dropped open. "I do not know what to say."

"I am sure that is a most rare occurrence for you, Miss Bly."

She huffed. "I am rarely without words, but not because I'm a flibbertigibbet. Because I speak only good sense."

He marveled at her, both in horror and admiration. It was a devilish combination. What was this strange thing that she evoked in him? He didn't like it at all. Yet he also did.

She made him…wish to argue with her, to lose control of his feelings. To treat her as his equal because, perhaps, she was. But the only thing that got him through this life was a sense of control, and if he let go of it—

Dear God, he didn't wish to think of the early years of his life when he'd barely been able to contain his rages, when he'd held on tightly, when so many school masters had made dire predictions about his future and his ability to be a duke.

No, he was in control. And he would remain thus.

Indeed, he well knew how to keep himself mastered. And he was not about to let some chit of a young woman, even if it was his future wife, tempt him away from the path of reason and the path that he had so intentionally forged.

Edward bowed his head. "Go home, Miss Bly. Please give my regards and wishes for good health to your parents and your sisters."

And with that, he turned and strode from the room, tempering his emotions, battening them down, ensuring that they could not rise to the surface again.

$$\cdots$$

"What the devil are you doing here?"

Andrew Althorpe, Laird of MacLiesh, Earl of Montrose, arched a russet eyebrow. "I came the moment I heard, mon. Thank God, I was already back from sea. Do you think I could let my dearest friend be shuffled off into matrimony without me returning immediately?"

"I'm not dying," said Edward as he took down a billiards cue from the wall. Even though he sounded terse, truly, he was relieved to have a friend. It was slightly assuring that he was capable of keeping a friend over the years. In fact, it was his friendship with Montrose that had convinced him he wasn't irretrievably broken. That there was hope.

"Might as well be, mon," said Montrose as he, too, snatched down a polished cue. "You've stuck your head in the proverbial noose and they're about to pull at any moment."

Edward inwardly did not disagree. While he was drawn to his future wife, most passionately, it was clear she did not like him. In any regard.

Aside from kissing, of course.

"You needn't make it sound so terrible," Edward said.

"Come now" — Montrose chalked his billiard cue — "you absolutely agree. This is the last thing you could possibly want. That chit of a girl, whoever she is, has managed to get you in her grasp. And you are now dancing the matrimonial jig of death."

Edward ignored Montrose, circled the elaborately carved wooden table, and took aim at the ball sitting on the green felt surface. "I refuse to condemn myself to such doom and gloom."

Montrose snorted. "You never feel doom and gloom, old mon. You just go on and on in stoicism, which of course I can appreciate. So, I shall go ahead and revel in doom and gloom for you."

Montrose placed the cue down on the edge of the table, threw his hands up, and in great drama, let out a cry. "The loss of such a bachelorhood is a travesty to this nation. Young ladies shall wail their dismay. The upper classes shall wail in horror that you have been captured by a maiden of such low esteem."

Edward tensed.

His friend's words sounded painfully similar to a few of his own, and the mockery of his future wife. "Now come here, she's hardly a shoemaker's daughter, Montrose. And even if she was, she's a young lady of virtue."

"Virtue?" Montrose said, his lips twitching. "How can she be if you're forced to marry her in such circumstances? I've never even heard you whisper her name. She's a total stranger to you."

Edward ground his teeth. The situation could hardly be borne.

"Brandy?" Edward asked, wishing to forget the difficulty of his visit with Miss Bly. She had been in his thoughts almost every moment since he had left her in the library after another thought-stealing kiss. He couldn't think effectively around her, and away from her, she was *all* he could think about. It was damned provoking.

"Of course," Montrose replied, "though I'd prefer a whisky." He looked at the cue then shook his head. "It's the only thing to do in such a circumstance."

Montrose threw himself down on the settee before the fire and propped a booted foot out before him.

Edward placed his own stick down, realizing neither of them was in humor for a game. He nodded toward his friend's choice of footrest. "That's ancient silk, I'll have you know."

"Never you mind," said Montrose. "I'll bring some back from my next journey to reupholster this ancient monstrosity."

"You're going to the East again so soon?" Edward picked up a crystal decanter and pulled out the stopper in one smooth action.

"As soon as I can," Montrose confirmed. "I loathe this island, as well you ken."

He poured out the deep amber liquid worthy of kings. "It's not such a very bad place. Shakespeare declared it a jewel."

"Shakespeare can sod himself," Montrose all but growled before he thrust a weathered hand through his thick, sun-streaked locks. "It might be a jewel, but jewels aren't particularly pleasant. They're a great deal of trouble and have to be polished to keep up their shine. England is a terrible place that causes trouble wherever it goes."

"*You* cause trouble wherever you go," Edward reminded, handing his friend a glass.

"That's true, but I'm Scottish." Montrose gave a devil's grin. "I'm allowed."

"Now why in God's name are the Scots *allowed* to cause trouble wherever they go?"

"Because it's in our nature and no one has been able to stop us. We like to be troublesome. We do it with a smile, though, and everyone thinks we're charming." Montrose took a long drink then winked. "And we like to wear a skirt."

"It's not a skirt," said Edward, keeping his face completely free of emotion. "It's a kilt."

Montrose threw his head back and laughed. "Indeed it is. Indeed it is. We mustn't let anyone think different, must we? I'm glad you passed my wee test."

"Well, it's not the done thing to wear kilts just now." Edward sighed, not wishing to remind his friend of the painful rules inflicted upon his homeland.

"But they're very freeing, you ken," Montrose said with false bravado, as if he hadn't been one of the loudest voices demanding the cultural return of his people from their Southern rulers. "If I could, I'd wear them every day, but sea air is a bit bracing."

"You spend most of your times in tropical waters."

"True, true. But the crossing over there." Montrose wagged his brows. "The nether regions can barely take it. And now here I am back in the North of England. You couldn't catch me and my bare legs out and about for anything."

"Weakling," he said.

"Ha! I'd like to see you climb the mountains that I have in various tropical lands. You would squeal like a wee bairn. The insects, my friend. The insects are as large as cats."

Edward shuddered. "Do you recall our days at school? You used to absolutely be terrified of the hordes of insects."

It was a truth that everyone knew but did not speak of. Schools for the aristocrats, one would have thought, would have been the height of luxury. They were not.

He and Montrose had attended the same school, a place where wealthy or titled young lords were sent to be taught by stoic, rather cross old men and ushered into that thing known as English gentlemanhood.

Neither of them had liked it.

Both of them had been given a great deal of trouble.

And the only reason Edward had survived it was because of the power of his future title. Everyone knew that one day when he inherited his dukedom, he could ruin all their lives.

Montrose, on the other hand, a Scot and an earl,

had been a great one for being cornered in various parts of the courtyard.

Given that Edward had known he was not at all like the other boys, he and Montrose had forged an alliance. When the Scot had realized Edward could not speak up for himself, he'd happily helped give his friend voice.

After all, Montrose had no trouble with words. Articulation of ideas was one of his finer points.

There had been times when Montrose's sheer volume and enthusiasm had been challenging for Edward, who generally preferred the world to be quiet and free of annoyance. But he'd become accustomed and appreciative of his loyal and determined friend.

Even though he wouldn't admit it, he was pleased that Montrose had come to assist him in a damned difficult moment again.

It was appreciated because Edward *did* feel in a corner.

"So, the lass does have you by the balls then?" Montrose asked before he lifted his brandy glass, ready for another measure.

Easily, Edward swiped up the brandy decanter and refilled his friend's snifter. "I wouldn't put it in quite such a way."

"Och, how would you put it?" Montrose leaned back, eyeing the brandy. "I heard you were kissing her quite passionately when discovered. You should hear old lady Trentham talk about it, that trout. She declared that you had half the girl's gown off and that it was a miracle you hadn't cast the chit aside as a complete and utter whore."

A wave of rage crashed over him, but Edward managed to carefully place the brandy decanter down on the mahogany sideboard without more than a dull *thud*. "Is that what's being said?"

"Indeed it is."

Edward folded his free hand into a fist, willing himself to stay calm. Willing himself to feel the pressure of his fingers into his palm. "I shall have to set that to rights almost immediately. Good God"— he forced his breaths to remain slow, steady—"the trouble this is all going to cause. None of it would have happened if I'd been married last year to... what was her name?"

"Gwendolyn Haverton," enunciated Montrose with an exaggerated shudder. "Thank God you didn't marry her. Beautiful but as curious as a trowel."

"Curiosity is not considered to be the most important thing in a young lady."

"It bloody well should be if one wishes to have children who love learning. Mothers who are curious about the world help their children to be as well," Montrose countered. "You don't wish your children to be without the spirit of inquiry do you?"

"No."

"And your intended, she must have a curious mind," Montrose intoned. "For she has got quite the better of you."

"She has not."

"Oh no?" Montrose's lips twitched.

Miss Bly had been quite fiery in his study but had made no advance upon him. She had stayed. And it had been he who had closed in on her, determined to make her leave.

Had she not intended to find him alone and to arrange for them to be caught together? No, certainly not. He didn't even entertain the thought any longer. Especially after their discourse this afternoon.

In fact, upon recollection, she'd assumed he was a poorly dressed servant.

"What the devil are you thinking?" Montrose asked.

Edward closed his eyes. "If you must know, she did seem to suggest I was a footman before I kissed her."

"A footman?" Montrose guffawed.

Edward found himself grinning. A most odd reaction. "She made comment about my ability to carry logs and the dubious state of my clothes."

"Did she, by God?" Montrose laughed. "So, you think she did not arrange it? She is as caught as you?"

"I don't know. The marriage is advantageous to her and her family. They would have faced a severe decline when their annuity was lost. Her mother is well enough, but her father?" Edward groaned. "If he bounces around me again, I might have apoplexy."

Montrose snorted. "You are not capable of apoplexy, Thornfield. You're far too serious for that. Nothing affects you."

"That's not true," Edward said solemnly, "and you know it."

Montrose was quiet for a moment.

They both knew it, indeed.

CHAPTER TEN

"He did *what*?" Elizabeth yelped.

Georgiana tucked up her night rail–clad knees to her chin. She barely believed what had transpired herself. "He kissed me again."

"In his library? During your lessons?"

They sat on Georgiana's bed in their small bedroom. They were lucky enough to have the one between them, the eldest sisters. A cheery but frugal fire, despite the summer, crackled in the hearth. Yorkshire summers were not warm, and the cold had come in that night. The damp walls were particularly chilly.

Elizabeth sat staring at her in wide-eyed silence until Georgiana couldn't bear the tension any longer, and tried to loosen it.

"Elizabeth, do not be so amazed," she teased. "We are to be married. And besides, he was an absolute bounder."

"The Duke of Thornfield, really? He's devilishly handsome, of course, and a rake, but you are not the sort of girl—" Elizabeth stopped suddenly, her mouth forming a perfect O then curving into a wicked grin, and she whispered dramatically, "He must think you are absolutely delicious. It's the only logical explanation."

Nothing her sister had said sounded logical.

And what a strange thought that was, that her future husband thought her *delicious*. She had never thought of anyone in such a way. As if one was something to be consumed.

But it *had* felt as if he was trying to devour her… and she had liked it.

Truth be told, before the duke, she could not remember a single time when a gentleman had looked at her with any particular interest. Most of her life, she paid little attention to gentlemen at all. They seemed rather foolish, in her opinion, only capable of talking about horses and hounds and their new coats.

She liked horses.

She liked hounds.

She could even appreciate a well-tailored coat.

But she valued books above all things, and as far as she could see, the vast majority of gentlemen had no interest in them whatsoever. Truthfully, she wondered if most had ever even opened one without the threat of a tutor.

And so, gentlemen had found her to be most vexing in turn.

Thornfield, on the other hand, was most definitely interested in books, and he had looked at her as if he might wish to eat her up like a dessert that one could never quite take enough of. Perhaps her sister was right. He did think her delicious. But why?

If she inspired no such feelings in others, why should she inspire such a feeling in him? Certainly, she inspired *some* sort of feeling in him.

Though it had seemed he'd been most distressed by her today, because he had left in quite a huff. Georgiana traced the hem of her night rail. "Well, his kisses are—"

"Yes?" Elizabeth asked, leaning forward, her eyes bright with curiosity.

"I cannot explain what they do to me," Georgiana said honestly, her breath growing short even as she recalled the touch of his lips.

She swallowed, then shook her head, not wishing to let herself be carried away. "But he was most rude. He said he kissed me to make me quiet, and at his ball, he kissed me to make me leave. I cannot think these are good things."

"I don't know," Elizabeth mused, but then her gaze brightened. "Perhaps he was only looking for excuses to kiss you, Georgiana."

That had never occurred to her before. Would a duke need an excuse to kiss a young woman? Perhaps they would if they fancied themselves above kissing unmarried young ladies.

"It is impossible to say what is in that head of his, but his kisses are marvelous." Georgiana scowled, annoyed that the thought of his kiss could distract her from his shortcomings. "He is exceptionally disagreeable, though. I do not think that I can like him."

"Well, it doesn't really matter if you like him," Elizabeth said. "You're going to be married to him and that's that. And you shall have to get an heir you know."

Oh, dear Lord. An heir. That was rather important. Duchesses did produce heirs.

Georgiana's heart slammed so hard and so quickly in her chest, she wondered if she was about to spontaneously combust with the realization of what was required of her.

It was one of the most important tenets of the aristocracy, the perpetuation of their lines.

Once she drew in several deep breaths, the idea was actually rather intriguing.

She knew about it, of course.

She'd read a great deal.

She'd seen several statues.

One knew about the Greek myths.

Her husband was a rake... And from all the myths, novels, and plays she'd read? Rakes were absolute bounders.

She did not like her state of affairs.

Was he going to continue in his rakish ways once they were wed?

That was a most disagreeable thought. The idea that he might be sharing his kisses with other women was appalling. How would she negotiate such a thing?

The very idea, though common amongst the *ton*, was most upsetting. For her parents had been loyal to each other, even if they were not the most reliable couple that one could think of.

"You look most distressed, Georgiana," her sister said softly. "What is it?"

"I'm thinking about his grace behaving in a way that Zeus might."

"Zeus?"

"Yes." Georgiana cleared her throat, completely stunned to be discussing such things at all with any relation to her future. "Hera must've been absolutely miserable with Zeus going about all over, being all god-like with ladies whenever he saw fit, with whoever he thought fit, and I don't think that I should like such a thing at all."

Elizabeth sat quietly for a moment, hopefully trying to find some bit of good to supply. "Simply tell him you won't be having it."

If only it *were* that simple. "I don't have a great deal of power in that regard. What if he tells me to, well, you know, politely tells me to hie off?"

"Well, then," Elizabeth said with her quiet firmness. "He's going to marry you, and if he did not it would be breach of promise. So, perhaps it would be a good idea to make it absolutely clear what your intentions are and what you require in a marriage, before you make your vows."

The idea of being forthright was rather appealing. It's something that she was rather given to anyway.

She beamed at her sister. "I think you're quite right. Just because he's a duke doesn't mean he's always going to get his way, even if he seems to think so."

"Oh, dear," Elizabeth said giddily, "I think your husband's going to get quite a surprise."

"He is indeed." Georgiana laughed, suddenly quite pleased. "Isn't it marvelous?"

. . .

The impromptu party held at Georgiana's home was a disaster.

There was no question—Georgiana wished she could slink underneath the carpet and hide for the rest of the evening, but since she was one of the primary guests, such a thing would be absolutely impossible.

Her father had what he assumed to be a remarkably good idea. Thus, a small dance in the duke's honor, since they were bound to become family, had come to pass. The small group of musicians played sprightly reels and jigs.

She wished she could take her father out to their pretty woodland and scream at him.

All of their friends had come. Their small ballroom was packed to bursting with all of the people of the county eager to see something they had never seen in such close proximity—a duke. But the truth was they were all in such a socially different strata that the whole thing was terribly strange.

It was very clear from the way the duke was standing on the other end of the room with two young ladies and a remarkably strange but gloriously handsome fellow that they did not belong together. The Duke of Thornfield peered down his nose as if the idea of dancing a reel was the most appalling thing he could ever think to do.

Georgiana bit down on her lower lip, feeling torn. This was the man she was going to marry, and he looked as if he might die on the spot from exposure to such *low* people.

Was he really so snobbish? Of course he was. He'd declared his own superiority!

Her father kept darting looks about the room, in turns grinning with delight and then all but wringing his hands. It was clear he was not entirely certain what to do next.

Charles Bly was ill-advised in many things, but one thing she could not discredit him for was the fact that he truly loved to make people happy, and he always enjoyed gatherings. So to him, a gathering would cause happiness. She wished the duke could see that, at least, and make even a small attempt to have a pleasant time for her father's sake.

She wound her gloved hands together, surveying the company from behind a large potted plant.

Elizabeth rushed up to her and whispered in horrified dismay, "Whatever shall we do? They all seem absolutely miserable."

"They *are* miserable," Georgiana said. "That's why they look as if no sugar has been added to the lemon punch."

"Perhaps we should pour wine into it!" Elizabeth teased. "And then they might appear a bit more jolly."

"Do you think so?" Georgiana queried, unable to hide her skepticism. "I do not think wine should improve them at all. No doubt the duke becomes morose and bad tempered with alcohol."

Georgiana blew out a breath. Really, this wasn't to be borne nor would she bear it! She seized Elizabeth's hand and pulled her through the crowded ballroom, carefully avoiding fans and feathers.

Everyone was tittering away, consuming large glasses of punch, all of them appalled by the duke's behavior and marveling at the fact that he was such an unpleasant presence. For generally, they, as a group, had such a lovely time. He was the veritable *thorn* in the side of the general company.

His name was apt.

Georgiana stopped a few feet in front of her future husband. She and Elizabeth both gave a small curtsy. "Your Grace," Georgiana said. "Good evening."

He looked down at her, perplexed. "We have already greeted each other this evening."

"So we have," she said with forced enthusiasm. "Shall we dance?" It was extraordinary that he had kissed her with such passion before. Twice.

He looked upon her as a statue might. A very beautiful statue, but an imperious statue, nonetheless. "I thought you did not care for dancing," he said.

All at once, her emotions were at war. That he remembered any of their previous conversation had her strangely thrilled. But she was still nettled by his behavior, tone, and the fact he was, in his way, telling her he did not wish to dance at an occasion meant for dancing.

Her smile was almost painful, but she continued at it, if only for the sake of her papa. "You are correct, I don't care for dancing," she said. "But it is the generally accepted thing to do at a ball, and since you and I are the guests of honor, perhaps we should set the proper example."

He peered at the empty dance floor.

He peered at the people gathered around the floor.

He peered at the musicians, arched a single brow, and said, "I do not dance reels."

"Well," Georgiana said through nearly gritted teeth even as she determined to be optimistic, "we could request anything that you please. A waltz, perhaps?"

"A waltz?" he echoed, his lip curling ever so slightly. "I do not think so."

She nearly threw her hands up and cursed his

fate, but such a thing, should she or any of her family wish to show their faces in any part of Europe ever again, was not possible.

The two young women, Lady Emma and Lady Gwendolyn, stood beside the duke, gawking at Georgiana and Elizabeth as if they were animals in a zoological exhibit. The women were exquisitely beautiful. Lady Emma, with red hair, pale skin, and a gown of emerald green, looked as if she had stepped right out of a canvas. It was almost painful, her beauty.

The other, Lady Gwendolyn, dark-haired, pink-checked, and blue-eyed with a gown of ruby, looked at them as if they were something that she had stepped in.

Something quite unpleasant.

And with a noxious scent.

"Your gathering is most interesting!" said Lady Gwendolyn. "What various people you do know, Your Grace."

"The various people," Georgiana put in, "include his future family."

"Yes," Lady Gwendolyn stated, her brows rising. "How remarkable."

Georgiana swung her attention away from the rather venomous Lady G and focused upon her betrothed. "Your Grace, is there nothing I can do to tempt you to dance?"

The duke's friend, a man with hair as thick as a lion's mane gave her a winning grin and announced boldly, "You must dance with me, Miss Bly! You look as if you are a great conversationalist, and I'm sure you will be light on your feet."

Thornfield looked at his friend askance. "You are mistaken. She declares that she is quite poor on her feet. Though, she did not step on me when we danced. Perhaps it was luck."

Georgiana just refrained from gnashing her teeth. It was very tempting to give him a good set down in public, but she knew that such a thing was simply a fantasy.

"Of course, I shall dance with you, my lord," Georgiana said with a cheeky grin. "But I think His Grace only refuses me now because I got the better of him in a discussion about Mr. Shakespeare."

"Thornfield, is that true?" asked Montrose, his eyes sparking with amusement.

She was pleased to see the duke's lips tighten into a frown.

"We merely interpret Shakespeare differently," Thornfield declared.

"I cannot agree," Georgiana said. "Shakespeare is a great man. He knew much about love."

"He knew about a great many things," Montrose agreed heartily. "Love, certainly, and the pleasures of love."

"I should be happy to discuss it with you!" she exclaimed, hoping all the while that Thornfield was growing irritated.

From the look upon her sister's angelic face, she must have been hitting her mark. The Duke of Thornfield shifted from dancing shoe to dancing shoe.

Montrose pressed on. "I shall enjoy that immensely."

"As it turns out, I think I am inclined to dance, after all," Thornfield broke in abruptly. "You may dance with Georgiana's sister."

"Why thank you, Thornfield," Montrose declared. "How very benevolent of you. And I think it should prove to be absolutely delightful, if the lady consents."

Elizabeth blinked in amazement at the rapid change of conversation, then smiled. "Of course, my lord. It would be a pleasure."

With that, Georgiana seized the duke's hand and allowed him to escort her onto the small floor. Finally, she noted from across the room, her father beamed with pleasure.

At last, things were going to turn in the direction he no doubt hoped.

"You are not to discuss love or pleasure with my friends," Thornfield said.

"Are you afraid that they shall corrupt me?" she asked as he began to lead her in the dance.

"Yes," he said frankly. "Montrose has been known to lead many a young lady astray."

"He's not a very good friend to you, then, is he?"

"He is the dearest friend I have," he countered, easily leading her about as more and more couples joined them. "I have known him since I was a boy. Nothing shall be said against him."

"Ah," Georgiana said, completely aware of the feel of her hand in his, and his palm pressed to her upper back. "It seems I have found something positive about your character."

"Have you?" he asked, clearly unimpressed by her esteem. "And what is that?"

"That you are loyal to your friends, and that is something I look upon with favor."

"Should I be concerned about what else you look upon with favor?" he drawled.

She narrowed her eyes at his frustrating reply. "Since I am to be your wife, I think it is a good thing that you do."

"I am not entirely certain I can appreciate your sense of judgment," he said. "We must resume your training and then perhaps I shall be concerned with your opinion."

She cocked her head back and leveled him with a hard stare. "If you must train me to be a better duchess, I must train you to be a better man."

He faltered a step and nearly tripped. She grabbed the duke tightly, helping to right *him* before he became acquainted with *her* floor.

Vindication coursed through her veins. At long last, she had shaken him and nothing could have felt better in this moment. Not even his kiss.

• • •

Edward's throat all but strangled at his future wife's extraordinary statement.

Train him?

Train him, indeed.

He'd spent most of his life in training, and he'd reached the age when such training was no longer necessary, *thank you very much*.

He clamped his teeth together so hard he feared they cracked.

But he was determined not to say another word throughout the dance. As they progressed down the line, weaving through their partners, he ignored the several pairs of eyes that studied him.

It was as if he was a remarkable artifact from some far off land on view. He hated it. As a duke he had become accustomed to being stared at, but this night it was particularly strong. And there was nothing protecting him from the crowd at large. Usually, he had at least a coach between himself and the onlookers. At his own balls, he managed to barely be present and then stay isolated, glowering at anyone who came too near.

Now his own wife-to-be was looking at him as if he had grown a second head. She thought he was appalling. He knew. Before this moment, he couldn't have given a blast for the opinion of anyone save himself and his beloved aunt, but much to his abrupt shock, he cared now that *she* was looking at him thus.

He couldn't really do anything about it. It was who he was. He'd tried years and years to be softer, more malleable, more pleasant, but it simply wasn't possible and she was going to have to get used to it. As he'd had to do himself. There was no other way about it.

After several moments, she snuck a glance at him. "Have you gone positively mute, Your Grace?"

"I think it is the safest option at present."

Her blond head nodded tersely. "I see that is to be your style."

"My style?" he echoed, doing all he could to keep his temper.

"Yes," she mused. "When faced with adversity, you retreat."

He all but recoiled at that. Retreat, did he?

Ha! She had no idea the adversity he had

overcome during his life. The tool which had served him best was to *regroup*, because the last thing he wished to do was say something he'd truly regret.

And from past experience he was absolutely capable of saying something that would cause someone incredible offense even if it was not his intention.

Over the years, he'd become very careful about what he let slip past his lips. Yet, still, he often blundered. It was like he had an albatross always about his neck.

"If that is what you think, Miss Bly," he began, astonished how many times they were required to go about such a small ballroom, "I think it wise we see each other but once or twice a year."

"That won't be possible, will it?" she asked, her brows furrowed together. "If we are to have children."

He nearly stumbled again. How in damnation did she do that to him? He was usually someone of great composure, but she had caused him to nearly lose his step twice. Children, indeed. He quite liked the idea of getting an heir with Georgiana Bly.

There was something about her that drew him. God help him, he *felt*...something he couldn't describe. Surely, it was simply irritation. But even as he thought it, he knew it wasn't true. This was a deep fire that she had lit and was slowly consuming him. Despite his good sense.

She was nothing like the women that he'd been with in the past. Georgiana Bly was tart. She wasn't outstandingly beautiful in the typical sense, though she did have a particular beauty to her. She did not attempt to put him at ease. As a matter of fact, he had a strong feeling she did everything in her powers to make him *ill* at ease. And she enjoyed it.

He wondered at that.

Did she understand what kind of person he was?

He thought perhaps she did. Or at least she *thought* she understood him.

When the music came to a close, he gave her a stiff bow. "Thank you for the honor of this dance, Miss Bly," he stated, as he knew he was supposed to do. But he couldn't help adding, "I see that we should have a great deal of work to do when next I see you."

"Work?" she repeated, her eyes all but dancing as she teased him. "How very trying, Your Grace. Surely, the prelude to marriage should be just the tiniest merry."

A muscle tightened in his jaw. Did she always make light of things? After several days attempting to teach her the finer points of being a duchess, he was beginning to suspect, much to his future misery, that yes… Yes, she did take things lightly. "You do not know enough about marriage if you think marriage should be merry. Clearly, you know nothing of *ton* marriages."

"Touché," she agreed with the merest shrug. "I do not. And perhaps I do not wish to know, if it is so dreary and bleak as you insinuate it is." The dancing faded from her gaze into utter seriousness. "I shall never be cold like you, nor shall I be distant as you seem so determined to be. Despite the fact that I know at your heart's core, you are warm through and through."

And with that, she turned from him and marched across the room in high dudgeon.

He stared after her, unable to formulate his usually dry response. *Warm through and through? That's what she thought of him? Where the devil had she gotten that idea?*

It was the first time in the entirety of his adult life that he could remember someone insinuating such a thing. He was usually thought of as one of the chilliest of them all. An aristocrat, a man to be won, a man apparently *more* appealing for his implacable nature.

He did not know what to think of her summation.

He turned away and headed back toward his party. It had been a great mistake inviting his young cousins, Lady Emma and Lady Gwendolyn. And his dear friend had shown up on his doorstep the night before, having returned from a journey to the Americas. Edward had to invite him along; he'd never think of doing otherwise. But no doubt Montrose would never let him hear the end of this night or his impending marriage.

Clearly, Georgiana's daily lessons with him were not enough. Drastic measures would have to be taken.

CHAPTER ELEVEN

Mr. Bly stared at the kipper on his plate as if he was definitely regretting the choice to put it there. His already furrowed brow creased, his lips pursed, and he slowly pushed the porcelain away.

He looked in deep despair at the idea of eating breakfast, and so he took his cup of coffee and sipped it slowly, his hand trembling ever so slightly.

Georgiana hid a smile.

Her father had had perhaps one too many glasses of wine the night before.

Fortunately, he had not been overly zealous or overly silly with the Duke of Thornfield in his cups. If he had, she wasn't sure she would have been able to show her face at breakfast this morning.

Sometimes her papa became quite merry at parties, something that most people quite enjoyed. Thornfield didn't appear as if he'd enjoy any sort of enthusiasm. She wondered if he'd prefer it if everyone was dead.

Well, perhaps that'd be a bit too far, but he didn't seem to like to see life in anyone, which was quite odd because his friend Montrose had appeared most jolly.

How peculiar people were.

She looked over to Elizabeth, who was staring at her breakfast with a much happier visage. She wondered if her sister was thinking of the Earl of Montrose. Georgiana wouldn't blame her at all, for he was a handsome devil if ever anyone had seen one.

Not as handsome as Thornfield.

No, no.

Montrose did not have that granite stoicism that made him mysterious and interesting, nor that superiority, which made her wish to throttle him... and then kiss him.

It was a most perplexing state of affairs.

A footman entered the room, carrying a small silver tray upon his gloved hand. He walked to her papa, showed him the letter, and her father's eyes brightened considerably.

"It is for you, Georgiana," he all but hollered, whereupon he groaned and clutched his head. He cleared his throat. "If I am not mistaken, it is from Thornfield Castle. Open it. Open it at once, my dear. You must. You must."

Georgiana took the note from the footman, broke the red wax seal embossed with the ducal coat of arms, and unfolded the thick parchment.

As she scanned the perfect, bold penmanship, her stomach sank. It was the last thing that she wanted to read.

Dearest Miss Bly,

It is the deepest wish of myself, my cousins, and my friend to invite you to stay at Thornfield Castle for a week. Aunt Agatha is desperate to know you better and thinks that it is only possible for us to come to mutual appreciation through an extended visit. Apparently, last evening my behavior was appalling and I am meant to make it up to you. We expect you no later than this afternoon. A coach will be sent. Please bring your sister Elizabeth as a companion.

Yours,

Thornfield

She nearly crumpled the letter and tossed it onto the scraps of her breakfast, but surely that would not do. "I am to go and visit," she said flatly to her father. "An extended stay."

Her father blinked then all but crowed, "At the Duke of Thornfield's?"

"Yes."

"Well, you are engaged, my dear," her father felt the need to point out, "and this is a wonderful honor."

"Elizabeth is to come, too," Georgiana said.

Her father's eyes all but sparkled. "Marvelous, marvelous. She shall have a chance at Montrose, then."

Elizabeth's gaze darted up, wide-eyed. And yet her cheeks were a lovely rose at the mention of the earl.

Her mother came into the room and kissed Georgiana, then Elizabeth, on the top of the head.

"Who shall have a chance at Montrose?" her mother asked as she lowered into her chair.

"*Elizabeth*," her father cheered.

"Oh dear," her mother said. "He seems as if he's far too charming for his own good. Elizabeth, I hope you don't have anything too serious in mind with him."

Elizabeth's lips tightened. She said nothing, only sipped her tea.

Her mother's face softened. "He is rather handsome, I agree, but, my darling husband, do not get into your head the idea that your daughter should marry him. A man like that can only come to no good, I'm certain, even if he is charming."

"An earl, my dear, though, think of it," Mr. Bly said, all but dancing in his seat. "An earl for our daughter. My clever Georgiana"—he inclined his head toward her—"I never thought you would marry, but look at what's happened. And now you are going to ensure that all of your sisters make excellent marriages, as well."

Her father drove her mad, love him as she did.

She sighed.

It did seem as if it was going to happen. She was going to sacrifice her own happiness. There would be no retiring to libraries with books of her own and a modest spinsterhood.

No, she was going to be a duchess, the most grand of titles save for royalty, and her sisters would all be wed well. Though she quite liked the idea of her own state of affairs at least making other people merry, even if she would not be.

Shaking her head, she wondered what her family would think if she told them the duke had been training her like a horse or a dog. She would just have to give her dear future husband as good as he got, then, and that was that.

• • •

Edward loathed giggling.

As another dose of the obnoxious sound traveled through his large library, he fought a shudder. It had been a mistake inviting his cousins down, but Aunt Agatha had been rather insistent a few months ago that it was time he did his duty and invite family.

And one, of course, always did their duty.

His connection would make it possible for them to achieve advantageous marriages, and the sooner they were married, the better in his opinion, because then he wouldn't have to worry about them or consider them much at all.

They were both intelligent young women, but they did have a tendency to let out horrific gaggles of sound.

It felt as if they were physically driving nails into his head. His shoulders tensed even further.

He wished he could go to his private study at this particular moment and sit in his own chair and hide away. But he knew he would hear no end of trouble if he did, for his future wife was to arrive at any moment.

As if his own thought managed to manifest her into the conversation, his cousin Emma declared, "Can you believe that frock she wore last night? My goodness. I have never seen anything so shockingly out of date. She will need a new wardrobe entire, lest she make us all a positive laughingstock. Can you imagine such a girl being the Duchess of Thornfield?"

His other cousin, Gwendolyn, let out a peal of laughter. "She could only ever possibly marry him because of scandal. Can you believe her gall?"

Edward ground his teeth together.

However, he was not surprised by his cousins' discourse. It was the discourse of all of England at present.

Emma lifted a hand to her rosebud mouth and giggled again. "She will be an utter failure, my friend, an utter failure. She shall embarrass our family to no end."

Edward snapped his gaze up. "Then I don't see why you're giggling, if she's going to embarrass you so thoroughly."

Gwendolyn's shoulders snapped back and she stared at Edward, shocked. "I thought you were as appalled as we were. I should never wish to displease you, Your Grace."

He scoffed. "You don't know what pleases me or doesn't, and you don't think or care anything beyond bonnets and lace as far as I am able to surmise."

"That's not true," she said. "I speak five languages, play the piano, sing, and—"

"Yes, yes," he said. "You are most accomplished, Gwendolyn, in all of the feminine attributes that are deemed important, but I am concerned you have little sense. You are talking about my future wife, you know, and would-be mother to the next Duke of Thornfield. I shall not hear another word said against her."

His cousin Emma gasped. "One would think you were in love with her, given your passion."

"Do not be absurd," he snapped, leaning back in his chair. "I barely know her. How could one be in love with someone one barely knows? Besides, such a thing does not matter for me to defend the future duchess."

Immediately, both girls gave quick curtsies. "Do forgive us, Thornfield?" Gwendolyn said, her face as pale as her muslin gown. "It was not our intent to displease you. Of course, we shall welcome her with open arms and do everything that we can to increase her chances in society."

Oh, he'd just wager they would.

He wondered what machinations they'd engage in to make Georgiana feel at home, so to speak, all the while gossiping behind her back.

"You will leave her alone," he said firmly. "She is not to be bothered or played with, you two. She is not to be a mouse to your cat's paws."

Both girls looked positively indignant. "We would never do such a thing."

He fought the urge to snort. His cousins knew how to live by the rules of the *ton*, and women of society had few weapons but words. Men, too, truly.

And the fact was he was very worried that Georgiana Bly would not be able to keep up with them. She had a sharp wit and a quick mind, but she had not had to endure the cruel echelons of England's highest halls. It wasn't that she wasn't their equal in discourse. If anything, she was superior in knowledge. Yet, the *ton* was desperately unforgiving, and he hated the idea of seeing her open, honest face crushed under the weight of people like Gwendolyn and Emma.

The Doncaster sisters were but a sample of the cruelty that awaited his betrothed.

He would do all in his power to protect Georgiana, but he supposed he was going to have to see how she handled herself, too. He wouldn't always be at her side to help.

The clatter of carriage wheels over gravel suddenly filled the air.

Gwendolyn's dark green eyes sparkled. "They're here!"

"Indeed," Emma said, her ringlets bouncing. "We

shall show you, cousin, just how capable we are of welcoming your intended."

Welcoming indeed, he thought to himself. He wondered what that meant, but he was not going to pass judgment until he saw otherwise. He would have ways of dealing with his cousins, if necessary.

Aunt Agatha, as though she had been ignoring the entire affair—but Edward knew better—suddenly perked up by the fire. She placed her book down, stood, and crossed to the window, like a grand old ship setting sail. A smile turned her lips up. "She and her sister do seem to be a good deal more reasonable than the rest of her family."

He sighed. "Yes, if we could but have them and not the others, all would be relatively well."

Agatha's lips pursed. "Her mother was rather interesting. She is daughter of an earl and all that. I do wonder how she came to marry such a man."

He wondered, too. And what Mr. Bly must've been like in his youthful days to attract Georgiana's mother. For he did not seem the sort of man to attract such a worthy lady now.

Mr. Bly appeared terribly foolish. At least so far as Edward could see. But there was little point in lamenting his future father-in-law. He had to accept it, after all.

Edward drew himself up from his table, placed his quill down, and got himself ready to face his future wife and her sister.

He hoped Georgiana was ready for such a trial as staying in residence where she would soon be mistress. She seemed capable, thank God. But he did wonder if she would bear up in the end. She had made such a declaration of disliking gatherings, and a duchess, well, that was her position, to arrange gatherings, to arrange political meetings for him, to endure the endless banal banter of politicians at dinner.

Could she survive it? She seemed to enjoy political discourse, but that might change when forced to hear it again and again and again.

He hated the idea of having a wife that he would have to retire to the country. But if he had to keep her away from London for her to be happy, he would.

Georgiana and her sister Elizabeth entered the long salon, both of them dressed remarkably plain. They stood side by side, unintimidated by the wealth and pomp before them.

He liked them both for it.

But he did have to give credit to his cousins' words. The frocks the Bly sisters wore… Well, they looked little better than servants, really, and that did not bode well if they were to be seen about the halls. He wondered if they'd ever had a proper gown, a gown that matched his standards, in their entire lives?

How the devil had either of them ever been invited into his household for his ball? They seemed so out of place.

It wasn't that he was a snob. He believed in inviting anyone who was worthy of interest, but it wasn't often that people of such low financial status were invited into his home.

The gowns looked careworn.

He wondered if Georgiana's gown had been turned over once before. Such a thing for the future

Duchess of Thornfield was almost incomprehensible.

Aunt Agatha offered her hand to both of the girls. "Come, come," she said. "We have cakes and tea waiting for you. Luckily the journey was not too far."

Georgiana laughed. "We would have walked. It seems almost silly to have required a carriage, the weather being so fine."

"Walked?" Gwendolyn asked, her gaze swinging from Georgiana to Elizabeth, certain they were jesting. "Surely not."

"Of course," said Georgiana. "Five miles is little to concern us. Why, we can cover such ground in a little over an hour. Don't you own a good pair of boots?"

"Boots," Emma echoed. "Do young ladies own boots?"

Elizabeth's lips twitched. "Indeed they do make them in ladies' sizes."

Georgiana eyed the two young aristocrats as if she couldn't decide which was the more odd. "Don't you like to go walking in the country?"

Gwendolyn gave a little shudder. "No, I like to walk about the house."

Georgiana cocked her head to the side. "How very interesting. It is a beautiful house, so I suppose I can understand that. But the Yorkshire Dales are exceptionally exquisite. You should give them a try."

"But my dear," ventured Emma, "don't you find the mud to be rather difficult to get about in? The state of one's dress, you know."

Georgiana grinned. "I do not overly worry about the state of my dress, not when there are such beautiful sights to be seen."

She was a bold thing, Georgiana, and Edward could not help but admire it. He loved the Yorkshire Dales, as well. If he had his way, he would have spent most of his life out upon them. Perhaps that was one thing that they could share in common.

Thank God that there might be one thing, and a general dislike of company.

Perhaps it wouldn't be all terrible.

He would have to take her out for the fresh air and see if they could enjoy a bit of stomping over the heather.

Quite suddenly and inappropriately, he envisioned himself laying her back in the heather, the purple flowers blooming, their fragrance wafting around them, as he slipped his hands to the hem of her gown.

He'd slide that hem upward, skimming her stocking knees until at last, he'd bare her pale thighs. He'd take her mouth with his, the world would disappear, and he'd slip his fingers into—

"My dear boy, are you quite well?" Aunt Agatha burst into his thoughts.

Georgiana cocked her head to the side. "Yes. You're looking, well, as if you're gathering wool. Pleasant wool, but wool all the same. Are you thinking of anything particularly interesting?"

If he had thought her to be a bit more experienced, he would have wondered if she knew exactly what he was thinking.

But she did not. Of that he was certain.

He was damned glad Montrose was out riding, because that devil would have known and Edward never would have heard the end of it.

"Oh, just considering the accounts of next year's coal."

"Do you consider such things?" she asked, puzzled. "I would have thought you'd left that to your man of business."

Clearing his throat, he took up his quill and sat abruptly again before his desk. "I do not leave any details to any of my people of business. I supervise everything."

"Oh dear. That committed to detail, are you? I must confess, I am not overly fond of details."

"That will have to be remedied," he said, "given that you are going to be a duchess."

"Oh dear," she said again, "so much to be remedied about my person. We shall have to find something to remedy in you, as well, so that I do not receive *all* the benefits of a good education."

Everyone but Edward gasped.

It should have been horrifying, and perhaps it was for everyone else, but he could not stop a smile from tilting his lips.

He never smiled in company. It was a shocking thing, but he could not stop himself. "I concur," he replied evenly. "I shall have to endeavor to be edified."

"I'm glad you think so, Your Grace." She arched a positively wicked brow. "And we shall, therefore, improve together, as one would hope a married couple might."

CHAPTER TWELVE

Georgiana stared at herself in the mirror, adjusted her pale blue bodice, and then shrugged her shoulders. Her gown was three seasons out of date, but it allowed for a bit more freedom of movement than some new fashions did, which she quite liked.

Besides, it was best as one could do when one's yearly income likely was not even equal to the boot black expenditures of the duke.

And even if she had funds for an elegant frock, there was little she could do about her general appearance. Her hair always refused to stay in a tightly coiffed arrangement. Her nose was a trifle too pert and her lips were always wanting to slide into a grin. Curls did insist on tumbling out, and she had little height to boast about.

So, she gave herself one more nod of encouragement, turned on her slippered heel, and headed out of the chamber that was larger than all of the rooms on the entire top floor of her home combined.

It was a bit intimidating, that bed chamber, what with its giant four-poster bed, silk hangings, and ancient ornaments. She hoped to goodness it wouldn't be her room in the future, for she felt as if she were to speak a single word, her voice might be lost entire in the cavern.

And she did not have a small voice.

In fact, the fireplace alone was so vast she could have stood up in it.

And that four-poster monstrosity of a bed? She was certain that all of her sisters and herself could sleep in it and still not meet each other in the night.

One did not need such a large bed, did they?

What possible purpose could such a large bed serve except to proclaim one's importance?

She headed out into the slightly dark corridor, looked left then right, and considered. Which way? A keen sense of direction was not one of her finer points.

She could walk quite well in the countryside without any fear of losing her way. For the sky, trees, hills, and rivers were good indicators of which direction she should head, but the house? If one could call such an enormous building a *house*.

Yes, the house was a mystery to her.

Should she turn left toward the painting of that Restoration merry cad, Charles II? Or should she turn right toward the series of paintings depicting the Glorious Revolution?

She gave it little thought and decided the only way to throw herself was in the direction of the Glorious Revolution. After all, that had been the moment of England's great change, and change was always a good thing.

Well, not always, but she was doing her very best to have a positive view of dramatic sweeps of circumstance. For her life had changed entirely and would certainly change more.

She charged down the hall, determined not to be late for dinner. She didn't like to be late for things, even if she was forgetful.

According to the golden French clock upon the

mantel in her chamber, she had left several minutes early… In case she did lose her way. Despite the fact that she had studied the plans of the house, she had yet to go into several wings. The guest chambers were one such area, and the castle was an undeniable labyrinth.

Her slippers pattered lightly along the woven carpet. It was a beautiful runner. A burgundy and blue. She nearly tripped, studying its patterns, she admired them so much. To think one could have a carpet that was more beautiful than the entire floor of her own home.

It was a revelation, and she wondered if it was a good thing or a bad thing, but she supposed in the end, it didn't matter. It was a work of art, that carpet, and she couldn't find any fault with it. And art was always to be lauded. Besides, it made her heart positively glow.

She wondered about the hands that had made it in a far-off place and how it had come to England.

It was an adventure she could not dream of. Not really. Only her imagination could let her slip away and think of such a thing. All of her life, it had never been possible, the idea of traveling to far-off places or having journeys. She'd been content with her books out of necessity, and she was still content.

But there was no denying she was on an adventure now. Of course, it was not the sort that she might've imagined for herself. Taking on the role of duchess was an adventure that she did not desire, but it was an adventure, nonetheless.

After she took one flight of stairs downward, she reached the landing and was met with another decision. There was a corridor leading left, and a corridor leading right. She closed her eyes for a moment then chose the one that led to the left.

But after several moments of walking through many rooms that opened one to another, she was no closer to where she was supposed to be.

What a bother. Would she spend half her life as mistress here just learning her way around?

She needed to find someone, she supposed, and ask if she was even headed in the right direction, lest she wander until she turned into a forlorn skeleton.

Upon further thought, however, she doubted she'd ever be covered in dust here, let alone be left to become a skeleton. There wasn't a single speck of dust anywhere that she could see.

If she was very lucky, then, a servant with an ever ready feather duster would find her in due course.

She barged her way down through a pair of symmetrical doorways, until at last she found herself in a beautiful room with green brocade curtains. She hesitated; it had such a beautiful, masculine appeal that she found herself wishing to linger and bask among the cherry wood furniture. Pastels were nice enough, but there was something rapturous about the rich, bold colors surrounding her.

Her mouth opened ever so slightly as she peered at the towering paintings of men dressed in red, green, purple, and blue. Earrings dripped with jewels and pearls.

And she realized that they were all men from the time of Elizabeth I. A time when a powerful woman had ruled. And then, much to her horror, she turned to the right and realized she was in someone's bedroom. There stood a bed even larger than the one in her room. If she hadn't seen it with her own eyes, she wouldn't have believed it possible.

It looked as if an entire regiment of soldiers might be able to sleep in it.

Curtains draped the elaborately carved pillars. Birds danced in that wood, surrounded by beautifully engraved leaves and berries. It looked as if the carvings might suddenly come alive. And she wondered, if she were to lie in such a bed, if she might spend hours upon hours studying those things, could she imagine them springing into flight?

"You're in the wrong place again."

Sheer horror crashed through her at the sound of that voice. The dark, richness of it sent a simultaneous wave of undeniable pleasure through her.

She tensed and turned quickly.

"Your Grace," she forced herself to acknowledge before she gave a shaky curtsy. "I do seem to be making a habit of it, don't I?"

"Indeed you do," he growled, his voice in his chamber moodier, stronger. More provocative. He stood before her in his unlaced linen shirt, his dark breeches clinging to his powerful legs. "We shall have to remedy that."

"There's already so much to remedy," she quipped, "but your house is extremely large. And I do find myself getting lost in it."

"We shall have to give you a more detailed map," he drawled, eyeing her up and down.

"Perhaps a tour instead," she offered, before licking her lips, "would be more helpful."

His gaze immediately went to her lips, and

something changed in his stance, as if he was some-how, bigger, stronger than just a moment before. "I can give you a tour, but will you recall it?"

"I have a rather good memory," she said, "if you must know. For instance, I can remember our altercation word for word in your private study."

"Can you indeed?" he asked, his voice a low rumble.

"Yes. And where is Captain?" she asked, feeling as if she was standing naked before him. It should have been alarming. It was not. It felt…exhilarating.

Still, she didn't wish him thinking her a complete wanton. She had to distract them both—and not with a kiss.

The question of his dog did not deter him as he narrowed his gaze and took her in from the top of her head to the tips of her slippers. "Captain is down in the kitchen, having his dinner."

"Oh. I've been rather hoping to see him."

"Captain prefers the kitchens," he stated. "He doesn't like to have certain visitors in the house. My cousins."

"Oh yes," she said, latching onto that as a means to escape the strange, incomprehensible need suddenly coursing through her. "I can see how Captain might not care for them. They do seem a bit high-strung. I don't think they would probably like a dog like Captain, given the fact that they don't like to truck in the mud."

Thornfield stood silent for a long moment, then said, "You're rambling."

"Am I?" she asked. "One cannot help their family, can one?"

"No," he agreed. "One cannot." He peered at her, as if trying to make sense of her quick speech. "Are you nervous?"

"I beg your pardon?" she laughed. "Well, I am not accustomed to being in a gentleman's chambers. This is your chamber, is it not?"

"It is indeed. I'm glad to hear you aren't in the habit of wandering into a gentleman's chambers."

"Of course not," she said curtly, offended that he wasn't sure of her character before she'd said it.

"Forgive me, Miss Bly." His dark gaze seemed to cut through any defense she might have made, but there was no accusation there. No, there was curiosity…and hunger. "But with you, one can never tell. So, I shall refrain from assumptions."

"I do apologize." She smiled, determined not to let him see how much she was flustered by his semi-clad body. Goodness, the way his linen shirt skimmed his muscled form truly was a sight to behold. "It was not my intent at all. I was simply looking for the dining room and heretofore, I have never been to the wings which hold the bed chambers. And, well, you see, I followed the Glorious Revolution, went down the stairs, made a turn to the left, went through this hallway and—"

"You found my room."

She nodded, opting to remain mute now lest she *truly* begin to ramble.

He took a step forward. "In many old houses, hallways are not halls at all, but rather the rooms connected."

"Yes," she laughed, winding her hands together before her. "I suppose I did know this. I have been in one or two rather large houses before."

"Have you?" he asked simply, taking another step toward her.

She cleared her throat. "Oh yes. You see, I've been to Chatsworth."

"Have you?" he repeated. Another step across the grand chamber.

"Yes." She swallowed, tempted to turn and leave. After all, she'd never been alone with a man in his bedchamber. And, frankly, Thornfield was no unprepossessing fellow. His very presence made her feel alive in a way she could scarce fathom. But she'd never been a coward and she wasn't about to become one now. "It is a marvelous house. I have been to Hampton Court, too."

"Mmmm," he all but purred, a remarkable sound coming from him. "Tell me about your experience."

"You see, I got particularly lucky," she began, finding she was utterly fixed by his gaze and unable to move from the spot as he closed the distance between them ever so slowly. "One of Mama's friends gave me a tour, which was quite kind, because I'm most interested in Henry Tudor."

"Are you?"

"Yes. He was a terrible, terrible fellow, you know."

His lips twitched ever slightly as he stopped just before her, the tips of his boots nearly skimming the hem of her gown. "Was he?"

"Well, yes," she said firmly... Or at least she intended to. Her words came out devilishly breathy. "If only some of his people had had the courage to tell him what a dunce he was being."

Suddenly, the Duke of Thornfield laughed, a rough, deep, rich sound that was so full of amusement the whole room seemed to shake with it. "Do you think you would have had the courage to tell Henry the Eighth what a dunce he was being?"

"Well, I don't know," she said, amazed at the way his laugh had rolled over her, awakening her body like the sun to the earth in early morning. "It's difficult to say how much courage one might have in such circumstances, but they would have saved the country a great deal of trouble."

He smiled down at her then, his eyes glowing. "If only you had the handle of this country, Miss Bly," he said, "then we would have no trouble at all."

"You're making fun of me," she accused lightly, rapt by his nearness.

"Oh, no," he returned as his broad chest expanded in a breath. "I truly wish the rule of this land was as simple as what you imply."

"But it is not simple, of course."

"No, and I think you know that already."

She nodded, but then burst out, "But I often do wish."

"If wishes were horses," he cut in.

"Beggars would ride," she agreed softly. "It is the country that we do live in, is it not? That beggars do not ride?"

"Are you going to take up the point of the poor?" he asked, lifting his hand to her cheek. As he twined a lock of her hair about his finger, he rumbled, "I shall not mind if you do."

Her lungs would not obey her. She could scarce draw breath as he caressed her errant locks. "You cannot fool me, Your Grace," she finally managed. "I've discovered that you take up the case of the poor quite often in the House of Lords."

He tensed, pausing his movement. "You've been investigating me."

"One should know as much as possible about their future husband, don't you think?"

"Some might argue it's best to know as little as possible," he returned quietly, "and then one won't be disappointed."

"I cannot believe you mean it. Or if you do, tell me at once," she said, feeling strangely drawn to him. He was so close. If she but leaned a few inches forward, they would touch, head to toe.

"For if that is how you feel," she breathed. "I shall run from England, you know. I'm sure I could survive in Naples if I had to."

He stared down at her from his considerable height, then laughed again. "How do you do that?" he asked. "You are such a surprise."

"I hope a good one," she replied as she tilted her head back to hold his gaze.

"You're novel. I shan't ever be bored."

She laughed then, despite her nerves at his strong, broad body within reach of her own. "I don't like to be bored either."

"Then we are of accord on more than one thing," he said, letting his fingers trail to her cheek.

Her heart slammed in her chest. No one had ever touched her thus. "A good thing, I suppose, for a marriage."

"Yes," he whispered, his thumb dragging lightly along her jaw. "And," he began.

"Yes?"

His gaze heated. "Our kisses…"

"Are quite nice."

"You liked them, did you?" His hot, dark eyes turned to her mouth, focusing upon it as if it were the most important thing in the world in that moment.

"Oh yes," she rushed, "but I don't like the fact…"

"Come now. You're always so bold, Miss Bly. Tell me," he urged.

She squared her shoulders, which only brought their bodies closer together. He noticed, his gaze flickering down then back up, but didn't shirk as he urged again, "Tell me what you don't like and I shall never do it again. A wife should be able to tell a husband what does and does not pleasure her."

His words caused her knees to wobble. Pleasure? How much pleasure could one woman take? Even so, she did as urged, and said bluntly, "That you use kisses to, well, bully me about."

"I," he rasped, shocked, "bully you?"

"Indeed," she said, fortified now that she had begun and at how he was listening to her.

"You do not seem to be the sort of person who can be bullied."

"No, I cannot," she said, relieved he had decided such a thing about her. "But that doesn't mean you don't attempt to bully."

"It is not my intention to bully," he stated. "It is simply my demeanor."

"That is not an excuse," she said. It was imperative she teach him to be kinder, to be a better man, even if he was already a capable one. "Just because it is your demeanor does not mean that bullying is not the result."

He stared at her for a long time, his palm now cupping her cheek ever so gently.

"I see your point," he said. "I don't know if I can take it, but I understand it."

She did not pull back, but neither did she yield. In fact, compelled by some strong force, she placed her hand gently on his arm. "I think you should take it, and I think you should attempt to do something about it. I don't really think you wish to bully people, but that doesn't mean you don't."

His gaze wandered over her face before he gave a single, subtle nod. "So, if I take your point and suggest that I kiss you again, would you care for it?"

"Since we haven't tried it before, how can I possibly know the result?"

"Well, since you approve of research," he stated, "I'm happy to oblige."

"Oh yes," she said, "research is of great import to me. I do think that consideration is the best way to discover one's true feeling on a subject."

"I like to consider you," he said, lowering his head ever so slightly.

"You do?" she asked, astonished.

"Oh yes. You are a most interesting young woman."

"Am I? Most people don't seem to think so."

"Most people are idiots," he drawled.

She laughed wholeheartedly at that. "I cannot disagree."

"Good," he rumbled. "Another thing we are in

accord of. Perhaps we shall not do so very badly after all."

"Perhaps," she said.

"But you're not sure?"

"How can I be?" she said, tilting her face into his palm. "More research is required."

CHAPTER THIRTEEN

Edward slid his hand to Georgiana's waist, pulling her to him.

Bloody hell, this was what he wanted from the moment she had stumbled so innocently into his chambers. He did not believe in fate. But if he had… This was what it would have felt like. Of that he was certain.

Driven by a need so strong, he scarce could countenance it, he slid his fingers into the soft curls at the nape of her neck. Stunned that he was so consumed by her, he tilted her head back, and took her mouth in a hungry kiss.

Damnation, he'd been thinking of this for days. This was the price of his future and it was worth it.

He knew it in his very core.

Even though she was not the duchess he required, this passion between them would make up for everything. It had to.

Somehow, he knew it would.

The very thought defied all reason.

It defied everything he knew to be right and good. But there was no denying that the kiss between them burned like the sweetest fire, like hot whiskey lit by a blue flame.

He wanted to kiss her forever, and she seemed to wish the same thing.

She moaned softly against him as she swayed into his body. He adored the feel of her skirts caressing his legs.

He wished to strip her naked right then and there, but knew he could not, for people were expecting them downstairs. A part of him was unaccustomed to roared for him to not give a damn and tear the clothes from her body now so he might discover her.

He let his hands roam over her back, pulling her harder, closer to his body. He savored the soft curves of her and he caressed the crease of her lips with a light touch of his tongue.

Her mouth opened ever so slightly in surprise, and he let his tongue slip between her lips. She gasped, the hot, sweet taste of her almost more than he could bear.

He pulled back and looked down at her. "Marry me," he ground out, feeling on the edge of control.

"I am going to marry you," she said breathlessly. "Remember? I have no choice, nor have you."

"Marry me now," he growled. He had to have her. He had to keep her in his arms. To know that this wild need for her could be made sense of.

She blinked. "I beg your pardon?"

"Marry me immediately," he repeated, holding her fast. "I don't wish to wait, Georgiana. I want us to be married. I want to have you."

"Surely, that would cause a great scandal," she whispered, her eyes wide not with dismay but with curiosity and desire.

"We can marry in secret now and then have a large wedding later as expected," he said quickly, convincing himself as well as his future bride. "One that will be the wedding everyone speaks of and knows of."

"Could we?" she asked. "Have such a thing to ourselves?"

A slow smile tilted his lips at her logic. A logic he liked well. "We can go to the little chapel on my land this evening, be married, and then we can…"

"Do more research?" she replied before she nipped her lower lip with barely contained anticipation.

"Yes," he said. "Then we can do whatever we like."

"You and I can never do whatever we like," she countered. "But I would like…"

"Yes?" he asked, a moment of tension holding him in its grasp.

"To feel more of this," she said as she slid her arms up his shoulders.

"Then marry me tonight," he said. "This is what we both want from each other, and there is no need to delay."

Indecision darkened her face. "Is this all that we wish from each other?"

"I do not know," he said honestly. "But for a husband and wife, it is a welcome place to begin. Be with me, Georgiana."

"I suppose I should be glad that I needn't fear you suddenly changing your mind."

"I'm not that kind of man, Georgiana," he assured. "I shan't ever change my mind. You are mine, and you will always be mine, as my wife." He stroked a lock of hair back from her cheek. "Say yes."

She eyed him carefully then. "But what if…"

"Yes?" he asked, studying her, wishing he knew the words that would allay her fears.

"Do you truly wish this?"

He gazed down at her, unwilling to lie. "I truly wish to kiss you," he said. "I truly wish to have you in my bed. And I truly admire you, even though I barely know you."

"That is a diplomatic answer."

He gazed into her intelligent eyes, eyes that wouldn't be fooled with false platitudes. "It is the best I can do because it is the truth."

"Then yes," she said. "I will marry you."

"Tonight?" he queried, hardly believing that he, the Duke of Thornfield was about to do something so rash.

"Tonight," she agreed firmly. "Whatever shall I tell my sister?"

"Surely, you're clever enough to think of something. It's not as if the two of you are sharing a room."

"We have shared a room since we were children."

"Not anymore," he said, holding her in his embrace. "Tonight you'll be sharing mine."

• • •

Edward wasted no time.

He dashed off a quick note to the bishop, who lived not but four miles away. He gave it to a footman and told him to take it posthaste. And, as he did so, he led Georgiana down to dinner.

The two of them entered the long dining room together.

He'd finished dressing without calling his manservant and she had watched transfixed as he'd donned his layers of clothing and tied his starched cravat.

It had amused him, that distinct fascination…
And it had made him think of when he would be
removing her clothing from her body in but a few
hours' time.

With his assistance, she had carefully righted her
frock and she had done her best with her wild locks.
The fact that they were both perfectly presentable
did not stop the curious stares of her sister, his aunt,
his cousins, and his good friend, Montrose.

Oh, why did he have to have guests right at this
particular moment?

Why had he thought it a good idea to invite his
cousins? Of course, he could not have known he
would be suddenly foisted into matrimony. He certainly wouldn't have believed that he'd now be
counting the minutes until the blasted ceremony
could take place.

The truth was he wished to have Georgiana entirely to himself.

She was such a strange, strange person. He found
himself longing to make study of her, to discover her
likes and dislikes, and to see what sort of young
woman she was, aside from what he knew about her
already, which was to say very little.

Of one thing he was certain. Georgiana Bly
evoked a deep passion and excitement in him no
one else had ever stoked before.

Wordlessly, for he never bothered with explana-
tions, he led her to the seat next to Aunt Agatha.
As his future duchess, she took the third most important position in the room, and he was happy to
have her close to him. Soon, only he would take

precedence over her.

But tonight, his aunt still held court at the opposite end of the semi-formal dining room.

Georgiana sat next to him across from the Earl of Montrose.

Her sister, Elizabeth, seemed to be holding her own next to Montrose, which was something that quite pleased Edward.

He wanted Georgiana to be supported by her sister. And given the nimble ability of Miss Elizabeth, he felt certain she would have it.

His cousins scowled at each other, shocked to be so out-played by someone so, in their opinion, beneath them.

The Earl of Montrose smiled, his eyes positively winking in the candlelight as he eyed Elizabeth. And Montrose gave Georgiana a curious stare.

"Your cheeks are most flushed, Miss Bly," the earl observed. "Is the room too warm for your liking?"

Georgiana's shoulders went back a little bit, but she met the earl's gaze easily. "Oh, no. Not at all," she replied without pause. "I just find myself to be in particularly good spirits."

At that, Edward found himself even more pleased. It had been on the tip of his tongue to rescue her from any potential embarrassment. After all, he knew exactly what Montrose was intimating. But Georgiana had not been put out of sorts in the slightest.

"Och, I'm glad to hear you're in such good spirits," Montrose enthused. "Thornfield here does'na always put people into a good mood."

"Indeed?" Georgiana queried as the servants began to do a silent, smooth dance of serving the first course. "I find him to be most pleasurable."

"You find him pleasurable, eh?" Montrose said.

"Indeed, I do," Georgiana replied, taking up her spoon. "He is a most intriguing fellow, and clearly believes strongly in certain things."

"Well, that's true enough," Montrose drawled as he sipped ruby wine from a crystal glass. "But isn't that true of everyone?"

Edward watched silently, curious as to how the two might get on.

"I think it's particularly true of the Duke of Thornfield," Georgiana affirmed. "He has a passion that cannot be denied."

Edward almost smiled, something that he was rarely given to do but had been more inclined to do so of late, with Georgiana around. He liked his future wife and such a declaration.

She saw him as passionate, did she?

She was perhaps the only person who did in the entirety of the realm.

It was a new way of thinking about himself, and a way that he discovered he liked. Very much indeed.

CHAPTER FOURTEEN

The Duke of Thornfield was a mystery to her.

At one moment, he was cold and distant, the next, passionate as any flame. Now, here at dinner, again, he was controlled, completely in his element, and everyone paid court to him.

Even his rather interesting friend, the Earl of Montrose, paid Thornfield his due.

She was very tempted to tease her future husband, to see how he might react, but such a thing would not be kind. There seemed to be something about him that just did not, in company, handle such oddity.

He was so used to being deferred to that anyone who might tease him, she suspected, simply did not. It also seemed to her, he was not given to the nuances of siblings and such banter.

Her sister, on the other hand, was having a most marvelous time discussing life at sea with the Earl of Montrose.

The Scottish man's wild mane had been tamed somewhat about his rugged face, which was a deep bronze, likely from hours on his ship.

Georgiana listened, agog at the very idea.

How exciting it must be to go on adventures as he did.

Likely, she would never do such things. Still, she'd have more adventure as the Duchess of Thornfield than as a girl in a library.

"You look suddenly perplexed, my dear. Is something wrong with the soup?" the duke's aunt asked.

"No, no," Georgiana said. "The soup is most delicious. I've never had such a delightful concoction. The lobster is truly wonderful."

"I'm so glad you think so," Lady Strathmore replied. "Some people do not like seafood."

Georgiana wished to say some people were silly, but she didn't wish to be rude. Even if, for all intents and purposes, it was something Thornfield had said earlier that evening.

Unlike some, she was generally excited to try new things. There was such little chance for it in her own home. They were not given to luxuries from far away or food made with such skill. She and Elizabeth had often had to do with potato soup or various broths that were within the reach of their cook's limited capacity.

It suddenly occurred to her she would be dining on fine and elegant food for the rest of her life. She looked over at her betrothed, who was glorious to behold. She wondered if he ate sweets at all. His body was so defined and so strong that she somehow could not envision him eating even one crumb of cake.

But then she thought of his mouth roving over hers, and, once again, she felt her cheeks flare.

Montrose's lips quirked in a smile. "There it is again. We must ensure you do not get too close to the fire, Miss Bly. You are perfectly pink-cheeked."

"Well, this house does seem to be a trifle warm," she said without thinking. "I am not accustomed to so many fires."

"My dear, my dear, it is almost the height of summer," said Lady Strathmore. "We barely have fires in this house at all at present. And in the winters, the fires barely warm the rooms. You shall be quite cold, I do warn you."

"Indeed?" Elizabeth asked between sips of soup. "It is such a fine house, one would have thought that it would be warm."

"It is a castle," said the duke's aunt with a smile, "and castles, no matter how fine, are frigid. One cannot heat stone easily, you know, so we all huddle about the fires wrapped in rugs and drinking hot tea or negus."

"It's true," Thornfield agreed. "It is a beautiful old place, but one does freeze."

"A bunch of weaklings, the lot of you," declared the Earl of Montrose. "Come and spend a winter upon ship on the Atlantic, and then we may talk about freezing."

"You do that to yourself on purpose," said Thornfield, without mercy.

"And you live in this castle on purpose," Montrose countered.

"Of course I do. It is mine, and therefore I must live in it."

"And my ship is mine."

"But you did not inherit it. This splendid old pile came to me," the duke said, "and I have no choice but to live in it."

"Ah," Montrose *tsk*ed. "We all have a choice, which is why I do not spend winters in Scotland."

"Do you dislike Scotland?" Georgiana asked, curious, for she'd never been to that northern country, and she found herself most curious about it.

"I adore it," he said, but his face grew serious. After a long, thought-filled moment, Montrose continued. "Much trouble has come to that place over the years, but it is a land of such beauty that one's heart might weep."

"That is very poetic," Elizabeth said. "Is it truly so beautiful?"

"I cannot put into words the beauty of it," Montrose said, turning to Elizabeth, "but I often find that I can no longer bear the ache of a country so destroyed by a war which—"

"No politics now," Thornfield said. "Montrose, we don't wish to become truly glum this evening. The ladies surely don't wish to hear—"

"The ladies," Georgiana cut in, "are most curious. After all, I've read a good deal about Bonnie Prince Charlie."

"Oh, dear," Thornfield said. "Romantic drivel, no doubt."

Montrose laughed. "It is true. A great deal of things written about Bonnie Prince Charlie really are a fiction, you know."

"Well, I am most amazed at the Highlanders," Elizabeth said. "If it is true that Bonnie Prince Charlie is but a fiction. I cannot imagine all the tales are false."

"The bravery that they showed?" Montrose hesitated then said, "They were very brave, and they paid dearly for it, that bravery."

"I've read about the clearances, as well," Georgiana said gently.

Montrose put his silver spoon down carefully.

"Yes. The lords of that land have been quite hard on the people there."

Thornfield grew silent as well, and Georgiana wondered if she'd hit some particularly sore spot. "I am so sorry. Have I been rude?"

"No," Montrose said, even as his voice grew thick with feeling, "but my land is one torn by war, and I am not an Englishman. I'm a Scotsman. But my allegiance, of course, is to the English king, so it becomes a bit challenging, dancing this particular dance."

"Which is why you spend so much time in the Americas with the newfound colonies," said the duke.

"They're not colonies," Georgiana said. "They're a country, the United States of America."

"Do be careful," Thornfield warned his friend. "Miss Bly is far too interested in revolution."

The Earl of Montrose's brows rose. "Och, a burgeoning revolutionary in the home of the Duke of Thornfield. This shall cause quite a stir at court."

Thornfield all but grumbled, "She is *not* a revolutionary. Duchesses of Thornfield aren't."

Lady Strathmore smiled knowingly and lifted her glass, "Well, my dear boy, you know duchesses are allowed to espouse some shocking ideas. Your great-grandmother, for instance…"

"Aunt Agatha, I don't wish to discuss it." There was a surprising note of plea in his voice.

"I do!" Georgiana leaned forward. "Do tell us about his great-grandmother."

"Well"—his aunt waggled her brows and began— "his great-grandmother was in the court of Anne the

First, and Anne was quite a difficult monarch, as you may have read."

"Oh, I have," Georgiana said. "Many, many troubles."

"It's all true. Now, Thornfield's great-grandmother was not overly fond of the Stuarts. It didn't matter if it was a Stuart daughter or a Stuart king. And so she made it quite known that she was eager for a change. While many agreed with her, one was not supposed to say it bluntly. When the time came, she was most happy to support the Hanoverians. As a matter of fact, she had no problem with the idea of Germans coming over. She learned to speak German herself. It was quite shocking, you know, an English duchess speaking German all of the time, in the hopes of pleasing the new king."

"That is most intriguing," said Georgiana, amazed at the influence and opinion a woman might have in a position of power. "Who would have thought it? The English are usually so very... *English*."

Montrose laughed. "You're English, you know."

"Indeed I am," Georgiana said quickly, "but I do like to look at our history. When I think of how Shakespeare talks about England, as if it is some hallowed heaven..."

"Do you not think it some hallowed heaven?" Montrose asked.

"Of course I do," she said, "but one must realize there's always room for improvement."

"Well said," the Duke of Thornfield replied.

They all turned to him, amazed. Georgiana most of all. Had she just garnered a public compliment from the Duke of Frost himself?

Lady Emma suddenly piped up. "There cannot possibly be room for improvement in England. It is the greatest country in all of the world. We are the greatest beacon of hope for all to see, and one cannot imagine a better place. Why, all the countries of the world are absolutely lucky to have our influence in them."

Georgiana turned to her future cousin slowly. "I'm sure you feel that is correct, but one cannot imagine we are correct all of the time."

"A good deal of the time," Thornfield said tersely. "But yes, you're right, Miss Bly. We're not correct all of the time. No one can be. Not even England."

Emma gasped. "Say not so, Thornfield. Don't you believe the doctrine that it is our duty, as English people, to ensure that our way of life is passed about the—"

"Look what's happened in the United States of America," the duke cut in sharply. "As my future wife points out, they have formed a new country without interest in our influence. I do think that perhaps one day India shall do the same, as will Canada, Australia, and Ireland."

Both Emma and Gwendolyn stared about as if they had all gone positively mad.

Montrose's eyes twinkled.

Elizabeth drank her wine, but still her face radiated with mirth.

Georgiana looked at Thornfield, her heart swelling with admiration. "You, sir, are all but preaching rebellion." She *tsk*ed playfully. "The Duke of Thornfield suggesting that one day the empire might not be so, well, empirical?"

"Oh, there'll always be an England, and England shall be free," he said. "I cannot doubt that in the slightest. England shall always be a proud island nation amidst the shining silvery seas, but one cannot imagine, the way this world is changing so quickly, that all things will remain as they are. We cannot even begin to imagine how they will be…"

Thornfield gazed upward to the celestial mural painted upon his ceiling. "Perhaps one day people shall even take to the skies."

His aunt gaped at him as if he was someone else entirely.

Georgiana beamed. "What a marvelous thought," she said. "da Vinci certainly thought that such a thing was possible."

Thornfield smiled slowly. "There are several scientists today who think such things are possible, that a man might take to the air."

"No," Georgiana said in shock. "Scientists, truly?"

"Oh yes," Thornfield said, taking up his wine. "I've met with a few of them. None of them have been able to make their ideas work as of yet, but it is a most intriguing principle, flight."

"Flight," Georgiana repeated, her eyes nearly misting at the idea that seemed like magic, and yet was being spoken of as if it would surely one day happen.

"Like a bird?" Elizabeth queried.

"I don't think it will be exactly like a bird," Thornfield replied. "We'll not be Icarus headed toward the sun, but who knows what it will be like? Perhaps one day we shall be amongst the clouds."

Georgiana smiled at her future husband then, and she felt a warmth toward him she'd never felt before. She'd been so certain she didn't like him. But when he spoke like that, he spoke as a man who was amazed by the wonders of a beautiful, promising world, and that?

That she liked a good deal.

CHAPTER FIFTEEN

Georgiana was not generally given to impulse.

A promise in the moment of passion was not something that she was accustomed to, for she was not used to passion at all. He was the one who knew about such things.

But he also did not seem to be a man who was given to impulsive behavior.

Both of them were leaping into the unknown... together.

And it felt right.

So very, very right.

As they crossed the dark grass in the moonlight, she wondered how the devil it had happened.

Tonight, they'd met at the foot of the servants' stairs at the back courtyard.

Captain was at his master's feet.

It was good to see the lovely dog again, who was the embodiment of sheer happiness. He'd greeted her with a wide doggy grin and a wave of his tail. They'd all gone off in merriment and...in shock.

If she looked anything like he did, she looked as if she'd been brained.

And yet it was wonderful.

It was all a complete daze.

Had she really agreed to this madness?

She had!

And she could scarcely believe that *he* had conceived of it!

The wildness of his kiss today had only flamed the embers of their first passion. And since she'd known they were to be wed in any case, she was more than happy to give in to the encompassing blaze.

They hurried to the small chapel tucked into the oak forest on his estate. The winding path was beautiful, lined with flowers that were now sleeping underneath the moon's silver rays.

Determined, hands entwined, silent, they walked up to the arched nave entrance. The vicar stood in his black and white robes by the doorway. For one brief moment, she felt as if she was in some ancient fairy tale where a young girl was running away with her lover to be married by moonlight.

It was a marvelous, adventurous moment of her life.

As she looked at the Duke of Thornfield's hand holding hers, her heart swelled.

He might be intimidating, arrogant, strange…but he was also beautiful and full of a vision for the future that few would ever have.

The Duke of Thornfield, for all his superiority, was full of wonder. And she felt certain there was more wonder within him to be discovered. He was a man that had more to him than he let other people see, and she was going to discover those depths.

What if… What if she might find love in her marriage, after all?

She doubted she could experience such passion with someone that she could not love, could she?

As they quietly whisked into the nave and headed down to the altar of the small chapel, her heart danced. She'd never planned on a marriage like this. She'd never planned on a marriage to a duke.

Truthfully, she'd not planned on marriage at all. Not once it had become clear that she preferred books to bonnets. But tonight she was going to embrace a side of herself she'd never dared to even believe could exist.

• • •

Edward Thornfield did not do clandestine affairs.

He did not do secret liaisons.

Hiding in the shadows was not for him.

But this, *this* was something he wanted more than anything.

He was married. *They* were married.

With a few short words, in a small church, in but a breadth of time, he'd changed from a bachelor to a husband.

Edward was not given to romantic flights of fancy, but it had been the ideal wedding for him. Calm, quiet, and nothing to take his riveted attention away from the woman he desired with an unyielding hunger.

He'd not had to worry about shouting crowds or the stares of hundreds of peers as they said their vows before a bishop. He'd not had to keep a tight control of himself as a cacophony rang around him.

No, he'd simply been able to say *I do*.

The marriage at Westminster Cathedral would still have to occur, of course. Georgiana had to be shown as someone who would be accepted by all of society, and a marriage at a great cathedral would do that. It would put the stamp of approval of his and all his family upon her.

But that intimate affair before a plain man of God, not some prince of the church, that had been for them.

It was the marriage they required. It was true that love wasn't important in a *ton* marriage. But the way he desired her was something that he could scarcely understand.

It wasn't reason. It wasn't logic. It wasn't controlled.

He was compelled. . .

He could not wait weeks for her to be his.

Hell, he could not wait days.

Anytime she was in his presence, he wished to consume her and to be consumed.

To be consumed… It seemed mad.

He'd never wished to be swallowed up whole or enveloped by anyone before. It didn't sound like a duke, but it was what he hungered for. She made him feel completely shaken, and he knew that he made her feel the same.

He was not what she would have chosen, either, he understood that now, but their bodies, their minds had been struck by a chord that insisted they meet and merge and meld and he would not pause.

As they headed back across the green toward Thornfield Castle, he swept her up into his arms, carrying her through the Yorkshire night as if they were secret lovers in some novel.

He loved novels.

He loved plays.

He loved the myths of old.

In most of them, love affairs ended in tragedy. But he would not think that far ahead. No, for tonight was to be a night of bliss, and that was all that mattered. He would not dare look ahead.

Quickly, he took her through the back courtyard, cradled against him as if she weighed nothing at all. He gazed down upon her and could not resist his smile. In her presence, he felt at ease and vulnerable.

It was strange. Most people he could not bear to spend much time around them. But Georgiana made him feel less a tumble. Indeed, she made him feel as if his world had gone still and pure and hot at once.

So as he strode up the servants' corridor, down the vast hall that led to his rooms, he did not allow his pace to slow. He did not care if anyone saw, but he also knew no one would. Not at this hour of the night, not on his floor. For on his floor, few servants were allowed to come, because he liked the silence so well. And they were only allowed at certain times.

For once, his idiosyncrasy would serve him, instead him serving it.

He nudged his chamber door open with his boot and took her across the threshold as if she were a young bride coming into a crofter's house. Easily, he shut the door behind them, then gently, he set her down, sliding her body along his.

She tilted her head back, catching his gaze. "Husband," she said.

"Wife," he said back, his voice rough with desire.

"This is so strange. How has this happened?"

"Because this is what we both wish," he replied, feeling completely captivated by her.

He wound his hand about her small one and led her across his chamber toward the banked fire.

He wished to look at her in the amber glow. It would show her to perfection.

She was already strangely perfect to him.

She was unique. She was plain. She was…herself without apology.

The strong lines of her face gave him assurance that all possibly could be well in this world, because she was determined that they would be. He felt it in the deepest parts of his heart. Georgiana was a rock.

And so was he.

The danger, of course, was that they might crash against each other and shatter. Surely, one of them needed to be water for this to survive, someone giving in to the other.

But he would not, once again, think that far ahead.

No.

They could both be strong together, and like two pieces of flint they would strike each other and produce sparks, sparks that would leap into flame and fire and all would be well.

And that was what mattered.

Gently, he stroked his fingertips along her cheek, savoring the silence, savoring the coolness of the room and hearing only her breathing and the crackle of the logs in the fireplace.

He drew in a slow, steady breath.

"Are you well?" she asked.

He nearly laughed. She was a young bride asking him if he was well upon their first night together.

"I am indeed. Are you?"

"Yes," she said, "only you seem different."

"Do I?" he queried as he slid her to the floor.

"Yes, you do, Your Grace."

"You must call me Thornfield."

"Might I call you Edward?" she asked with a quirk of a smile. "I know people of your standing use titles in intimacy, but it seems so odd."

"You may call me Edward," he said before he considered the strangeness of barely ever using his given name. "For that is who I am. I don't really like to be called by my title. It seems so…"

"Thorny?" she said playfully.

"Yes," he said, pulling her toward him in a great embrace that turned warm and soft.

"Aren't you thorny?" she asked, as her hands pressed against his back. "You do seem to try to make everyone believe so."

He shook his head. "I cannot explain why I act so. I have always done. My parents tried to assist me, but it seems to be my nature. But with you, the world seems to still a bit, and I can focus on you, on the lines of your face, the light of your eyes, the tilt of your mouth, and the way you defy convention. It makes everything go away."

"Everything?" Her eyes narrowed as she clearly tried to understand.

"Yes," he said. He closed his eyes for a moment, trying to describe how he felt so often. "You help the rattle of this world, the buzz of it all, the shaking of it…dim."

Her brow furrowed, and he wondered if he had said too much.

"I am glad."

"You and I, Georgiana, we are who we are without alteration and without artifice."

And he wondered how long that could remain. But he would enjoy it and keep it as long as he could.

CHAPTER SIXTEEN

If anyone had asked Georgiana but a fortnight ago if she would be a spinster or no in less than a month's time, she would have guffawed in their face…after she rolled her eyes rather hard at such an asinine question.

Of course, she'd be a spinster. From the night of her first card party she'd known that the general life of a married lady was not for her. But now, not only was she not a spinster, she was a young wife swept up by connubial enticement and conjugal vows.

No bloodless, dry marriage for her.

Edward, even if he seemed in complete control, gazing down at the world with judgment, was a man who held an inferno of desire at his very core. Much to her surprise, it burned for her.

"Are you afraid?" he asked softly, tipping her chin back with his thumb and forefinger.

It was a kind question, but fear had never been an emotion she'd given much sway. Fear, in her opinion, caused a good deal of trouble, for it made people act in the most terrible of ways.

His touch stirred such powerful feelings inside her, but fear most certainly wasn't one of them. "Should I be?"

"Some young ladies are, as I understand." He eased down beside her, stretching out his long legs. It was a languid unfolding of limbs and a captivating display of masculinity. "Shouldn't like you to run screaming into the next room because I had not had this conversation with you."

She gave him a look of mock horror. "That you think me even capable of such vapors is an insult."

He blinked rapidly, then a hesitant smile curved his sensual mouth. "Forgive me. I should have known you would not be easily overborn."

"I have read of it. I am no stranger to anatomy books and novels, as you know."

His eyebrows rose ever so slightly. "You are an excellent theorist, then."

She considered this. "Excellent is too strong a word, but I am not ignorant."

His gaze fell to her lips, the look of a man who had not eaten for days spotting his favorite dish. "Then shall we put theory to practice?"

She rather liked the way he used reading and study to ease her into this, for if she was honest, she was *nervous*. Only a foolish person wouldn't be, and foolish she was not.

He was not a small person, and while she found the way he dominated a room with his remarkable physical power most fascinating. She was a tiny bit daunted that they were about to… Well, no matter how much she wanted him, it did give one pause.

Georgiana drew in a calming breath. She wasn't a ninny and she wasn't about to begin acting like one. The action drew his gaze to her bosom. Oh so slowly, he lifted his large palm and skimmed the slightly calloused tips of his fingers over her breasts.

She gasped at the subtle onslaught. No one had ever touched her so boldly and gently at once.

"Tilt your head to the side for me," he urged, his

voice delicious.

Bracing her hands on the soft woven rug beneath her, she made herself comfortable, leaning back, and did as he bid. She had no idea what he intended and gazed at him through slitted eyelids. Wary, but desperately curious for this awakening.

Something in his face changed, then. The usual sharp intelligence warmed with hunger and he lowered his head, kissing the curve of her neck. His lemon, leather, and cinnamon scent surrounded her. She drank it in, delighting in the masculine freshness of it. She felt surrounded by him, and the kiss…

It never would have occurred to her that the brush of his lips over the place where her neck met her shoulder might be so enticing, but the pleasure of it raced through her blood straight to the rather fascinating place between her thighs.

As he trailed open-mouthed kisses with agonizing slowness down to her clavicles, her world spun. She'd expected him to kiss her as he had done before. On her lips.

Not here.

He lingered over her breasts, gazing at them with an admiration she'd never seen in a man before. Then he lowered his head, skimming his mouth over them.

Her elbows trembled a bit and she found herself tempted to lay all the way back before the ruby glow of the fire.

Edward swept her up into his arms, and with utter ease bore her to his bed, the great bed that was the largest she'd ever seen. Gently, he placed her down onto the soft counterpane. He stilled in his ministrations and gazed at her. "Follow your instinct, Georgiana. And I will follow your desire."

She swallowed.

What the blazes did that mean?

Given her vast inexperience, she really couldn't know, and oh how she longed to know. So, she followed his suggestion and paid heed to her inner voice.

The silky fabric beneath her felt cool against her back as she settled down. The soft goose down embraced her as she allowed herself to trust him… and more importantly, herself.

And she did trust both of them implicitly in this.

Edward easily slipped free the hidden ties at the front of her bodice and then slid her gown over her shoulders, and shimmied it down her legs.

She made no comment about the ease in which he did it. In fact, within moments, her stays and chemise were in a snowy pile beside her gown and she was in nothing but her pale stockings before him.

With him still fully clothed, she bit down on her lower lip, feeling tremendously exposed. Daring herself, she cleared her throat and ventured, "I-I'd like…"

"Yes?" he whispered, stroking his strong hand along her forearm then up to her shoulder, where he traced his forefinger down the valley of her breasts.

She could scarce draw breath.

Her nipples tightened, though he had yet to touch them, and when his fingers teased over her stomach and stroked her hips, it was impossible to weave two thoughts together. "I should like to see you, too."

He paused, his dark eyes suddenly alight. "Whatever the duchess commands."

Duchess.

The word echoed in her head and she could barely wrap her mind around it. From Miss Bly to the Duchess of Thornfield in but a few unexpected hours.

But even more intriguing was the fact that she liked the word uttered in his rumbling tones.

Edward locked gazes with her, as if he could caress her from within. He worked his cravat free. Slowly, he unwound it, then he reached for his linen shirt and tugged it from his tight fawn breeches.

In one smooth stroke, he pulled it up and over his head. It joined her chemise.

Without looking away, he undid the buttons at the placard of his breeches and once again, the garment and his boots vanished in an instant.

He was remarkably graceful in his movements as he joined her on the bed. The full sight of him was breathtaking. Of course, she'd seen representations of the male form in art, but she had never seen a real man nude.

She marveled at his hard body.

Velvet skin poured over taut sinew.

The hills and valleys of his chest were captivating. All the defined muscles leading her gaze down... down...down.

What the devil? It was nothing like the statues she'd seen.

"You look perplexed," he said.

"I do not know what to call it."

"Ah," he replied without embarrassment. "The

education of ladies is not particularly thorough in this area."

"I agree," she breathed. "And why... Why is it like that?"

He answered her question easily, as if it was the most natural thing in the world. "My cock is upright because it cannot wait to be inside you," he said.

Georgiana swallowed. "I see."

"Let me show you."

Gently, he took her hand and placed it on his chest. The power he was giving her was unquestionable. He was letting her dictate this. Licking her lips, she decided, she might as well go about this as she had decided to go about everything else. Boldly.

Georgiana savored the feel of his warm skin beneath her fingers. The living, glorious feel of him. The intensity of it amazed her, for she could hear her own heart beat, and her breath came in faster and faster takes as she let her hand trail lower...and lower...until at last, she let her palm slide over his erect length.

A hiss slipped from his lips and she yanked her hand back. "Did I hurt you?"

His lids fluttered shut. He did look pained. "Your touch is heaven, Georgiana."

"It doesn't appear thus," she protested.

"It is also torture," he said, opening his eyes.

"How can that be?" she demanded.

"Describing it is rather pointless." And with that, he bent forward, placed his hands at her hips, and slid her down onto her back.

Her thighs trembled as gravity assisted her knees in slipping apart. "Whatever are you doing?"

she whispered.

"Showing you heavenly torture," he drawled. He paused. "Do you trust me?"

"Yes," she breathed, stunned that she truly did.

"Then allow yourself to have this."

What the blazes did he mean, allow herself to have—

His mouth kissed the inside of her thigh and then— *Oh!*

His mouth was upon the most secret part of her body, eliciting sensations that she had never experienced.

Was this possible?

She wasn't dreaming. Of that, she was certain. She was not going to suddenly wake up at home. She was truly in his chamber. But the sheer pleasure dancing through her seemed improbable.

A hungry, pleased sound rumbled from him as his tongue teased her folds.

She gasped and a feeling so intense shot through her that she reached down and wound her fingers into his hair. Unthinking, she tossed her head to the side and sucked in a breath.

Surely, she shouldn't be allowing him to do such a thing! But he was her husband, and a duke. Who was she to tell him he must be mistaken?

And more so…she liked what he was doing.

Like was not the word.

This was beyond all things imagined.

Edward kissed her again and again, his mouth and tongue circling over her sensitive spot until she thought she couldn't bear it another moment.

Her thoughts slipped away until all she could do

was feel, and feel she did. Higher and higher, she searched for something. Something she did not know.

That was indeed heavenly torture.

Edward slid a finger over her opening, teasing it even as he kissed her between her thighs. A cry tore form her lips as pleasure burst through her body in wave after impossible wave.

She arched against him, but he didn't cease, until she lay desperate for air. Once her body was relaxed and warm as molten wax, he knelt before her and said, "This may hurt a bit. Do you wish—"

"Please," she rasped. "I want to know."

And she did.

She had uncovered a whole new world of knowledge and she could not wait until the rest of it was hers.

• • •

Edward had never felt so alive or so seen in his life.

The way he desired Georgiana was indescribable. What was occurring between them went far beyond passion. Far beyond reason. Whatever it was, it made him do things he would have considered mad.

For instance, a midnight marriage was far beyond his usual approval.

Not only had he approved it, he had done it.

Now, he had watched her crest in pleasure, and he felt a surge of pride that was the greatest he had felt in his life. He wished her to love what happened between them. Given the way he hungered for her, his need was going to have no end.

He wished for her to need him as much in turn.

But, in this instant, he had to hold himself in check.

She looked up at him with only a hint of apprehension. He never wished to see pain in her perfect eyes, but this moment, as he understood, could be difficult for an inexperienced young lady. He slid the head of his cock along the slick folds between her thighs, until she arched against him and a moan of desire escaped her lips.

Edward braced himself on his arms and rocked ever so gently at her opening.

Her cheeks flushed and she reached up, her hands holding onto his shoulders.

Then her eyes flared in surprise as he thrust forward, and she yelped.

"Are you hurt?" he asked, stopping immediately.

"It is most strange," she replied.

She panted for a moment, wiggling underneath him as she tried to adjust to having him within her.

The feel of her body moving thus nearly undid him, but he held perfectly still, taking deep breaths, keeping his bloody brain and body on task. He could cease if he had to, but damnation, he prayed she would not ask him to.

Instead, her brow furrowed in concentration and she rocked her hips.

"That feels much better."

"Indeed, it does," he said. The way her body wrapped around his cock was a glory heretofore unknown.

Slowly, he began to thrust again, carefully and attentive. Studying her for any sign of distress, he increased the pace of his hips, driving deeper into her body. And when he felt his world begin to come apart, he stroked his fingers between her thighs, seeking the place he knew would send her to perfect heights.

After a moment, she tensed. Her core rippled around him, and he could no longer hold himself back as he cried out her name.

For the first time in his life, he let himself go entirely.

He did not think of the past or the future. He only thought of Georgiana, this moment, and a pleasure so wild he knew that his world had forever changed.

CHAPTER SEVENTEEN

Edward rolled off his bed, feeling completely at ease with the world.

Or as at ease as he ever had.

His feet hit the cool wood floor and he strode over to the fireplace. Crouching down, he did not bother to call for a footman and added another log to the dying embers. He grabbed the poker and carefully jabbed at the ruby red wood that was only beginning now to spring back to a fire. As he hung the brass poker back, he contemplated what he should do next.

He had quite a long list of things that had to be done.

Quietly, he headed over to his dressing gown, slipped it onto his shoulders, and picked up one of the ledgers from his desk. He hefted it in his hand, took his traveling desk, and moved back to the fire, for the room had quite a chill.

He felt content in that moment.

Things were going exactly as they should, even if he had not planned to be married.

The night had been a success and he was glad they had married so secretly and in such quick action. It had been exactly what he needed and exactly what he desired.

And now this morning, it was a relief going back to the tasks necessary to the smooth running of his estates and his dukedom.

"What are you doing?" Georgiana asked.

He did not even bother to glance back over his shoulder; he was so absorbed at the task at hand.

"Edward," she called rather loudly.

Had she said his name more than once?

He was not certain.

He flipped open the ledger, determined to finish this task. It was absolutely necessary he do so. And he began jotting figures in the book. If he did not sort this particular aspect out, several of his tenants would not be able to have a proper roof this fall when the bad weather came.

Such a thing was unacceptable.

"Edward," she called again.

"Hmm?" he muttered, realizing some response was necessary.

"What are you preoccupied with?"

"Work, Georgiana," he stated, his eyes still transfixed as his gaze flew over the ledger. Ten roofs to be repaired. How many builders would be required? What exact amount of material?

Facts and figures began to fly though his head, the room disappearing in a whoosh. He blinked as a strong voice cut through his thoughts.

"But," she said, "we've just—"

"Yes?"

"Don't you think perhaps you should stay with me?"

"Should I?" he asked, lowering his quill to the inkwell, dipping it, and cleaning the nib of excess. "I have a great deal to do."

"But we've just been married."

"So we have," he said, writing numbers tidily in a

satisfactorily perfect column. "And it was most pleasurable. Did you not feel that it was pleasurable?"

There was no reply, and the silence gave him
pause. It struck him louder than words and he lifted
his gaze from the ledger, an almost painful task, for
the need to complete whatever he started was a
powerful one.

"Yes, I did," she said at last, "which is why I don't
understand what you are doing."

A strange twist of a feeling shot through him.
Her face didn't match her experience. She had been
pleased...but she did not look pleased. Or so he
thought.

He stilled and forced himself to focus on her
downturned lips and wide eyes. When so driven, he
often forgot he needed to carefully assess the faces
of others to know if he had gone amiss.

From Georgiana's face...he most certainly had.

She sat, still naked upon his bed, the linen held
tightly around her. Golden locks tumbled about her
face, spilling down her back. How could he make her
understand? When he had to work, he had to work.
Numbers needed to be aligned. Columns had to be
sorted.

Work had to be completed, no matter what was
at hand.

Slowly, he cleared his throat. "I have a good
many things I must do, Georgiana. And it's simply
how it is. It is my life as a duke." He smiled then,
hoping to assure her all was well. "Now, you may
rest as long as you wish."

Then he considered and his smile faded.
"Though, with the encroaching light of day, you

may wish to go back to your room, unless you wish everyone in the house to know that we have consummated our marriage."

"I beg your pardon?" she queried.

He put his quill down for a moment, not quite understanding the note in her voice.

She sounded different than usual.

Not her usual sort of defiant, quirkiness, but something hollow, something harder, something strange. "Georgiana, are you angry with me?"

"I am not angry with you," she said so calmly it was clear something was about to go very wrong. "I am furious. We have just married. We have just spent our first night together and you are leaving me to go and do your tasks immediately? Without even a good morning?"

Had he not said good morning? He supposed he hadn't. Was that so very terrible?

"It is what I must do," he said, at a loss. "I'm a duke, after all."

She gazed at him as if he was a complete lunatic, a most unpleasant sensation.

Others had looked at him strangely in the past, when they didn't understand him. Somehow, seeing that upon *her* face was deeply upsetting.

"But surely you could take but a few moments to stay here with me," she protested. "To get to know me a little better, for us to have our first hours together as man and wife?"

"Is it truly necessary?" he found himself asking. "We are going to have years together."

He was shocked when she threw back the covers, bounded out of bed naked, and grabbed her clothes from the floor. "This, sir, is appalling. I find that I am your wife. And if this is the sort of marriage that we are to have, this is unacceptable and you must know it immediately."

He blinked at her. "I don't follow."

"You just made love to me."

"Yes," he agreed, though he winced at the word love. "I did."

"Are we to have no affection outside of bed?"

"Affection?" he queried. "I don't follow."

"I can see that you don't," she bit out, "and this is a very important problem. I *require* affection if we are to have any sort of relationship." She yanked on her chemise. "You have just shown me so much, and to take it all away in a single instant—I don't know what to do."

"Well," he said, eying her wild movements as she pulled her clothes on rather ineffectively, "I'm sure that I can find you something to do. There is a great deal that must be done."

She threw her hands up. "This is absurd. You are being thoughtless."

He tensed. "Georgiana, it is who I am. I cannot help it."

"Of course you can," she hissed. "You can make an effort."

He drew in a slow breath, the room starting to feel like it was humming, a bad sign. "I make an effort at a great many things."

"No," she countered, "at this. You can make an effort at being a kind person. I have given myself to you as your wife and I have been remarkably vulnerable with you. And I have never shown anyone my naked body or engaged in such intimate actions in all my life. And you have already left me alone by myself. And it feels most, well, unpleasant."

And with that, she shoved her feet into her slippers, stockings in hand, and headed for the door.

He stared at her, the sound of her voice ringing in his ears.

How to stop her and make the ringing stop at the same time? "Georgiana," he called.

"No," she said, whipping around and leveling him with a hard glare. "If you feel this way, we shan't talk again until you've had some time to reflect upon your actions and decide if you are able to change. And if you are not, our marriage is going to be an absolute misery. Of that I am certain." She drew herself up and stated, "I also need to collect myself."

With that, she headed out the door. Amid the buzz that had begun to spin around him, he heard her feet thumping through the hall. It was not the reaction he had expected. He looked about then stormed to the window. He threw it open and stuck his head out into the cold air.

As if on cue, Captain bolted into the room and sat down beside him. His warm body pressed into Edward's leg. He stroked the dog's fur, sucking in cold, fresh air.

Did she not understand him at all?

No, of course she did not. They'd had little time together. And though he had warned her time and time again that he was distant, she had insisted that he was not.

Finally, after the world had stopped buzzing, he let out a slow sigh. It had already gone horribly wrong. He shouldn't have been surprised, but it was a bit dismaying.

No, not a bit. The ground beneath his feet had opened and he'd fallen into a black abyss. Was this to be how it always was with him? Was he to disappoint everyone he brought into his inner circle?

He would just have to stop, because he kept failing so intensely. It was terrible.

Gazing down at his wiry, trusting wolfhound, he swallowed back a wave of pain.

He'd had such hopes and things had seemed so perfect. But then he'd attempted to do as he wished, to be himself.

And she'd left him, as most everyone always did.

CHAPTER EIGHTEEN

"We're leaving."

Elizabeth rolled over in her bed. "I beg your pardon?"

"Get up!" Georgiana exclaimed, storming to the bedside. "We are leaving immediately."

"Why?" Elizabeth asked, sitting up so quickly she swayed.

Georgiana hated the way she felt. She hated that she was so full of emotion. And she hated that she couldn't explain it adequately to her sister in this moment.

Even more so, she hated that she was not in Edward's arms. But she didn't want to be in the arms of a lout. How could she?

"I have to marry him," Georgiana declared as she marched to the Chippendale dresser and threw it open. "But I don't have to spend any more time with him than absolutely necessary."

Mindlessly, she began thrusting Elizabeth's clothes into the trunk next to the bed. "It is time to go home and have the last days before my horrible marriage in a place that I can at least enjoy."

Elizabeth gaped at her, a look of alarm darkening her usually bright eyes. "What has happened? Everything seemed perfectly well last evening, and now you are in—"

The sleep fell entirely from Elizabeth's eyes, and with a gasp of horror, she gestured to Georgiana's state of dress. "Where have you been?"

"It matters not where I've been," Georgiana huffed as she folded another gown rapidly and tucked it away.

"It does matter, indeed," Elizabeth retorted, swinging her legs off the side of the bed and rushing to her feet.

A wave of panic washed over Georgiana. "If you must know, I have been with him."

Elizabeth's eyes could not widen any further with her shock, but they did. "You've *been* with him?"

"Yes." Georgiana closed her eyes for a moment, wondering how it had all gone so terribly wrong. "But he is my husband."

"He's not your husband!" Elizabeth whispered so loudly half of Yorkshire might have heard her.

Slowly, Georgiana squinted her eyes open and a wan smile parted her lips.

"Oh my goodness," Elizabeth said in hushed tones, "He *is* your husband."

"He is," Georgiana confessed, feeling such a tumult of emotions she did not know where to begin.

"You two married last night?" Elizabeth's mouth dropped open as the full ramifications of Georgiana's news hit her. "In secret?"

Now, in the cold light of a gray Yorkshire morning, Georgiana did not feel the romantic adventurer she had been the night before.

"It was a terrible mistake, because now I absolutely cannot go back." She turned to the dresser and busied herself again with Elizabeth's things. "There's nothing to be done."

"Would you have tried to go back?" Elizabeth

asked carefully.

Georgiana's hands stilled and a sorrow crept through her, then. "If I knew yesterday what I know now? I very well might have convinced mother and father that a life in the Americas was far preferable to my marriage to that man."

Elizabeth's face softened. "Oh, Georgiana. I'm so terribly sorry. Is he truly that awful?"

"Yes. He truly is," Georgiana managed to say. How had she been so very foolish regarding him? She knew. It was all that chatter about flight and man taking to the sky. She'd seen the wonder in him…

Georgiana sucked in a steadying breath. "He has no idea how to be a husband."

"Of course not," Elizabeth said. "He has never been one."

Elizabeth's practicality struck Georgiana so forcefully she could scarce draw breath. Even so, when she had attempted to make a request of him, he had ignored her. She'd all but had to shout at him to gain his attention. She nibbled her lip then ventured, "He could not see that he should at least consider the fact that this morning…was different. It was our first morning together."

Elizabeth reached out to her. "I am so sorry. Perhaps he knows little of such interactions. After all, everyone does as he tells them."

Tears stung Georgiana's eyes before she quickly blinked them away. It had almost been as if she wasn't in his room at all, and she'd certainly seemed a nuisance. "It was horrible."

Elizabeth winced. "Oh, well, they do say the first

time is not particularly—"

"No, no," Georgiana rushed. "Not that. That was actually quite, well, marvelous. But come morning he all but leaped out of bed to get away from me. There was no kiss, no good morning, no embrace. I can't explain it."

"Oh, dear," Elizabeth said, wrapping her arms about Georgiana. "That isn't very romantic, is it?"

"He could not tear himself from his work. I understand he has a great duty, but…"

"Perhaps no one has told him how cruel such behavior can be," said Elizabeth.

"I have." Georgiana groaned. "But am I supposed to educate him daily, on the hour?"

Elizabeth gave her a squeeze then leaned back. "I think you must be blunt and honest with him as often as is necessary. You're going to be absolutely miserable if you don't. For as you said, there is no going back now."

Georgiana hated Elizabeth's good sense just now. In her frustration, it was the last thing she wanted to hear but likely what she needed most. Even so, she needed time to formulate some sort of plan for life with her new husband. And she wouldn't be able to do that at Thornfield Castle.

Elizabeth laughed softly. "You know, I do not think that we could run away to the Americas. How would we ever have paid for the travel?"

Georgiana laughed, too, though it was more a sound of vexation. "I don't know what's to be done. I've tried assisting him and teaching him not to be so arrogant and unfeeling. But it hasn't taken."

"Well," Elizabeth said with her firm sort of

gentleness. "You mustn't give up. You can't. You're married now."

"I do not think he's capable of learning," Georgiana bit out, her heart sinking as she remembered him studying his ledger, ignoring her in his bed.

"Everyone is capable of learning," her sister said sagely, "if you take the time."

• • •

"Scared her off, did you?" Montrose drawled, his Scottish burr particularly rich this morning.

Edward made no reply to Montrose as he stared at the bleak sight of his wife running away from him.

He let out a derisive sound, hoping to hide the fact that he was deeply affected by Georgiana's abrupt departure.

Edward had made no attempt to stop her. If she so wished to be away from him, he wouldn't trap her in his castle. He wasn't a bloody gargoyle.

Gripping the windowsill, he dug his fingers into the stone as he watched the coach race down the immaculate drive and out onto the foggy Yorkshire moors. She had wasted no time in going home. She certainly hadn't said goodbye to him.

No… She wasn't going home.

This was her home now. She belonged with him. Here. But it had all gone horribly wrong.

Edward ground his teeth together, fighting the pain cutting through his gut. Damnation, he had not felt such pain since—

He wouldn't allow himself to even contemplate it.

How could he have been such a bloody fool?

The night between them had been heavenly.

The morning had become hell.

Why hadn't he pretended? Why hadn't he forced himself to behave as most people did? Edward winced. It was so easy to think now what he should have done. He should have had a plan. When he had sent the note to the bishop for the special license, he also should have arranged for breakfast to be sent up to her. Hot tea. Flowers. Something. Anything to show he was not a cold lout.

It was the gravest mistake, allowing her to see him so preoccupied without some sort of plan in place. He always had a plan, but she had shaken him from his usual course.

Over the years, those that had seen him as he'd been this morning assumed he was rude, unfeeling, thoughtless. They believed the worst of him, just as she had done. But that side of him, the side which drove him to rise from his bed and go straight to the list of tasks inside his head could not be denied.

If he tried, and he had tried, it caused a visceral pain he could not shake. Why had he thought she might be different? He had not weighed the danger of it. And now he'd lost her good opinion of him, as well as lost *her*.

He shook his head and forced himself away from the painful image of her disappearing over the horizon. He'd see her again at Westminster in a few weeks.

The marriage was final. She already belonged to him…and he to her.

Edward swallowed the discomfort burning through his body. The way she had looked at him, as if he was the worst of men. He wasn't thoughtless or cruel. Truly.

Montrose eyed him carefully. "Are you well? You look a bit green there, mon."

"Perfectly fine," Edward said without looking at his friend.

"Hmmmm. A young lady hasn't put you in a twist, has she?" The sound of Montrose's newssheet flicking shut filled the breakfast parlor.

Edward eyed the toast and eggs in their silver chafing dishes on the cherry wood sideboard and scowled. He had no appetite. In fact, the feelings, *bloody feelings*, racing through him coated him with such displeasure that he rushed out of the breakfast room.

He couldn't stay and make niceties. Not with the morning's memory pounding in his head.

"Thornfield," Montrose called from behind him.

But Edward did not turn back. Not when he was like this. Not when the storm inside him threatened to break loose.

He strode as quickly as he could through the wide hall, down the winding stairs, and out into the crisp Yorkshire morning, which never quite felt the heat of summer.

South.

He needed to go south.

There was only one place that might improve him in the tumultuous turn after his brief moment of happiness.

His stables at Richmond.

There he could forget the way she had looked at him after their first night together. The certainty in her eyes that there was something truly amiss at his core had shone so intensely that his mind hummed with it now, repeating again and again how disappointed she was.

Edward shook his head sharply, desperate to rid himself of the echoing thoughts.

He stormed across the gravel drive, his boots crunching. He wasn't going to linger to bid Montrose, his cousins, or his aunt goodbye. He'd send them an apology and ask them all down to London.

After he'd found himself again.

Yes, once he'd regained control, he could face them.

Once, he'd stilled the riot of distress pounding through him, he could face her too.

Even though he knew, he'd never be able to be himself with anyone.

Not even his wife.

CHAPTER NINETEEN

"My dear, you do not have to marry him."

Georgiana stared at her kind mama in the single candle's light. Her throat tightened. "I do. I absolutely do."

"No, you don't, my darling," her mother assured, as she sat upon Georgiana's bed in her night rail. "Somehow we will overcome. Yes, the entire country knows what transpired that night at his ball. But you have been most miserable since returning from his house. And you came home post-haste. You were supposed to stay at least a week and you stayed but one night. I can only imagine the disaster of such a visit, and I would not condemn you to such a marriage of deep unhappiness. I myself have not always known the felicity of a happy marriage, though your father is a good man. I would not wish to bestow the same upon you."

"Mama," Georgiana whispered. "I have been very, very foolish."

Her mother cocked her mob-capped head to the side. "Foolish, my dear?"

Georgiana wound her hands about her linen sheet then rushed, "Mama, I have already married him."

"Married," her mother repeated flatly.

"I confess it to be true," Georgiana stated, her heart heavy. "He convinced me. He's most persuasive. And to be honest, Mama, I desired him very much."

Her mother took her hands in hers and looked upon her without recrimination or disappointment. "I can only imagine how much you desired him, my dear, for it was a desire for him that got you into this in the first place. Do you think perhaps you could love him?"

"I do not think so, Mama." She shook her head as she thought of their encounters. "He's not the sort of man one can love or who loves. He is very beautiful, though. And he knows how to…"

Her mother smiled. "Yes, my dear?"

Georgiana felt her cheeks burn and she coughed. "Let us simply say that I do think he has done a good deal of study in the carnal arts."

"Yes, my dear, society does seem to suggest that he is a rake. And rakes generally have done a good deal of studying. You enjoyed yourself, then?"

"Mama, there are no words to explain how I felt."

"I'm glad to hear it," her mother said. "At least on that score things shall be well. Many women do not have that luxury."

"No?" Georgia queried, surprised.

"No," her mother said plainly. "Many women have never experienced any sort of pleasure at all within matrimony. They go from wedded wife to their deathbed without knowing bliss. So at least there is that for you."

"At least there is that," Georgiana agreed before she sat up a little straighter. "But he is so strange, Mama. He does not seem to have an ounce of affection in him, even if he is capable of, well, pleasing me."

"My dear, perhaps you can like his other points."

Georgiana scowled. "What other points?"

Her mother smiled. "He is a skilled duke. He is respected throughout the land, and he's extremely intelligent."

"But am I expected to go through my entire life without affection and intimacy?"

A look of regret deepened the shadows that the candlelight threw upon her mother's face. "You will have children, and they shall give you a great deal of affection."

Georgiana fought a sigh and a feeling of frustrated resignation. That wasn't what she'd planned on. It only made her think that she really, truly should've stuck to her spinsterhood.

There was something to be said about independence and the ability to not have to look outside of oneself for assurance.

"Since you have no other choice but to go forward," her mother said, "you must make the best of it. And he will make the best of it, too. Would you like me to have a word with him?" In her deepest heart, Georgiana knew she had to simply accept the fact that she was marrying a man who would likely never love her. Who might not even know how to. Still, it was…hard.

"No, Mama," she said, lifting her chin. "I think I am capable of handling this."

Her mother leaned forward and patted her hand. "I am glad to hear it, my dear, and I do not wish to think you have given up. I did not raise a daughter to give up in the face of adversity, even if it happens to be in the face of a duke. You mustn't be intimidated by him. He is your husband now."

"I've never been intimidated by him."

"Good," said her mother. "Now start acting thus. I don't like to see you downtrodden. You mustn't let it get you down, my dear. I think you will handle this quite marvelously as long as you do not mope about."

Georgiana scoffed. "Mama, I have never moped about in my life."

"Good." Her mother pressed her forehead lightly to Georgiana's. "Do not begin now."

And with that, she kissed her daughter on the head and went back out into the hall.

Georgiana stared at the closed door and contemplated her mother's words. *Moping*. She had never moped before.

She certainly would not begin now, as her mother suggested, but what did that mean?

She knew exactly what it meant.

She needed to take charge of her affairs, be the best duchess she could be, and not let Edward get away with protestations of lack of feeling.

And that was that.

• • •

Edward could not outrun the mistakes he had made. It did not matter how much he wished or longed to change what had happened between himself and his wife, he could not.

All he could damned well do was get on with it. And when the time came to see her again, he'd...

He'd what? Be different than who he was? He was almost certainly going to make the same error over and over, because in all the years that he had tried to change, he'd never succeeded.

Dark defeat loomed in his mind. It was a place he did not tolerate himself to go. It was far too hard to come back from that. And so he faced the new horse and willed himself to be still.

His stables at Richmond were a special place, the only place in which he could truly bring himself back from the brink, when the world seemed to fall apart. And it surely had fallen apart. If he allowed himself to think of the look upon her face, as she stood naked beside his bed—

No. He closed his eyes. He could not think of it. Not if he wished to accomplish anything this day.

The horse stamped his hooves into the earth, clearly sensing his agitation.

Edward turned to the gelding and met his wide but wary eyes. The horse reared his head a bit, and Edward let out a soothing sound. Oh so slowly, he moved closer. The beautiful animal had had a rough year. The reports had been full of unkindness. And so Edward would need to take even more care than he usually did.

He circled round the horse's side and reached out and stroked his shoulder. The gelding gave him a look through his angled lashes as if to say, who exactly do you think you are?

Edward wanted to tease, The Duke of Thornfield, of course.

But horses did not care about titles. They only cared about feelings.

And if Edward allowed his thoughts to wander in the wrong direction, his feelings would go with them. Pointedly, he managed the thoughts inside his head, kept his gaze upon the horse's beautiful face, and said, "You are safe here. I am safe here. Together, we are safe and I shall help you to find a bit of peace, my new friend."

The horse considered him.

His tail flicked back and forth. But then, the horse did just as Edward hoped. He lowered his head, a sign of relaxation. A sign not of yielding or supplication, but acceptance that Edward might indeed be his friend.

"There you go, my lad," Edward murmured, firmly stroking the horse's withers. "That's the stuff. No more trouble for you."

Edward smiled to himself.

He loved it here.

If he could throw all of his inheritance away and not have to worry about the duties of being a duke, something he rarely thought about, he would choose to keep this place. All the hard work and attention to the details of so many animals that needed specific care was worth it for these moments, these moments of stillness, these moments where he could ease the pain of a horse that had been taken advantage of.

And they gave him something in turn, too. A temporary peace.

He'd come here for that today.

He stroked the horse's neck, refusing to allow his mind to wander to difficult waters.

No, he would not think of his wife.

He would not think of the pain in her voice and the shock tensing her features.

The horse's withers trembled beneath his hand, once again, the fellow clearly sensing that he was in a moment of disturbance.

"Forgive me, forgive me, old boy," Edward whispered. "I had a recent run of bad luck, but who knows? Perhaps it will prove good. One never knows what bad luck will bring. Look at all the bad luck you had and now you're here."

The horse let out a whickering sound as if to agree.

With that, Edward rested his forehead against the animal's warm neck. The horse shifted his weight from hoof to hoof. Then as if one, they relaxed together, both exhaling the weary woes they held.

CHAPTER TWENTY

Standing outside Westminster Cathedral, Georgiana wondered if she had gravely miscalculated in her offense at Edward's insistence that she might be ill-suited to the role of duchess.

There was a crowd.

It stretched toward parliament and the cheering was positively deafening. Thousands of Londoners stood outside the famed entryway to the ancient religious house. She gazed over them, astonished. In this moment, she realized she had not understood the scope of Edward's power. Not truly.

Oh, she knew he was one of the greatest men in the land, but it had never occurred to her that half of England would want to come out and see her wed.

They had.

She stood in her wedding gown, a beautiful, soft-yellow silk striped with ivory, her hair coiled in soft waves about her face, spilling over her shoulders.

Pearls had been studded into those locks. The diamond coronet Edward has given her had been woven into her curls, the weight of it a reminder of both the splendor and seriousness of her new position.

She felt dressed in a way that only a princess might, she supposed, for all her life she'd known nothing but muslin and cotton, and sometimes gowns passed down by her mother. This was a gown made just for her and it fit her in a way no other garment ever had.

She adored it.

And she knew it did wonders for her figure.

Once she had donned it, she'd understood why her husband had sent Madame Yvette to her home in Yorkshire to take measurements and create a series of frocks for her.

Edward stood beside her, seeming undaunted by the cheering masses, a pillar of perfection in his morning coat.

His dark hair was brushed to a sheen that made it seem obsidian in the morning light. His cheekbones were just as chiseled as ever. He held one arm behind his back, and with the other, he offered his forearm to her.

She placed her palm upon it.

She had not seen him in a month, and it felt terribly strange.

As he gazed out over the ribbon waving crowd, she thought he looked exactly like a king might. Only he was far more handsome than any king ever could be. That she knew for certain. For she'd seen pictures of monarchs and English monarchs were always rather disappointing when it came to their looks.

Whereas her husband? Her husband was more handsome than any man she'd ever seen and felt she would ever see again.

She was not beautiful. She knew it. But she was unique. And she would cling to that with every fiber of her being.

Georgiana lifted her chin.

Indeed, she wouldn't concern herself with what

other people thought. She was more interesting on the inside and more capable than the members of the *ton*, surely.

Edward led her down to and inside the coach as the crowd continued to applaud loudly and cry out over and over, "Hurrah for the Duke and Duchess of Thornfield!"

They pulled their way through the mass of Londoners. On pure instinct, she leaned toward the window and waved at them all for several minutes.

As they continued west, Edward observed, "You are doing very well."

She turned to him and arched a brow. "Thank you. It is not particularly difficult to wave one's hand."

"You'd be surprised," he countered. "Many people become overwhelmed by the sight of so many people."

"I find that this doesn't trouble me," she said honestly. "As opposed to Society, they're simply people who are excited to see us."

"Very true," he said. "You're not worried if they approve of you?"

She contemplated him, weighing her answer before she replied, "As long as I act in a good way, then I have nothing to fear."

"Oh, Georgiana," he said, leaning back against the brocade squabs across from her, "you are naive."

She refused to take offense. After all, he was not wrong. "I'm only naive because of lack of experience, but I am incredibly well-read and shall make the most of it."

"Theory," he said, "is not reality."

She shrugged, feeling her bosom press against her tightly cut bodice. "I cannot help the fact that I do not have a great deal of real experience. I shall simply have to wait for that to come."

He merely studied her at that.

The silence stretched between them, and she was brought to mind of that strange morning after they wed. Did he always fall into such silences?

"And you," she found herself asking suddenly. "Are you not afraid of what they think of you?"

"Not particularly," he stated, gazing toward the polished window. "They know what to expect from me, a steady hand in an uncertain time."

A steady hand could be a welcome thing at such a time, she had to agree.

The newssheets were full of terrifying accounts coming from France. Most of the English aristocracy was frightened that such a thing could happen to them. And instead of easing their tactics and giving help to the poor, many of them wished to crack down and simply make more rules to ensure that none of the people who lived so far beneath them could ever attempt to rise up and take power.

Georgiana stared at her new husband and leveled him with a hard look. "I want you to know I intend to be a good duchess, despite your dire predictions."

His jaw tightened, but then he pointedly leaned back against the brocade squabs of his coach, extending one leg out in front of him, the beautiful cut of his breeches stretching over his muscled thigh. "I'm glad to hear it. We shall endeavor to make it so."

She cleared her throat and said boldly, "While I do not have the opportunity of as much polite company as you, I think I shall actually do better in it, for I have seen how rude you can be."

His eyes narrowed ever so slightly. "Still upset, are we, over that morning?"

"Indeed, I am." Her teeth gritted at his audacity. "And you do not seem to have taken my words into effect."

He shrugged his shoulders ever so slightly.

"Edward," she said bluntly, "you must listen to me and attempt some affection if we are to have a pleasant marriage."

He stared back at her. "Affection," he repeated.

She nodded encouragingly.

"Is it really so very necessary?"

"Yes," she said.

He sighed. "If it is required, I shall endeavor."

"Good," she said, feeling a rush of optimism at his relent. "Let us practice."

"Practice affection?" he queried, his brows rising, which seemed a veritable storm of emotion for him.

"Indeed," she said.

"How the devil does one do that? Do you wish me to kiss you?"

"Kissing is not all there is to affection," she said, wondering at the life of a duke.

"Affection is intimacy and kindness."

"Intimacy," he repeated, with a slight curl of his lip.

"Have you not known intimacy?" she asked gently, shocked at how her heart suddenly hurt for him.

All her life she'd been surrounded by love and the kindness of those ready to assure her, take her hand, or hold her. Had he not known those things?

"Of course, I have," he scoffed.

"No, no," she corrected, realizing he had not taken her meaning at all. "Not carnal. Not that kind. But did no one comfort you when you were a child or take care of you? Do none of your friends?"

He made no reply. In fact, his lips pressed into a disapproving frown.

"No," she ventured, feeling all the more for her husband who had apparently known a lifetime of distance. "I suppose not. English boys are not well-known for intimacy and friendship, are they?"

He laughed, a dry, manufactured sound. "Indeed we are not. And as to my childhood..."

His gaze grew unreadable, but there was a sudden vulnerable and intense pain about him as he whispered, "My parents died when I was but a boy." His voice hitched. "But while they were living..." He sucked in a sharp breath and his hands fisted on his knees, his knuckles whitening. "Simply know that they loved me deeply and their loss was monumental."

"I am sorry for it," she said gently, wishing she could offer more comfort but seeing that he would reject it harshly if she made the attempt now.

"Thank you." He took three slow, distinct breaths. "They understood me in a way no one ever will, and that's an end to it."

She studied him.

Whatever could he mean by that?

But she had to take him at his word. And so she

decided not to push him in this. The death of one's parents had to be a very painful thing indeed. She could not even fathom such a loss. Nor did she wish to upset him. Not today. It wasn't a memory she wished to make on her wedding day.

"Well, then," she said, with forced cheer, "let us see how terribly the wedding breakfast goes."

"Indeed." He locked gazes with her and abruptly asked, "Is there anything you look forward to? In being my wife?"

How the blazes could she answer that, given the tenuous state of affairs? With truth, she supposed. And so, she stated, "There are many interesting people I wish to meet."

A muscle tightened in his cheek. "Such as?"

"Mary Wollstonecraft, Edmund Burke, Richard Sheridan."

"Good God," he said, "you have a list already prepared."

"Of course I do," she replied brightly. "I would never have the opportunity to meet these people as Miss Georgiana Bly. But as the Duchess of Thornfield? I have realized I can meet them all."

He laughed, his eyes warming suddenly with a boyish animation. "Yes, you can. And if you like, I shall arrange it."

"Truly?" she asked, barely able to breathe through her excitement.

"Truly," he said. "I can arrange for you to meet Mrs. Radcliffe, too."

"Mrs. Radcliffe?" She gasped with surprise. "Do you care for horror novels?"

"Indeed, I do," said Edward. "I quite enjoy the

drama of them."

"B-but you are so…so…"

"Yes?"

"*Serious*. And you don't seem as if you'd enjoy a novel in which the heroine is kidnapped and taken to a faraway castle."

"Perhaps it is you who is misreading me," he said, his lips curling into a tentative smile.

And just as that passed between them, the carriage rolled to a stop in front of an immense house. The square was quite large, and she realized that the house itself was wrapped around it.

Good Lord. This was no regular town house.

Town house was barely the proper term for it.

This was a *palace*.

This was something that stretched along the banks of the Thames and declared itself to be a jewel of the past, something that she had never dared to anticipate.

Of course, she'd read about the great old houses along the Thames, houses that had been built in the time of Henry VIII, Charles II and George I.

This most definitely was a house that had been built in a time when a family had become extremely powerful and wished to declare that power.

And now that family was hers.

She could not even fully countenance the immense wealth it would take to build such a house in London.

As the coach slowed, Edward pounded on the roof. "Take us round to the back."

She stared at her husband, wondering what the devil he was about. She felt the coach sway, and instead of slowing, it picked up speed as it turned the corner of the street that was lined with people.

Even here, people had come to applaud and to see them, but there was a look in her husband's eye that she did not quite understand. It was a fantastical mystery to her. Whatever it was, it caused the most delicious sensation of anticipation to dance through her.

Once they'd disappeared to the isolation of the drive behind the house, away from onlookers, he twined his fingers about hers, then pulled her across the way onto his lap. The heavy skirts of her gown splayed about her legs, the silk rustling.

Her bottom bounced against his hard thighs as he pulled her to his chest.

Gazing down at her, he said softly, his chest rumbling with the depth of his voice, "We have not time to practice the sort of intimacy you speak of. I do not know if I can do it, but I will try. You see, you are entirely unique to me, Georgiana. And despite how odd you might find my behavior, I confess, I never wish to let you go. I may never be the man you want, but I desire you entirely, and I know you desire me. Let that be enough."

Enough?

He slid his hand up to her face and caressed her cheek, stroking it with his thumb. Then he slid his hands into the soft locks of her hair, tilting her head back, waiting for her to deny him.

Despite the fact that she wished to protest, she found that she could not. For he was correct, she desired him just as much as he did her.

Her mouth opened slightly, anticipating his kiss,

offering herself to him.

Perhaps they were destined to disappoint each other. Perhaps they were destined to fail, but they could at least have this, and this, as he said, would have to be enough for now.

When his mouth came down upon hers, she was eager for him. She wrapped her arms about his shoulders as if she was clinging to a future that might not ever come to pass. Oh, she longed for it more than anything; enough to forget all of her arguments, all of her points, and to simply give way to his kiss in this moment.

It mattered not if that made her a fool.

His mouth worked over hers passionately, his tongue teased the corners of her lips. She opened to him and the hot, velvet stroke of his tongue touched hers. She gasped against him, their bodies taut against each other, the silk of her gown rubbing deliciously against the perfect wool of his morning coat.

As though nothing else mattered in the world, Edward managed to pull down the window coverings and they slowly rolled toward the isolated entrance she assumed was used by tradesmen.

Though she was still uncertain as to their future and how they would navigate each other, she could not deny how much she desired him.

Or how he clearly had a need for her.

Edward found the hem of her silk gown. He clasped it in his hand and worked it up her calf. Its voluminous folds floated up toward her waist as his hand traced the now bared skin above her knee.

When his fingers slipped under her chemise and

deftly slid between her thighs, she bit down a moan of sheer pleasure.

He kissed her with unyielding intent to make her drunk on him. Of that, she felt certain.

The way he stroked her body was the most glorious thing and also the most maddening. She shook with anticipation.

His fingers skillfully slid over her slick folds until she parted her thighs, eagerly. She held tightly to his shoulders, desperate for the pleasure that could unite them.

Surely at any moment, he would part her thighs farther, take down his breeches, and fill her with his hardness. But then Edward sat back on the bench.

She opened her eyes and gazed at him, perplexed.

Making quick work of his breeches, Edward bared his hard length, which had filled her with pleasure the night of their wedding. Their *real* wedding.

He held his hand out to her.

Not knowing what the devil he was up to, she still placed her hand in his. After all, in matters of pleasure, she trusted him entirely.

He swept her onto his lap and eased her over him so that her core was pressed against his hard shaft. Her knees splayed over his hips and pressed down into the cushioned seat.

As he guided her into place, understanding struck her. "Truly?" she whispered, awestruck.

"Truly," he growled.

And with his hands upon her hips, she lowered herself, taking him deep inside her body. The power of it filled her with passion. It took her several moments, but he did not try to force her to his rhythm. Rather, he allowed her to find hers.

Her head dropped back as she undulated her hips. That part of her body which overwhelmed her with intense pleasure pulsed with promise. As she rocked, she bit down on her lower lip.

"Look at me," he said.

Georgiana blinked, then met her husband's dark gaze. The intense hunger in those eyes declared one thing and one thing alone.

Mine.

Yes, she was his. By law. And in this moment, by pleasure.

But...he was hers as well. She knew it from the way he held her, relentless in the power and pleasure he could give her.

A gasp of sheer bliss passed from her lips and the tight coils of release shocked her with their strength.

His eyes fluttered closed, and he shuddered. Even as he thrust against her, he held her to him so tightly in that moment, she felt certain he might never let her go.

When their breathing slowed and she rested her forehead against his, she wondered how they could be so perfectly matched in this, yet veritable strangers—opponents, even—in other ways.

The coach rolled to a final stop and he helped her off his lap. Arranging her skirts and then his breeches, he carefully tucked one of her curls behind her ear.

His thumb trailed along her jaw, then teased her lower lip.

"Come then, Duchess, let me introduce you to

your adoring crowd."

"Adoring," she said, laughing, though her entire body was liquid from the lovemaking they had just shared. "I think they might all wish to murder me. For I have taken the greatest prize in the kingdom, without even trying."

But was he, she wondered, the arrogant prize everyone thought? Or was there, by some sheer chance, something more?

CHAPTER TWENTY-ONE

The crush of people inside Edward's town house was completely different than the crowd outdoors. The people outside had been eager to approve of her. Those in the ballroom? They stared at her as if she was a strange creature brought from the bottom of the sea that might infect them all with some insidious disease.

It was most shocking, their obvious skepticism, and more to the point, she discovered that she knew *no one*. And it quickly became apparent that in the English aristocracy, knowing one another was the key to the kingdom.

As she was trotted about the room by Lady Strathmore—or rather, Aunt Agatha now—she was introduced over and over again to people who were a complete mystery and who greeted her with feigned approval. It was obvious from their ferocious smiles that many of them wished to say something cutting, to all but eat her alive, but Edward lingered just behind her, glowering all the way.

She could not deny the feelings for him that filled her heart, because he stared with such intensity at the ladies and gentlemen at their wedding breakfast.

As if he was her private guard, not only her husband.

Because of Edward, not a single one of them would dare say something unkind to her. But she could not always be under his protection or Aunt

Agatha's wisdom. No, she was going to have to face these people at some point on her own, and she knew exactly what she was going to have to do to survive it.

After several hours of being paraded about like a dubious pony, she pulled Aunt Agatha aside into one of the myriad hallways. Even from the more isolated corridor, the ballroom buzzed loudly with gossip.

Aunt Agatha peered at her with sympathy. "Are you holding up, my dear? You must brace yourself. There will be much of this."

"I can see that," Georgiana confessed with no self-woe. "It is a bit daunting, but I shall overcome."

Aunt Agatha nodded her silver hair, which was perfectly coifed. "Edward and I were concerned."

"You needn't be."

"Oh no?" Agatha asked, though she did not appear convinced. "You are not overborn?"

"Certainly no!" Georgiana forced a smile, holding her mother's advice to her heart. "I am made of stern stuff."

"I am glad to hear it," Agatha said. "I did think so, but one never knows how the strain of so many people who consider themselves to be so—"

"Superior?"

"Yes," admitted Agatha, patting her curls with her emerald-ringed hand. "You see, I did not know how they might have an effect upon you."

"I wish you to hire several tutors at once," Georgiana said simply. "There is to be no delay."

"Tutors?" Agatha echoed with a pleased smile.

"Indeed," Georgiana confirmed, folding her hands before her. Determined. "You and Edward have taught me many things. But I need more. Much more. You will continue to be invaluable, of course, but I need people who can dedicate their time to teach me the intricacies of *ton* gossip, of the rivalries and histories of the great families, not just the titles and their precedence. I wish to walk into a room, know who's about, know the scandals, and if I wish, to be able to skewer them."

Aunt Agatha's eyes lit with delight. "My dear, how splendid."

"I think so," Georgiana said, glad to be met with equal enthusiasm. "I should also like to hire a dancing master. I may not be good at it, but I can at least improve. Also, you and Edward? Your manners are so ingrained. I do not think you know how to teach them. I need someone who can help me negotiate the strange manners of the *ton*, for they are a bit more nuanced than the ones of my set."

"I'm glad you've noticed, my dear." Aunt Agatha sighed as if it was terribly tiring. "You certainly aren't an embarrassment, of course, but the *ton* does behave in specific ways."

"So, I've observed," Georgiana replied ruefully.

Agatha cocked her head to the side. "We shall begin at once."

"Marvelous," Georgiana confirmed, relieved. "I wish Edward and I to have a chance at happiness."

Aunt Agatha smiled again. "As do I. You know, your ability to be happy in his world will greatly affect his happiness, too. He likes you a great deal."

"Do you think so?" Georgiana found herself asking, attempting to resolve his strange behavior with someone who *liked* her.

"Oh, yes," Agatha said. "I have not seen him have such an affinity to someone as I have to you."

Georgiana laughed, barely able to hide her disbelief. "If he shows me affinity, I can only imagine what he is like to someone he does not care for."

Aunt Agatha waggled her brows. "My dear, you have no idea."

Georgiana stared at Agatha for a moment, then swung her gaze back to the ballroom filled with people dressed in silks and brocades and sparkling jewels. "They're all cowards, aren't they?"

Agatha blinked. "I beg your pardon?"

"Cowards," Georgiana whispered. "They're all quite terrified of Edward. They want to mock me, but they won't because he's there."

Agatha nodded. "It is true to a degree, but be careful. Some of them are great men and women. They work hard to further the causes of independence and progress throughout this world. They fight tyranny and do their very best for the country, even if they are all power mad. But yes, many of them have very small minds."

"They think they are so grand," Georgiana said.

"Yes," Agatha agreed easily, as it was the most natural thing. "They were veritably born that way. From the moment that they burst into this world, wailing away, they were told that there was no one like them. It is only being told daily that they are special that makes them so certain they are so. It is truly something that cannot be learned, that ingrained belonging."

"You do not think I can learn it?" Georgiana asked, disappointed.

"Not what they have," Agatha warned. "I would not bother to try to be truly like them, my dear. You will fail. No, you must be yourself and you must be it boldly. But I agree with you. You must still also know the way of the land, lest you be caught in one of their traps."

Georgiana grinned at that and took Agatha's worn hands in hers. The older lady blinked in astonishment, clearly surprised by the touch.

Taking courage in hand, Georgiana declared, "I am glad that I have you."

"And I am glad to be of service to you," replied Agatha. "You may not have been born to be a duchess, my dear, but you certainly have the heart of one."

At that compliment, Georgiana felt her heart swell, for she agreed.

"Now," she announced with more confidence than she truly felt, "let us return and show them that I am not bothered a wit by their snobbery."

CHAPTER TWENTY-TWO

Lords and ladies frolicked in the impressive and extensive gardens of the Duke of Thornfield's London townhome.

Her townhome. Well, townpalace. Georgiana grinned. She couldn't help herself.

She had never seen such a sight.

Men and women dressed in the most beautiful shades of lemon, rose, lavender, robin's egg blue, and hues of every spring flower filled the lush but manicured gardens.

She could scarce believe the sights before her. Lords and ladies giggled amongst the fountains as they raced about the sculptured topiaries, playing like children.

Was this how it was to be? People who ruled the world acting as if they were at a children's birthday party?

It certainly seemed so. It was most astonishing to her, their amusement at the delights Georgiana had arranged for them. Some of the ladies looked remarkably like what they no doubt thought dairy maids or shepherdesses looked like.

Oh, it was true that the fashion for full skirts had gone out just a few years before, but the ladies still looked as if they wished they could live some sort of bucolic life in their soft linen gowns.

Georgina doubted that any of them had ever met a shepherdess in their life, or a cow...or a sheep, for that matter. Georgina had met several of them out on her walks. At present, she wasn't entirely certain as to which she preferred, but there was one thing that was unquestionable.

So far, her first garden party was a resounding success.

Nerves had rattled through her all morning and into the afternoon. They were still there, but as she gazed at the happily jaunting *ton*, drinking champagne and tossing flower petals at one another, she felt relieved.

At several moments, old fears had threatened, and she'd been quite certain that she was going to turn over the lemonade bowl, but somehow, with Agatha by her side for several of the first minutes of the party, she had not yet managed to jostle the refreshment table.

Quite the opposite, she had been most successful in navigating the guests, the shrubs, and the drinks.

Dozens of servants moved about, dressed in light livery, delivering hosts of glasses filled to the brim with crisp, bubbling champagne to the thirsty *ton*.

Georgiana had barely seen Edward, aside from a firm assurance this morning that she would do well.

He had then appeared for a brief moment on the stone balcony before he headed back inside the house.

He had not lied.

Edward did not like company and seemed to avoid it if he could. It was most interesting.

Clearly, as his duchess and hostess, she was not allowed such a thing even if she did not like company, either. She had no choice. No, she had to be at the center of everything. And much to her delight, people were not treating her as if she had the plague, so at least there was that.

A few comments about her accent had been made, however. An accent she could not eschew. She had tried and realized it was foolish to do so. She would always sound like someone from Yorkshire. She *was* someone from Yorkshire, and she wasn't going to apologize for it any longer.

As she traced her way across the immaculately raked grass, her soft kid-leather slippers barely leaving a print, she allowed herself a sigh of pleasure at how well it was going.

"Pleased, are you?" Edward asked from behind her.

She nearly jumped at that deep, rumbling voice caressing her, but then she turned and smiled. "I am, thank you. It has gone off without a hitch."

"Yes," he agreed, his hands folded behind his back. "I can see that. Well done, you."

She inclined her perfectly coifed head—the curls had taken an hour to arrange—amazed that she could still feel so completely alive at his nearness. But he was so handsome, in his taut faun breeches, navy waistcoat, and tailored cutaway. "Thank you, Your Grace."

"You must call me Edward," he whispered, tilting his head toward her so that his dark hair lightly skimmed his chiseled cheekbones.

"But we are in public," she pointed out, "Surely we must abide by all the rules and regulations to which you have assured me are necessary."

Slowly, he arched a dark brow, a glint of playfulness

dancing in his intense gaze. "I like to see that you are so interested in those rules and regulations, but we are allowed a little bit of intimacy, as you call it, given the fact that we are husband and wife."

"Husband and wife," she echoed whilst they crossed the green. "As far as I can tell from *ton* marriages, that is more reason than ever not to be intimate in public. Husbands and wives showing each other affection is very unfashionable."

He laughed, a rich, booming sound.

Half the company turned to stare.

He did not seem to notice it, but she did. Was it such a rare thing for the Duke of Thornfield to laugh in company?

She rather guessed it was. An immense wave of pleasure washed over her at the realization that she could cause him to laugh when others could not.

As they strolled to the end of the green, she spotted one of the amusements she had arranged, and an idea struck her.

"Edward," she began, "will you play with me?"

He looked down at her as if she had lost her wits. "Play with you?"

"Yes, a game of bowls," she explained as she gestured to the line of special, weighted bowls.

"I do not play bowls," he said, blinking. "It is a game for ladies."

She gasped with mock affront. "It is not a game just for ladies."

A crowd began to gather at their end of the lawn, witnessing their banter.

"It is," he insisted. "It is a way for ladies to make certain that they attain a certain level of exercise and do not—" He paused. "Glow."

She *tsk*ed, barely able to contain her laugh at his silly assertion. "You know that I am quite capable of a good long walk, and therefore a bit of a glow, but bowls are not meant for simple sport. They are a sport that has been outlawed and forbidden to the most excellent and capable of men! It is a game of fascinating facts!"

He stared at her again as if she had lost *all* her wits now. "What the devil are you talking about, Duchess?"

"Do you not know?" she queried, though she found herself lighting up as he called her by her title. "There is something that my husband does not know?" she teased lightly.

He gave her a droll look. "There are a great many things I do not know. I've never claimed that I am a knower of all things."

She smiled up at him. "Of course, my dear. I do not wish to give offense. But I do think we can all agree you know many things."

He stared her again, clearly not quite following her playful commentary.

She smiled up at him again, realizing he might need a bit more help in such discourse before their growing audience. "It is most endearing. I do not mind it at all. It is one of the things that I have grown to like about you, your sense of self."

His brow furrowed. "My sense of self."

"Indeed, but you must indulge us mere mortals and play."

He looked about, his eyes darting. He looked uncomfortable. And yet she was certain that there was a part of him that wished to indulge her.

"It would mean a great deal and certainly show your"—she leaned in—"affection for me."

His jaw tensed before he said quietly, "As you know, I am attempting to work on that."

"I do know," she murmured. Georgiana hesitated for the briefest of moments then decided to be bold, for she had promised herself that she would teach him to be a good husband. "Will you do this?" she asked softly, so that no one else might hear. "Your acquiescence will show you are taking some of my suggestions at being a—"

"Don't say it again," he said.

"Say what?" she asked, batting her lashes.

"Affectionate...and intimate," he said under his breath.

Georgiana swallowed, determined. "I am working very hard to be a good duchess, am I not? Therefore—"

"Yes, yes," he cut her off. "And you're doing a most admirable job."

She nodded, pleased he noticed. "I shall endeavor to be what you wish just as you are now endeavoring to be what I wish, and we shall both be mutually happy."

"Fine, fine," he relented. "We shall play bowls."

"Good," she said, clapping her hands together. "How marvelous."

She looked out to the small green, which was kept open for the event. Bowls was one of her favorite games. Happily, she collected the small white ball, the Jack, from the stack of bowls, and rolled it far into the field.

"What are you doing?" he inquired.

"You truly have never played bowls?" she asked, first collecting four bowls for him and four for herself.

He cleared his throat as he took one of the weighted bowls. "I have had far too many other things to do."

"How sad for you," she said. "One should always have time for a bit of fun."

"Dukes rarely have time for a bit of fun."

The growing crowd of aristocrats clearly strained to hear as they seemed to lean forward as one.

"You are being very stoic, my dear," Georgiana said brightly. "I appreciate said stoicism, but I also like to see you smile."

"Humph," he muttered, before he paused and confessed with apparent difficulty, "I do like to make you happy. Therefore, I shall make an attempt to smile."

She laughed. "I'm glad to hear it. Now hold the bowl easily in your hand," she said.

He gazed at her askance, but then did as she bid before the host of people who were always awaiting his every move.

"Now," she said, taking on a mock serious tone as she instructed him. "The goal of the game is to try to roll one's bowls as close to the Jack as you may. And whoever gets all their bowls closest to the Jack wins."

"This seems like a game for infants," he pointed out, but there was something in his gaze she couldn't quite read.

Was he nervous?

"Do try," she urged. "It is such a fun game."

"Whatever my wife requires."

And much to her pleasure, he hauled his arm back and rolled the ball...too far.

It skittered across the green, well past the Jack.

A titter of comments went up amongst their guests and then soft applause, despite the lack of dexterity to his roll.

She smiled, for she knew this game quite well. "My turn now, Edward."

She eyed the Jack, eased her arm back, and artfully rolled the bowl. It settled very near the Jack.

A round of applause surrounded her and she beamed.

"Now," she said, "we must each roll three more and see who is closest in the end!"

He rolled again and missed, but once again, she noted a slight gleam in his eyes, as if this gave him satisfaction. Which was most curious, given his reticence.

She smiled encouragingly at him, pleased he would play on with her, learning something new. She rolled again, and came far closer.

"This game is not quite as simple as I had imagined," he observed.

"Few things in life are ever as simple as we imagine, Your Grace."

He cocked his head to the side. "Is there a technique that you should like to teach me, since you are clearly far superior at this game than I?"

His seemingly honest compliment surprised her. "It is nice to know that there is something that I am far superior at," she replied. "And since it is something as amusing as bowls, I feel quite good about it."

Another laugh tumbled over his lips. "My dear wife, you're superior in many things. I could list them…" His voice trailed off and then he whispered. "But I do not wish to cause your cheeks to glow an astounding shade of pink in front of our guests."

"Pink?" she echoed. "Whyever not?"

"Because," he breathed. "They might think that it's from pleasure of another kind."

Ever so gently, he placed his hand upon her back and guided her back to her bowl. "Though I love to give you pleasure of that kind," he murmured.

"I love to receive it," she replied. "But I also love this."

And with that, she rolled her last bowl. It danced along the green, knocked one of his to the side, and then stopped right beside the little white bowl.

Edward lifted his hands and clapped.

She gave him a quick curtsy and handed him his last bowl.

He took it, their fingertips caressing ever so slightly.

Slowly, he turned, closed his eyes, then rolled. The bowl went wild.

"You've let me win," she said with faux horror.

He closed the distance between them, towering over her. "Never. It is I who have won, for your face shines with happiness."

Suddenly, she had a very strong feeling that this was not his first game of bowls. He had allowed her to teach him something. And the feeling that filled her heart at that moment was most decidedly, hope.

• • •

"To the new Duchess!"

The dozen men sitting at the long mahogany table covered in crystal, silver, and porcelain imported from China stood. As one, they raised their chargers high and let out several shouts of approval.

Edward remained seated but lifted his own glass in a more dignified manner. Georgiana had been put through her paces over the last weeks. Ball after ball, party after party, she had faced the wolves of the *ton* with growing confidence. And now this. His hosted political dinners. She was rising to the occasion with aplomb.

Wine had been drunk for hours. Bathed in the golden hue of beeswax candles in ornate silver candelabras placed on the outer edges of the dining room and table, speech after speech skewering the opposition party had filled the air.

The general merriment of the politicians was exuberant. Edward sat at his end of the table, amazed at how easily Georgina took it all.

Over the years, he'd always found the excitement of politicians to be rather difficult to deal with. He'd enjoyed taking part, of course, because he found the modern issues of the day quite pressing, but after bottles and bottles of wine and brandy were consumed, he often had difficulty maintaining enthusiasm or putting up with the increasingly ludicrous comments of the politicians that he supported.

The Whig Party was his party, and he agreed with all of their important points, but he didn't necessarily like eating dinner with them. The hours of boasting, shouting, and clanking of his crystal were often hours he endured.

Politicians were a necessity, but they weren't necessarily good company.

Georgiana seemed quite in her element.

He admired her for it.

Her eyes sparkled as the gentlemen lifted their glasses to her, and rather than being intimidated by them, she had given as good as she had gotten.

Lord Parker turned to her, his eyes gleaming. "It is such a pleasure to hear from a lady with such an intellect, Your Grace. Such a pleasure."

Her lips twitched, and her diamond ear bobs danced against her neck, as if she wasn't certain of the compliment. "Lord Parker, I am surprised that you would consider my intellect or opinion at all."

"Whyever not?" boomed Lord Altonby, his cheeks red and his wig slightly askew.

Georgiana leaned forward, with her emerald bracelet, the same shade as her silk gown, winking in the candle light. "I cannot vote, my lord."

Lord Altonby and Lord Parker both harrumphed as if her point was most worrying, but neither had the fortitude to suggest ladies should have the vote, as Edward believed they should.

He leaned back, realizing that his wife could take on any gentleman in the room.

The gentlemen, despite their cups, were quickly realizing this, too, and much to their good sense, they did not attempt to humor her.

Edward felt a dose of pride. He did not think Georgiana could be humored, and he found that singular. He would never make such a foolish attempt as to humor his wife.

No, she was a creature of remarkable sense, and so he would listen to her. It seemed the politicians admired her for it, too.

The gentlemen began listing off compliments to her, some of them quite silly.

One rather wobbly politician who was forced to lean against the table, Edward could not recall his name, made some comment about Georgiana's fine eyes.

Mr. Fox was much more clever and declared boldly, "It is wonderful that His Grace has married a woman of such excellent mind."

Georgiana beamed at the esteemed politician's praise and returned, "It has taken some skill to hone it, sir, but I am greatly appreciative to my mother for ensuring it is sharp enough to cut through foolishness when necessary."

Mr. Fox's dark, bushy brows rose, but then he lifted his glass and looked around the table. "To Her Grace's mother!"

The toast was met with a cheer and an echo, "Her Grace's mother!"

The gentlemen around the table pounded it.

Silverware rattled. Glasses clinked. And Edward folded his hand into a fist beneath the table, willing himself to be calm in the din, but then, much to his amazement, Georgiana stood.

She lifted her own glass and said, her voice strong, "To the gentlemen of the Whig Party, whose principles I admire and shall strive to encourage. I am grateful to be embraced and taken in. We shall endeavor together to improve the quality of life of those who are struggling the most. We cannot allow children to climb down dark holes to collect the coal that feeds our fires."

She drew breath, lifting her chin as if laying out an edict as boldly as any prime minister. "We cannot allow them to climb up our chimneys to clean them, simply for our own convenience. We cannot allow young ladies to be shoved into misery because of the circumstances of their birth, for all young women are ladies."

There was a moment of silence at her shocking comment.

The idea that all young women were ladies? It was not something that most of his set would give credence to, but then they all stared at her and erupted into applause.

"Well said, well said," one member of Parliament cheered.

And Edward's heart lifted at the sentiment. Perhaps he was more of a revolutionary than he had thought.

He looked across the table at his wife, stood, and then lifted his own glass and said, "Here is to the Duchess of Thornfield, a woman determined to make the world better, and I shall do everything I can, gentlemen, to support her in that."

The members of Parliament cheered their enthusiasm. Georgiana beamed as she locked gazes with Edward. "We shall all do it together," she insisted, "for it is the only way for it to be done."

Edward took a long swallow of his wine then inclined his head. For he could not agree more. As he held her gaze, though, his heart pounded with trepidation.

There was something he needed to do.

And it was time he did it, if he could simply gather the courage.

CHAPTER TWENTY-THREE

As the days of his marriage passed into weeks, Edward was uncertain if he was ever going to see his bride during the day. Georgiana was always working, just like he was, and it was astonishing to be met with someone who had the same sort of dedication and passion as he did.

It had never happened before.

Oh, he was surrounded by lords who worked quite hard to keep their estates running and intact and the country going, of course, but Georgiana's dedication was such that he rarely caught sight of her. She was always going from one lesson to the next or bent over a book and sipping her tea.

He was proud of her. So much so, he had no idea how to express it. And along with his pride had come an emotion he'd never needed to address before.

Doubt.

Even in his deepest struggles, his parents had loved him. He'd known he'd been born to be a duke. And power had always been his.

Georgiana was his by law, but as he watched her ascend obstacles, overtaking anyone or anything which stood in her way, he'd begun to wonder if she could ever accept his true self. Not the distant, controlled duke he had forced himself to become. But himself. Did he dare begin to show her?

The little time that they did spend was in the

evening together before the fire in their chamber. His chamber, in truth, but it had become theirs. She had a chamber of her own, but by the light of the moon and candlelight, they found the time to be together and with few words, unite.

It was a time that he loved. He had never felt so much in his entire life.

In fact, he feared he might rattle apart with the power of the emotion. He was coming to *need* her. His body hungered for hers, driving him to seek her out and pull her to him when the sun slipped below the horizon. Frankly, it terrified him, for he'd never thought to need anyone so intensely.

Needing her was dangerous. What if she turned out like all the others that had known the truth about him? What if she thought...

He closed his eyes, willing the wave of volatile emotion away.

Georgiana was the most remarkable person of his acquaintance. And with every day he found himself longing more and more for her admiration. He did not wish her to seek his. Far too many were always seeking it, and he loathed that.

No, he wished to find *hers*. But could she?

She'd called him despicable not so very long ago.

He'd studied the idea of *affection and intimacy*, trying to understand ways in which he could please her so that she might change her summation of him. And because he did wish her to be happy in their marriage.

Even though he knew he might never be the man that she wished, he could, as he had promised, at least try to give some semblance of it so that she could be content.

He arranged for there to be fresh flowers in her room every day, for her favorite black currant jam to be served with her breakfast, for the tea she seemed to like most steeped for her every morning on her tray. And without her knowing, he had been writing letters inviting people to come for a dinner party soon.

It would be his great surprise for her.

The greatest literary minds in the land would gather in their house. For her. He hoped with a hope he'd never felt before that she would like it. He wasn't entirely certain it would please her. After all, he didn't always know what would best please people. But she had made it clear that her deepest hope as his wife was to meet famous writers. That, he could truly supply her with, and he wasn't going to shirk on his promise.

Edward glanced down at the bouquet of violets in his hand, wondering if she would be like the small, yet bright flowers. Wondering if he told her everything…that she wouldn't recoil from him.

He lingered before her morning parlor, a room she had picked for herself and was currently decorating to her tastes. There was really only one way to find out.

He slowly walked to the door and peered through it. They did not bother with closing doors in this house. There was no point. Secrecy was something that was difficult to keep from servants. And as he studied her, he felt his heart do the strangest thing. It seemed to fill his chest and ache… ache with longing.

But for what?

She poured over a book, and her curls banded with a rose silk ribbon were falling about her face. Even though he knew her maid had likely spent an hour at her coiffure, it had already become a bit of a riot, for she was always errantly pulling at a curl here or tucking a lock there.

It all amused him greatly to watch her do so. She cared so little about the perfection or lack thereof of her appearance and he found it…refreshing.

She leaned over the book, took a sip of tea from her delicate blue cup, and smiled. What line had caused such pleasure, he knew not, but he liked to see her so happy. Though he knew he had appeared full of arrogance to her, he had been deeply afraid she would not be content in his house. But he had been mistaken. And in this case, he was so grateful to be mistaken.

In fact, he was discovering that he loved being proved wrong by her.

Edward strode into the parlor and, recalling his plan, he leaned down and kissed the top of her head. He had read that it was a good thing to do, that ladies liked such things. Gently, he laid the bunch of violets before her. She lifted her face to his and smiled. Her eyes shone with a deep contentment as she picked up the bouquet and brought it to her nose.

Her smile deepened with profound pleasure at such a small thing. "Good morning, Edward."

"Good morning, wife," he replied. "You look most pleased by your book."

"I am," she said, tucking the bouquet into the

glass of water in front of her. A small but strange gesture for a lady. "I am learning the most fascinating things about the Earl of Sandwich."

"Indeed?" he queried, delighted she wished to keep his gift alive so much that she did not even bother to call for a vase.

"Yes." She placed her red ribbon in her book then closed the leather-bound pages. "Did you know that the sandwich was created because the Earl of Sandwich gambled far too much?"

Edward laughed then nodded. "I did, I confess," he said. "The Earl of Sandwich's gambling exploits were legendary. If I am blunt, they are one of the reasons I stay far away from the tables. I like logic, odds, and statistics," he continued, warming to the topic and her interest, "and statistics tell me that games of chance are not a logical way to spend one's money."

She beamed up at him. "I am glad to hear you are a man of such good sense, for I do find that many men of your station do not have sense at all."

"Agreed, dear wife."

"And what shall you be doing today? Are you going to the House of Lords?" she asked, taking up her teacup.

She did not recriminate him with her question. As a matter of fact, she seemed eager to know what he might be about. He often did go to the House of Lords, and he was rarely in her company during the day, for he had meeting after meeting after meeting. It was simply the way of things, something that did not seem to bother her, thank goodness.

But not today.

Today he had a different plan. He drew in a

steadying breath.

"No, Georgiana," he said before he cleared his throat, a shocking wave of nerves traversing his system. It was a very unfamiliar feeling and he wasn't quite certain what to do with it. "I should like you to come on an outing with me."

"An outing?" she queried. "But I have so many things to do."

His nerves stirred and a hint of disappointment curbed his enthusiasm. But he continued, "I'm sure you do, but do you think, by chance, for this particular day, you might miss all of your appointments and come with your husband?"

"When you put it like that," she said with a slow smile that lit her entire face, "I might be able to arrange a delay in my education."

"Oh dear," he said with exaggerated seriousness. "That sounds terrible. But I promise what we do shall be edifying also."

"Then," she said, pushing her book away and drinking the last of her tea, "I will not regret it in the slightest. I shall make my apologies to my tutors and all shall be well."

"Good." His relief was so palpable he was tempted to crow with triumph. "Be ready in an hour and wear attire that will be suitable for riding."

"Riding?" Her face paled. "I am not particularly good at it."

"That will be part of your education," he said, eager to take her out. There was a slight wariness to her countenance, or so he deduced from the way her brow furrowed.

"Are you afraid of horses?" he asked.

"Not afraid, exactly, but I am not accustomed to them. We did not have the money to keep horses for riding. We only had horses for our carriage."

"Do not worry," he said. "Horses are the most magnificent creatures in the world. In fact, aside from dogs, I find them to be far preferable to humans."

She laughed, then. "Well, I do quite like dogs. Therefore, if you say horses are as lovely an animal, I'm sure I shall be won over."

"Indeed you shall," he declared, wondering if he should have Captain brought down from the country, since she clearly liked dogs so well. But it was a poor idea. The wolfhound would be miserable in the city.

And with that he pivoted on his booted heel and left her to get ready.

As he traversed the halls, he felt quite pleased that the endeavor had gone so well. Perhaps this was something he could do, this affection business. She'd been rather insistent that she required it for their marriage to be a success. And he found he did wish it to be a success.

Edward wished her to be happy…

Much to his amazement, he wished it with all his heart. But most of all, he hoped they could find happiness together.

• • •

The crimson riding habit clung to her form in a way that Georgiana had never quite experienced before. The fact that she had skintight cream-colored breeches on underneath the skirt was a revelation.

Georgiana did not ride. At least not well. Still, the frock had been made for her on insistence by Madame Yvette. Now she knew why.

Madame Yvette, the French seamstress who had also made her wedding gown, clearly had an understanding of the Duke's needs in a way that she had not. She had never thought her husband might ask her to go for a ride.

No, a curricle drive perhaps in the park, certainly, but a ride? Then her lack of foresight dawned upon her. Of course, as a duchess, she would be expected to do such a thing as ride. No doubt, like all things, she was expected to ride *well*.

Was Edward going to teach her to ride today? Was the list of her inabilities to never end? No matter how many strides forward she took, it always seemed as if she was missing her mark. Would she ever know enough to be a proper duchess? She bit her lower lip. She'd worked incessantly, trying to fulfill her role. And she was proud to take on her duties. But she had begun to worry that she might never meet Edward's expectations.

She felt a moment's trepidation as she sat atop the well-sprung curricle seat as they headed out of the city and into the countryside. Resting her hand on the side of the curricle, she willed herself to rise to this next lesson. He wished her to ride? She would boldly make the attempt.

She had made a decision that she would do whatever was needed to be one of the best duchesses in the land. If it meant facing a four-legged creature that could pound her into the earth, so be it. Besides, surely, if Edward thought so highly of them, they couldn't be too terrifying. Could they?

No. She wouldn't allow doubt to creep in. She had enough worries without equine ones. She forced herself to think positively. Edward liked Captain, a great burly wolfhound, and she adored the dog. Could a wolfhound, which stood as high as her waist, be so different than a horse?

Her attempts at purely optimist thinking died as she envisioned the horses that traversed Rotten Row every day.

Of course they were different. Horses were massive, sinewy, beautiful creatures with eyes as wide as owls and tails that lashed back and forth, snapping at the flies around them. And they had teeth that were considerable. Dogs had teeth, too, of course, but they were generally bared in panting and lolling their tongues.

Horses, she knew, could literally chomp one quite powerfully. Still, she was not about to act the coward now.

And why should she? Her bold determination with Edward had been reaping rewards. Oh, she might never know enough to be the duchess he desired, a thought which often kept her awake in the darkest hours of the night, but he had listened to *her* instructions. Over the last weeks, he'd shown her hints of affection and care. From the fresh-cut flowers, to new teas, to books brought to her daily, Edward was trying to please her and give her what she had stated was necessary to her happiness.

He went out of his way to hold her in his arms during the few hours they were able to spend together in their chamber. Oh, he was still an arrogant, all-powerful duke, but he was an arrogant, all-powerful duke who was trying to be intimate with her in genuine ways.

He was living up to what she required. She only prayed she could do the same for him.

As they drove farther from the ever-growing West of London, she wondered where the blazes he was taking her. She'd assumed it would be a stable block close to his house, and then they would go for a gentle ride in the park.

Regardless of her lack of knowledge, she drank in the fresh air and his good humor. The fact that he had a surprise for her had put him in a shockingly chipper mood.

They drove in companionable silence toward Richmond. The hills were still beautiful, covered in rolling trees and meadows. Deer roamed through the woodland. At one time, this had been the great hunting park of kings. Now, it was slowly being encroached upon by the city. She wondered how long it would remain wild.

It was almost impossible to say, what with the progress that was being made. She admired progress, of course, but sometimes she wished the wild things of this earth could remain untouched.

"There," he said triumphantly.

She swung her gaze to the direction he pointed. In the distance were several adjacent fields and in those fields were several horses of various colors. But all of them…all of them were shining, their coats sleek and well cared for under the morning sun.

The paddocks were fenced in by beautiful, thick

Hawthorne bushes, flowering with their perfect white blossoms. Adjacent to the fields was an immaculate Tudor-style stable block.

"What is that?"

"It is mine," he said proudly.

"All of it?"

"Of course."

"Well, I'm not surprised." she said. "I believe you own half the country."

"Not half. But close."

She hid her smile at his response. He was so factual about the way he'd stated it. No teasing at all, and she realized that meant it was true.

Edward *did* own close to half the country.

He was a marvel to be sure, and no wonder he spent most of his days from before sunup to sundown, organizing and managing things. His devotion to columns and ledgers was really quite amazing when one thought about it.

And she truly did admire him for his dedication, even if it meant that sometimes he barely knew she was in the room. It was something she was becoming accustomed to, for he had tried in so many other ways to make up for his obliviousness to anything but his endeavors. At pointed moments, there'd been soft touches, long glances, and all the other small but important things he did to show her affection even when it seemed he felt little for her.

Would she ever gain his full affection? But she couldn't deny the importance of his work or the fierceness with which he helped so many in the hours he spent at and preparing for The House of Lords.

His body veritably vibrating with his excitement,

he drove the curricle up to the stable and quickly jumped down to the raked earth. In a single moment, he was transformed.

Georgiana nearly gasped. She looked at her husband and he barely seemed the same person. His whole face became light, relaxed, free. His shoulders stretched, becoming even broader, taking up more room under his perfectly tailored black riding coat, if such a thing was possible.

His height even seemed to expand.

He simply looked completely at ease. Far more at ease than she'd seen him either at Thornfield Castle or his town house.

As he held out his hand to help her jump down, the air about him filled with his anticipation at whatever was about to come.

"I have never seen you look so pleased," she said, pressing down upon the top of his gloved hand as she descended.

"Do I?"

"Oh yes," she replied, beaming at him, for it was impossible not to be caught up in his rare enthusiasm. "Very much so."

"I am proud of this place."

"Are they your racehorses?"

So many lords had horses they took to New Market every year.

"No," he scoffed before he turned to look upon the beasts prancing across the green. "These horses will never race. That is not what they're intended for. They are intended simply to be here."

"I don't understand," she said, as they walked toward the edge of the nearest field.

"You see," he began, his voice rich with the clear joy the horses gave him, "this is a place where I bring horses who have had very hard lives, and they come here and they heal."

"They heal?"

He was silent for a long moment before he gazed down at her and said pointedly, "Yes, a bit like me."

She stopped then, her own gaze riveted to his usually implacable face. There was nothing implacable about him now.

"A bit like you?" she said gently, her whole body suddenly humming with awareness. This was important. This moment. This place. She knew it instinctively, and so she focused on him most carefully.

He turned toward her, towering but vulnerable. "I wish to explain something to you, Georgiana. Something I think might help you understand why I am the way I am and why it will be difficult for me to change." He smiled, a rusty smile, but a smile nonetheless. "Though I am making my best attempts."

"Please tell me," she urged.

He gazed to the horizon and a muscle in his throat tightened, as if he was bracing himself. Then he launched himself into speech, his words rapid and tense. "When I was child, it was clear that I was different from other boys. I had trouble."

"Trouble," she repeated, wondering what he could possibly mean, he was such a seemingly perfect adult.

"Yes." Edward stepped forward abruptly, whatever he had to say driving him toward the field where the horses were running back and forth.

As a matter of fact, the moment they spotted him, the horses perked up their ears, lifted their heads, tossed their manes, and almost as one came running toward him.

The whole herd of animals was overjoyed to see her husband. They thundered to a stop before him, each of them maneuvering the other gently, trying to reach his attention. Edward murmured to them, caressing their muzzles and necks. Patting here, patting there, stroking one black horse, another roan, another pale horse with dark mane; he eased them and made each one feel cared for.

It was an astounding sight.

She waited patiently, watching him care for each horse, her entire view of him changed, and she blinked back tears of amazement.

Edward was not cold. He was a gentle soul. And now she realized something had happened to him as a child and that was what made him so in tune with these animals who had known travail.

Because he understood them.

As he stroked a black mare's mane, he said, "I was born unable to see the world as others do."

"I don't understand." she said. "You had trouble with your sight?"

He shook his head firmly. "Let me explain another way. When I was four years old, one of my nannies told my mother that I was destined for a madhouse. Another told her I was possessed."

"What?" she gasped.

She did not repeat his comment about madness or possession. She wouldn't even countenance the absurdity. But such a supposition must have had a profound effect upon him as a child.

"You see, I would throw myself on the floor and scream."

"Many children do such things," she said, shocked by how intensely she wished she could defend him.

"But not like I did," he corrected quietly, all the while keeping his attention on the horses before him. "I would scream for hours and I could not be contained, and I was angry all of the time. The slightest sounds could set me off. Or being touched the wrong way. Or being surrounded by a group of people. None of this bode well for a future duke."

His chest expanded, stretching his coat, as he took in a deep breath. "My mother and father could not bear the idea of sending me away. Thank God, they refused to take the advice of my nannies…and even a doctor who insisted there was something mentally wrong with me, that I was going to be a stain upon the family's honor."

He swallowed and said with pride, "My mother and father refused to believe this was true, and my mother never left my side from that day forward. She became my tutor, my nanny, my governess. And I will never forget the power of her love."

It was then that he turned to her and met her gaze.

"My mother gave me love, even when I did not wish to hug her or to give her the affection she likely longed for. I simply did not like it. It is the truth of it, Georgiana. I do not always like to be touched or to be hugged or to converse. But she never gave up."

"I wish I could have met her," Georgiana replied,

her heart going out to the mother and boy so long ago.

"She would have liked you and your practical nature a good deal. But I must explain fully. I… withdraw sometimes and unlike people, these horses understand my need for silence. They feel it, whatever strangeness that is my nature, and accept it. And so, I do all that I can for them. Many of them have been abused by masters who are unkind to them. Together we survive this tumultuous world."

"I see," she said, though she didn't. Not entirely. But she knew it was imperative to listen. It was remarkable that he was telling her this.

"So your mother took you under her tutelage?"

He nodded. "And somehow we found ways of managing my inability to take on the world as others did. As I said, I retreat. I often have to be alone. I must fortify myself before going into company. I have ways of clenching and unclenching my hands that make certain I do not rattle apart before a host of people. I have a way of breathing, which stops panic from encroaching upon me, and I also sometimes must be silent."

He looked away then, his voice catching. "Th-that silence appears as a vast arrogance and rudeness to many people. But, truthfully, it is just myself doing my very best not to come apart at the seams as I stand in a situation that nearly drives me mad."

As his story raced out of him, her heart ached for all that he had endured and the worst that she had assumed about his nature. "How long have you felt this way? How long have you had to be alone because people did not understand? Why did you not tell me this before?"

For several moments, he said nothing, but the look upon his face was the look of someone who had endured pain for a long time.

"Do you remember the morning after our wedding?" he asked softly. "Our true wedding."

"How could I forget it?" she asked, her heart beginning to beat rapidly, wondering what he was about to proclaim.

"I was being myself," he said, his voice almost a whisper. "Truly myself." He blew out a long breath, then continued. "That is how I behave, Georgiana. I become engrossed and swept up in a world I cannot explain to others. My mind riots with numbers and figures and facts, and I must complete the tasks that suddenly come to me, because if I don't... It is the most infuriating, terrible feeling. You felt as if I was ignoring you, but I was not. I was so engrossed by the need to do what had to be done, that I could not look away from it. It was not my intention to be unkind or rude, but...it is physically painful to me if I cannot do what my mind requires of me."

She nodded, trying to show she understood, though she was astounded.

"And as in pain as you felt," he said, reaching out now to slip his hand around hers. A decisive gesture to bring her closer to him. "If I am honest with you now as I intend to be from this moment on, I felt rejected that morning, too."

"What?" she gasped, tempted to pull back, but she did not.

"You felt as if I was ignoring you, and I felt as if I had failed once again, with someone I cared about, that the person who I hope cares about me would not be able to accept me…for myself."

What he was saying dawned on her and she held onto his hand then, a lifeline in a wild world. "I am the person who cares about you," she said softly.

"I hope so," he murmured. "I pretend that it doesn't hurt when people don't understand. I show a great face to the world because it is important I appear strong, but I let few people see the real me."

She stepped toward him then and slowly raised her hand to his jaw, allowing time for him to shake his head if he didn't wish it. But he did not move away, and so she caressed his beautiful face that was so haunted. "Forgive me. I didn't understand then. I couldn't. But now that you have explained it to me, I understand it is no small thing to you. That what you did? It was not just some disinterest on your part."

His eyes closed and the tension drained from his face. The worry he had been carrying for so long faded away and her heart leaped, for she had helped him to remove that.

"Edward, I am honored you would share this with me, that you would share the pain of your childhood."

"Only Aunt Agatha knows." He turned his lips to her palm and said against her fingers, "No one else."

He kissed the soft hollow of her hand then drew it down to his shoulder. Pulling her close until her body was pressed to his, he laid his cheek against the coiled tresses of her hair.

"She has been my support since my parents

died," he said. "When they died, my God, my world fell into darkness. I did not know how I would survive, for they were the only people who truly understood me, and I have been alone since then."

He had overcome so much. All this time…all these weeks, she had judged him so harshly, making assumptions about him and his behavior. She'd allowed herself to often think the worst of him without daring to discuss it with him.

Her husband? Her husband had walked through fire over the years to arrive at this moment where he bared the trials he had fought through.

He was a man to be greatly admired. What had she fought through? What had she overcome? If not as privileged, her life had been one of love and ease. She saw him in a new light now, and she wondered, in her haste to judge him and the little turmoil that she had faced, would she and her family truly be capable of matching his spirit.

She hoped so. She would endeavor to live up to his strength. As she thought of the small boy who had struggled alone, she ached for him. She ached, knowing that she had not seen him as he truly was. But now? Now she would try with every fiber of her being to shore up what mattered most to him, his family honor and name. No matter what it took.

He'd given up so much to make his parents proud, to uphold the dukedom with honor. Surely, now she could do the same. She held on to him tightly, as if she could save him from all those years of pain, even though she knew she could not. "You are not alone now. You have me and you're correct. I care about you deeply."

He tilted her head back. "And I, you, Georgiana. Now, will you trust me to teach you to ride?"

"Yes," she said firmly, her heart daring to care for him. Daring very much.

"Good, because I have a friend just for you."

CHAPTER TWENTY-FOUR

The relief coursing through Edward's veins increased exponentially with every moment. He led Georgiana into the immaculately kept stables, so proud of the place he could barely contain it.

Horses that no one else would wish to own were a strange thing for a duke to be proud of. Most would have had the animals shot. But he understood broken things, and the power of patience.

So many others of his class were proud of acts in Parliament, houses built, jewels obtained, but no, this was his crowning glory.

This place and the gift the horses had given him in turn.

The stable block was long.

Several horses were able to simply be here with no expectations put upon them. Some, when they arrived, were wild, kicking at their stables, attempting to bite the stable workers' hands. But over time, they all came to understand that no harm would come to them in this place.

Only green fields awaited them where they could frolic and graze to their heart's content.

Here, they could simply be horses, free of human brutality, free of the demands so often put upon such perfect creatures. It was in gaining their trust and riding those that enjoyed it where he found his greatest peace.

When he was not in Yorkshire out upon his

estates, here, adjacent to London, he could find peace. Eventually, London always leached his resources. This haven was his salvation where he came to renew himself and his strength.

Slowly, he walked down toward the final stable and stopped before a beautiful black mare. He had spent a great deal of time with this particular horse over the years. She'd come here skittish and uncertain of people, but over time they had built a rapport, and he had taken her out almost every day for a year. The other hands easily took her out, too, and she was happy with any rider as long as they were gentle.

Now the mare was happy to see him, and he beamed at her. She nickered away gently, and he slipped a carrot from the bin by her stall and fed it to her. She gobbled it up happily.

"And who is this?" Georgiana asked.

He patted the mare's neck. "This is Beatrice. Indeed, she is feisty and steady, just like the Shakespeare heroine you so admire."

Georgiana laughed, and the horse lifted her head up and down, as if enjoying their good humor.

Beatrice eyed Georgiana for a moment, turning her head slowly, then gently blowing air through her lips, a sign that Beatrice approved of Georgiana. He'd known that she would.

"Come," he urged gently. "Do not touch her face. It's just like with a human. When you go up to a human, you do not immediately stroke someone's cheek."

Georgiana grinned at that. "Oh, dear. How terribly inappropriate I've been with horses over the years."

He nodded. "Most people are. They think that's what you do, but it isn't. You may stroke her neck, of course. And she adores a good scratch."

Georgiana approached Beatrice slowly. He kept a steady hand on Beatrice's shoulder, ensuring a good meeting of the two.

His wife met gazes with the horse, and much to his astonishment, she said, "How do you do, Beatrice? It is a pleasure to meet you. I understand you are a friend of my husband's and, therefore, you shall be a friend of mine. I hope you agree to this."

Beatrice, much to his pleasure, drew in a breath through her nostrils and then gave a lovely sound of pleasure, that gentle nickering a horse made when happy. Ever so carefully, Georgiana reached her hand out and stroked Beatrice's soft neck. Beatrice leaned into that touch, her lids heavy showing that she was relaxed. Georgiana instinctively scratched.

Beatrice gave a tremble of pleasure and leaned into Georgiana's hand, despite the stable door.

"She likes you," he concluded, pleased he'd been correct in his prediction.

"I see that," said Georgiana. "And I am very glad."

"Good. You shall have to ride her. The two of you will get along famously."

"Well, I'm glad you think so." A wide smile parted her lips. "Mayhap if you believe it, I can, too."

"I believe a great deal of you, Georgiana. You've surprised me, and I am loath to admit it. You are clearly a capable woman."

"Thank you, Edward," she said.

A strange look crossed her face for a moment. It

was so fleeting he was almost certain he had been mistaken. Before he could ask, Georgiana glanced about and queried, "Are there no stable hands or stable boys? Surely, it takes several to run this place. It's in such good order."

Her subtle compliment was a balm. He loved that she could see how much care he ensured was taken here.

"There are. At present, they are in the far pasture, tending to several of the horses who are new. I wished us to have this place alone for some hours. I shall saddle Beatrice for you."

He opened the stable door and easily guided the mare out. He made quick work of the leather saddle and bridle. In one swift, smooth swing, he helped Georgiana atop Beatrice.

She sat rather rigidly for a moment.

"Though I know it is easier to say than to do," he said, "relax. Allow yourself to feel her beneath you and trust her. Beatrice is an excellent mare and a good friend, if you let her be."

Georgiana gave a nod, even though he could see this was far beyond her usual comfort. He adored that about his wife. Whatever she did, she did fully. No hesitations.

Georgiana drew in a deep breath through her nose, blew it out threw her mouth...and visibly relaxed. She was an excellent study. Her whole body seemed to soften as she allowed herself to become more at ease.

He would not torture them both with a sidesaddle, and he was glad he didn't care about such things. One day, if she rode on Rotten Row, she'd have to make use of one. But not now. Not on a day when they were attempting to feel so free.

As he gazed up at his wife, he could not express the joy building inside him. She had so easily taken the truth about his past. Some might've recoiled. He had decided it was worth the risk to confess it. He could not spend a lifetime hiding from her.

No, he wished to go boldly through it with her, just as she seemed to be doing with him. Which was also why he had brought her here, to the secret place that had made him well over the years since his parents' deaths.

Quickly, he went over and picked one of the more energetic but still safe horses, Antigone. Edward didn't bother with a saddle. He liked the feel of riding without the accoutrements of man too well.

He swung up onto the black mare, who sometimes still liked to take the lead, and he was content to let her have her head whenever necessary.

He subtly urged Antigone to walk out of the stables first, allowing Beatrice to follow gently behind. He stroked Antigone's shoulder, allowing his body and the horse beneath him to become as one.

His tensions floated away.

They rode out into the field at an easy pace. Georgiana followed, laughing all the way at Beatrice's rolling gate. It was what he liked so well about his wife, the fact that she met life and its challenges with such joy.

After a few moments, they were circling the pastures easily.

"It is like flying," Georgiana proclaimed, her face

positively glowing.

It wasn't exactly how he would have described it. But her enthusiasm was catching. In his estimation, horseback riding was probably a bit more bumpy than he imagined a bird at wing, but he was glad that Georgiana was enjoying herself so very much.

Time rushed by quickly and soon the sun was high overhead. Edward led them back into the barn. "You understand why this place is so important to me?" he asked, as he jumped down from Antigone.

"Indeed, I do," she replied, adjusting her hands upon the reins.

She had an instinctively light touch and little fear.

"Would you like to have a moment of rest? Cook prepared a basket for us."

"Oh, yes." A pleased smile tilted her lips. "I am most surprised by how much strength it requires in ones limbs. Walking has prepared me, thank goodness."

He had observed her morning ritual of a good five-mile walk in Hyde Park. Most people went to be seen. Georgiana went to make ground. It certainly had assisted her today, keeping her seat.

He led Antigone to the small corral where she could walk for a few moments, and then Edward returned to his surprising wife. He savored the feel of his hands about her waist as he helped her slip down off Beatrice.

A look of indecision creased her features for the barest instant as she shifted weight in the stirrups and swung her leg over the mare's back. Then she was bracing her hands on his shoulders, their bodies pressing together.

They stood like that, gazing into each other's eyes, their bodies aligned, slowing. Without mention, their breath seemed to come at the same pace and her lips parted ever so slightly.

Beatrice, wise mare that she was, walked over to Antigone, and though Edward hated to slip away from Georgiana, he secured the horse behind the gate.

He turned back to Georgiana, uncertain as to what would transpire now. "Thank you for coming today," he said.

"I'm glad you invited me." She folded her gloved hands behind her. "I feel close to you in a way I never thought you would allow me to be."

"I want you to be close," he said. "I want us to find that. I didn't think I could allow myself to do it, but you are teaching me that I can."

"Thank you," she said.

With that, she reached up, grabbed his head, and pulled him down toward her.

He returned her kiss happily, eagerly, their bodies entwined. Before either of them could say another word, he guided her into one of the empty stables, the floor scattered with soft hay.

He was damned glad he'd had the foresight to send the stable hands out to the fields today. Pressing her against the wall, he gave way to passion. Oh so slowly, he dragged her heavy skirts up her thighs and met her bare skin.

The scent of grass and fresh air and the country surrounded them. It was an invigorating moment.

A perfect moment.

"Put your arms about my neck."

Eagerly, she did so. In one quick and easy heft, he positioned her against the wall and wrapped her legs about his waist. The folds of her skirt pooled around him, and he freed his cock from his breeches.

"This is most remarkable," she exclaimed, her cheeks pink.

Her words filled him with a hunger so intense he could barely fathom it. Unable to wait, he thrust deep inside her.

A moan of abandon tore past her lips and her hands dug into his shoulders.

"Kiss me," she demanded.

He was more than happy to oblige. Angling his mouth over hers, he took her lips in a wicked kiss, one in which he meant to scorch her forever with his memory.

He wished her to always think of him as they were now. To desire him every moment. To never let him go. Just as he would never let her go.

For the first time in his life, he'd had the courage to be free and this was his reward. He couldn't think of anything better.

Her core tightened around him and his knees nearly gave way, but he bolstered himself up and pounded into her welcoming body. Her hand wove into his hair at the nape of his neck and tightened.

The sensation and proof of her passion nearly undid him, but before it could, he slid his hand between them and teased her until she clasped him tightly and called, "Edward!"

The sound of his name, rough upon her lips, sent him over the edge.

And he joined her in bliss.

CHAPTER TWENTY-FIVE

Georgiana could barely contain the joy in her heart. Watching her husband ride wildly about the pasture this morning, she'd felt as if she was watching a boy. The gruff man that she'd known for a little over a month had vanished entirely.

The grand duke had slipped away, replaced by a young man, happy and at ease.

Seeing him so free had freed her, too. The man who rescued horses, who was most alive in the country, he was the man she was married to, and he was the man she'd been longing to meet. This was the man she could love and fall in love with.

She *was* falling in love with him.

Yet, she couldn't deny that Edward was a man of many parts, and she would have to love them all, not just the easiest ones. But she was overjoyed he had allowed her into his secrets, because now she was absolutely certain they could build a future.

She would continue to work hard to be a good duchess for him, just as he was working hard to be affectionate toward her. Yes, they had a great future to look forward to, and she could not wait.

Georgiana all but danced about her chamber as she slipped a diamond ear bob into her lobe. She still was not entirely accustomed to her lady's maid, Greggs, who was fluttering about, desperate to keep Georgiana's gown from rumpling. But Georgiana was so excited she could not sit still.

"Your Grace, Your Grace," Greggs implored her, clapping her slender yet wrinkled hands before her equally wrinkled but kind face. "You shall ruin your hair!"

"I don't care, Greggs. Do you know how excited I am?"

"I can see, Your Grace," Greggs said, sighing with dismay. "You shall ruin your frock, as well."

"It is impossible to ruin it," declared Georgiana as she twirled about, eager for the forthcoming dinner party. For this night was the night she was would meet some of the greatest writers in all of England.

It was the greatest present anyone could ever give her, and Edward had arranged it. He was such a good man and attentive to her interests. How could she have ever thought differently?

And he was so caring.

He specifically went out of his way to find things she liked. He had been so insistent that he wouldn't be able to learn to be affectionate or intimate, but how mistaken he was, and how mistaken she had been to doubt it. He had applied himself with great vigor to making her feel happy in many aspects of their life. Throughout the night and throughout the day, she had not missed all of the little ways in which he tried to make her feel well…cared for.

And tonight was the culmination of it all.

In an hour's time, a host of writers would descend upon the town house! It would be a most fascinating evening, for she knew some of them did not get along well at all, and she would have to be that which smoothed the difficulties between them or enjoyed the conversation that arose from such discourse.

Truly, it was going to be splendid.

Christmas had no appeal compared to this night.

Finally, she stopped her all but skipping feet and eyed herself in the long polished mirror beside her dressing table. She nearly laughed aloud with her own approval.

The elegant crimson silk gown skimmed her figure to perfection. A golden belt emphasized her rather, if she dare say, voluptuous breasts. They were plumped up quite nicely with barely an inch of fabric to cover them. No doubt, the cake served with tea in the late afternoons had caused her breasts to increase in size. Whatever the case may be, the cut of the gown certainly flattered her.

Though Yorkshire would have found it to be scandalous, it was the height of fashion.

The wisps of fabric at her shoulders were embroidered with golden thread and the skirts were voluminous, wrapping about her legs in the Grecian style. The fabric was so light, she felt almost naked.

Georgiana absolutely adored the gown, and though she herself was not what the height of fashion cried for, she knew that she looked quite well, and it made her feel very good about herself, indeed.

She could not wait for Edward to see her in it, because she was certain he would also appreciate how she looked in it.

That moment when his eyes lit up, spotting her, full of passion and hunger and excitement? She adored it beyond measure. He had no such look for anyone else. No, that look was reserved purely for her and she delighted in it.

Greggs went to the ivory dressing table and began sorting the hairbrushes and perfume bottles, sorting all of them back into their proper places. Collecting her pressed gloves from her bed, Georgiana drew in a deep breath, ready to descend and revel in the evening. But before she could cross her chamber, the door swung swiftly open and Aunt Agatha slipped in.

Georgiana stopped, beaming, ready to share her enthusiasm with her aunt by marriage.

But the words of excitement died on her lips.

Agatha's face looked as if she had seen death.

Georgiana's heart slammed in her ribs. Something had happened.

"What is amiss? Is Edward hurt?" she demanded.

"Not at all," Agatha said, her voice tight. "It is not Edward. He is quite well and I believe dressing. I have come to tell you something altogether different."

"Greggs," said Agatha, "you may go now."

Greggs swung her hazel gaze from Georgiana to Agatha, filled with curiosity, no doubt, but knowing she could not stay. She gave a quick curtsy then hurried from the room, her gaze full of apprehension as she went.

Agatha cleared her throat and gestured to the chair before the fire. "Come, my dear, you must sit."

Georgiana shook her head, her entire body tense. "I don't wish to sit. I can tell that what you have to say is ill. Please do not torture me with delay."

Agatha nodded, her shoulders drooping under

the immaculate green brocade of her gown. "It is about your father."

Georgiana's world whirled around her and she whispered, "He's died."

"No!" Agatha exclaimed, crossing the burgundy and blue Axminster carpet. "I'm so terribly sorry. I should not allow you to think thus, but, my dear, he is in a great deal of trouble."

Georgiana was able to draw breath, knowing her father still lived. But what could be worse than death? For from the grave pallor of Agatha's face, it felt so. "I don't understand."

"Let me show you." Agatha lifted her hand from her skirts, revealing a small, folded piece of news-sheet. Her hand, worn with time, reached out, shaking.

The wink of her jeweled rings did not hold a luster tonight. In fact, they felt mocking.

Georgiana tentatively stretched her fingers to it, hesitating, as if it might burn her. Once she forced herself to take it, she pored over the paper. As she read the words, her mouth dried and she collapsed into the chair beside her dressing table. She did not even know how her legs had ceased to support her. Lifting her free hand, she covered her mouth to stifle her dismay.

The truth, for it had to be true, or Agatha never would have presented it to her, crushed her usually implacable spirit. If she'd been asked a moment before, Georgiana would have insisted that nothing could, except for the death of a loved one could break her heart.

She would have been mistaken.

Her father was involved in a financial scheme and apparently had lost a great deal of funds and was responsible for the loss of the funds of others.

Speculation.

The word sent a veritable shudder of horror through her.

She scanned the block print words again as if re-reading them could somehow change the meaning of the contents of that report. But no. Even as the words blurred whilst her eyes misted, she couldn't deny the truth.

Mr. Bly of Yorkshire had lost every penny speculating on villas in Italy. The company had been false, a pretense. And all the men who *owned* it had done a midnight flit, leaving a few men like her father to take responsibility for the ruination of dozens.

The horror of it struck her.

The words in black ink condemned her father as a fool. Worse, he had convinced others of the soundness of the proposition by mentioning that he was the father-in-law of a highly important and influential lord. One of the greatest lords in the land.

They did not explicitly say the Duke of Thornfield, the paper daren't use his name so boldly, but everyone would know exactly who it was. Her father had brought disgrace to the Duke of Thornfield and to herself. And he'd ruined her mother and her sisters.

A jagged breath tore her before a terrifying realization hit. She lifted her gaze to Agatha and asked, "Does Edward know?"

"No," she said said softly, "not as of yet. Though he may hear at any moment. I truly thought you should be the first to know…and there is more."

"More?" Georgiana rasped. "How could there possibly be more?"

"Do not tempt fate, my dear. It loves to show us how brutal this world can turn." Agatha laid her hand gently on Georgiana's shoulder. "I have heard from your mother. Your father has disappeared."

Georgiana winced as she gazed up at Agatha's worried visage. "You have heard from her?"

"Do not be hard upon her for telling me first," Agatha said. "I think your mother did not wish you to read it in a letter and did not wish you to be on your own when you heard. Likely, she was not entirely certain how you would take all of this. She was also concerned that you might have seen the paper before learning of the fact that your father has vanished. He must be terribly ashamed, my dear."

Ashamed.

Dear God, shame was slipping over her, too, its black, oily fingers coating her with shock and disappointment.

Whatever was she to do? How could she break this scandal to Edward?

By facing him and getting done.

Georgiana drew her shoulders back, something that felt positively Herculean, and stood. "I must go to him at once." Tears stung her eyes and she dashed them away. "What will he think of me?"

"You are his wife," Agatha replied kindly, "and that is all that matters."

Georgiana nodded, but the assurance felt hollow.

It wasn't all that mattered. Edward would be horrified and appalled. In the end, her fears were proving correct. She was never going to live up to Edward's expectations.

Tears choked her throat and forced her to swallow them back. How could she live up to him? How could she ever be enough? She was going to prove as much a disappointment to him as he had expected. Her family was going to shame him just as he knew that they would. And she could barely keep her chin high with the guilt of it.

She was so proud of her husband and all that he did, the state of her own family's disgrace coated her with the most vile emotion. If it had just been her father, alone, losing all his funds, she could have borne it with some comfort. But this? This was beyond all imaginings, for she could not shake the images of families being cast from their homes, of children losing bread, of widows losing all security because they had invested in her father's scheme.

She swallowed back the acrid sorrow and strode toward the door. She wouldn't hide from this. She couldn't.

But neither could she ignore the fact that she had likely just lost Edward's love before she had truly found it.

CHAPTER TWENTY-SIX

Edward gave the last touch to his starched cravat and turned away from his long mirror.

Quite glad to be done with dressing, he went back to the high stack of beautifully bound, and well read, books upon his secretaire to make certain he could repeat all the titles and authors with ease.

He excelled at such things. Memorization was one of his skills. But tonight was particularly special and he didn't wish to make a blunder. He wouldn't shame his wife in front of her favorite writers.

That was imperative.

The door to his chamber opened, and he did not immediately look up, assuming his man, Hoyt, had forgotten something. The rushing steps were not that of a man, though. Edward looked up to the sight of his wife rushing across the large chamber. He smiled in pleasure and welcome. "Come here, my wife, it is good to see you. I did not think I would until we were both downstairs."

As he caught sight of the way her mouth was pressed in an austere line and there was no spark dancing in her usually mischievous gaze, he stilled.

A dark foreboding slid over him.

"I have something to tell you, Edward."

The feeling of dread increased at the tone of her voice. It was different, not full of the sprightly enthusiasm she so generally had. No, there was a tension to it he had never heard.

The floor beneath his feet felt as if it were moving as that dread built inside him. Whatever was worrying her, he would fix it. Somehow. Surely, as a duke, he could always fix her troubles. He clung to that thought as he held his hand out to her.

"Come," he urged.

But she did not give him her hand. Quite the opposite. She flinched then she stood stock still before him.

Her hands gripped a piece of paper.

"What is it, Georgiana?" he said slowly.

"I have news of my father," she said.

"Oh?" he queried, determined not to react with fear.

Her hands began to shake, but she also lifted her chin, possibly to give herself courage. "He is involved in a scandal."

"What kind of scandal?"

Her eyes darted away before she let out a small cry of pain and continued. "A financial one. As part of my marriage settlement, you placed a stipend aside for Papa and my family?"

"I did," he said simply, not wanting to anticipate some dire strait, but from the tortured look upon Georgiana's face he began to fear the worst.

"He has lost it all and more," she said, her voice breaking before she rushed, "He encouraged others to invest into a scheme that has failed. And, Edward, he used your name to increase his influence and encourage others to believe the speculation to be respectable."

Edward said nothing as her words unfurled in his brain. The air around him felt thick. So thick he might have cut it with a knife. He did not feel shock as Georgiana so clearly did.

It was exactly what he had feared with such a man as her father.

There had been a brief hour in which he had hesitated in giving her father an allowance of significance. He had feared Mr. Bly would not be responsible, that he could not resist his nature. But to see the pain on Georgiana's face, Edward wanted to go find her father and shake him until the man could not speak.

Edward shoved such impractical emotions aside. Such an action would not help her or her family at all.

"Georgiana," he said quietly, without rancor, "where is he now?"

"No one knows," she cried, dropping her hands to her sides. "Apparently, he has run off. My mother is unaware of his location. I do not know what to do, and all I can say is that I am so terribly sorry. Please forgive us."

"Georgiana, I do not wish to hear apologies," he stated flatly. "They will do no good. Do not think another moment of it. Now, I will go and I will find him."

She gave a nod, though tears shone in her eyes. She sucked in a shaking breath. "I am so very so—"

He raised his hand, refusing to let her apologize again. Why, in God's name, should she? "I do not wish to hear it, Georgiana. I will not hear an apology on your lips."

And with that, he strode to her and pulled her into his arms.

"Wait here," he said. "I will find your father."

She nodded against his chest. He could feel the fear and the pain vibrating through her. Damnation, he wished he could take that all away. But he couldn't force the feelings from her. And she was stiff in his arms, unwilling to take his comfort.

That filled him with a terror he never thought to experience.

"My family is everything you feared," she whispered.

There was nothing he could say, because she was correct. But how could he make her understand that none of that mattered?

First, he would find her father and ascertain his safety.

Edward let her go, though he was loath to do so. Without a backward glance, he headed out into the hall.

He would make things right. For her, for them both.

It was, of course, within his power, and for once he was going to use his power in a way he never thought he would. He was going to save an absolutely foolish man, because in the end…it just might save himself and the woman he loved.

• • •

Georgiana carefully removed her diamond ear bobs then stood still as Greggs slipped the crimson gown from her shoulders. The silk rustled as her maid swept it away.

Her heart was breaking. She nearly snorted at

her own drama. A heart could not break. But it hurt. It hurt terribly.

How could this truly be occurring? How could her father, who had always been harmless, if exasperating, have done such a thing?

Georgiana knew one thing above all else. She must go to her mother at once.

If she, herself, could not bear the heartbreak of it all, she could scarce imagine how her mother felt or how her sisters were bearing up under such conditions. They would be sitting alone in their small house in Yorkshire, wondering what their fate was, wondering the condition of their father…and praying not to be abandoned by the Duke of Thornfield.

She knew without hesitation that Edward would not abandon her family.

He was a man of too much duty.

The price would be high. So very, very high. For she could not believe that he could ever look upon them with respect again. The Bly family had played out exactly as he had foreseen, and it was agony. It burned so intensely, she could scarce draw breath. She clung to that pain. Her fear for her father was too much to even consider for longer than a terrifying moment.

Standing now in her chemise and stays, Georgiana shivered, though it wasn't cold in London at this time of year. She didn't move, for this was a costume change.

Every part of her longed to burst apart. Surely, she would sob at any moment. But something else had taken her over. Now she was driven. Driven to go to her home. Driven to ensure her family did not suffer any more than necessary as she waited to find out if her father was safe.

The silence was so intense, Georgiana ground her teeth just to break it.

Greggs rushed back to her with a simple green traveling frock and Spencer. Wordlessly, she let Greggs dress her, until at last her matching green bonnet, flocked with black ribbon, was placed upon her head.

She nodded at her lady's maid. "Let us go."

In just a few moments, Greggs had prepared all that she needed to depart. She admired the efficiency of the older woman. At present, it was a godsend.

Greggs collected her small traveling valise, then they both swept out into the hall with only moonlight to guide them. They rushed down the stairs and out through the cavernous foyer.

Aunt Agatha called to her across the foyer, her voice high over the clatter of their steps. "My dear, you must not go,"

Georgiana turned to the lady who had been so kind. "I must indeed. Please accept my apologies, but I cannot leave my mother alone."

"But you must wait," Agatha protested, aghast. "Edward will come back with news."

"Please tell him to send a message posthaste." She glanced toward the waiting coach in the courtyard. "He will understand duty to family."

"Yes," Agatha said woefully, "but he is your family now, too, my dear."

"Something he is no doubt ashamed of," Georgiana replied, before she swallowed the acrid truth of it.

When Aunt Agatha did not contradict her, Georgiana's heart only sank lower.

But she would not be completely broken by it, even if her heart was bleeding from the knowledge she had almost certainly lost Edward's respect forever.

She squared her shoulders, turned to the carved, thick wooden doors, and headed out to the pavement. She rushed into the coach without looking back.

Greggs followed behind her, a surprisingly sympathetic presence. And as the coach jolted forward, leaving London behind, Georgiana prayed that Edward would be able to find her father before it was too late.

Only Edward could find the man. Of that she was certain. But even so, even if he did set everything to rights, Georgiana felt in her heart of hearts that the great void between their families was one to vast to be breeched. The Blys would never be worthy of his great name.

Oh, Edward had not said it. He did not have to. After all, it had been clear from the night when they'd been caught kissing in his private library that he had felt his life ruined to be linked to such a family as hers.

In the end, he was right. Edward was almost always right. And the great disparity between his family honor and her family? Had been proved without question this night. All that he had struggled and fought for? Her father had made muck of it in a matter of weeks.

Georgiana swallowed back stinging tears. She

had almost certainly lost the happiness and the hope and the love that she had begun to believe would be hers.

All the tutelage in the world mattered not.

In the end, she was still a Bly.

CHAPTER TWENTY-SEVEN

Dashing down from the coach, without awaiting assistance from a footman, Georgiana raced into her childhood home. She whipped her cloak off, her gaze darting for any sign of one of her sisters or her mother.

The house was silent. No servant came to greet her, which only sent a new wave of alarm through Georgiana.

Had her mother and sisters been abandoned in the scandal?

Greggs staggered behind her, her legs weak no doubt, after so much time traveling. The lady's maid gawked at her surroundings in complete shock. Likely, she'd never had an employer who had lived in such an unremarkable dwelling.

Georgiana did not take time to assure Greggs that they would indeed be able to find a place for her to sleep that was not in the back chimney. She had far greater concerns. Even so, she was grateful to the maid who had accompanied her on their wild ride.

"Wait here," Georgiana instructed, handing over her cloak.

Greggs nodded wordlessly, too astounded to make reply. Georgiana left her standing in the foyer, small though it was. She started for the stairs and called out for Elizabeth. A great racket and mixtures of female voices ensued up above.

Elizabeth raced out to the landing, her cheeks drawn and pale. "Thank goodness you have come."

"Where is Mama?" Georgiana demanded, swooping Elizabeth into a quick embrace.

Hugging her back mightily, Elizabeth whispered against her bonnet, "She is in her room, at her desk. She has been writing letters for days, desperately hoping that someone, anyone we know, might have information regarding Papa's whereabouts."

The news did not shock her. Her mama had always been a woman of action. "And where are our sisters?"

Elizabeth pulled back, her shoulders easing as if just the sight of Georgiana had repaired her a good deal. "They're all with her. Everyone is in a worried state. No one has been able to sleep. I think we're all surviving on cups of tea."

"Take me to her."

They rushed up the stairs, leaving Greggs standing alone. But Georgiana was quite certain that Greggs was capable enough to find the kitchens. Greggs was capable enough to lead Wellington's Army.

Georgiana all but ran through the narrow hall and to her mama's room.

She crossed the small chamber swiftly and fell to her knees before her mother, who was indeed sitting at her writing desk. In all her life, she had never seen her mother's shoulders bent. But one glance told Georgiana that she had aged a good ten years in a matter of days.

Her mama's usually rosy cheeks were hollow, her eyes were gaunt and her fingers were stained black with ink. Her dressing gown of deep rose was rumpled, and her braid was coming undone, strands flying about her shoulders.

"Oh, Mama," Georgiana exclaimed.

"My darling girl," her mother breathed, lifting her gaze with painful slowness from the letter she was currently scribbling.

Her hand shook slightly as she cupped Georgiana's cheek. "Have you traveled all night, then? We must get you a cup of tea."

Georgiana swallowed back tears at how her mother still thought of others in her own pain. "I have traveled for three days straight to be with you. We did not spare the horses and we had to change at coaching inns along the way, but here I am now, and we shall make sense of all this."

Sorrow filled her mother's usually knowing eyes. "What shall be done?" Her lips trembled as she fought back tears. "He has ruined us, but I care not for that. I am most worried about his well-being. You know how dark moods can take him."

"Mama," Georgiana said, holding her mother's hands fast. "Edward is looking for him."

"Edward," her mother repeated, before her shoulders shook. "Of course he is. Dear boy. He is such a good man. Is he not?"

"He is, Mama." Georgiana took her mother in her arms, holding her carefully, willing her not to give in. "He is better than any man I have ever known."

"But how shall we ever repay him?" her mother asked, holding onto Georgiana like one lost at sea. "If he finds him, my God, what if he does not?"

"Mama, we must stay calm." Georgiana forced herself to speak with the same sort of steadiness that

Edward often employed.

Her mother pulled away then took Georgiana's hands again in hers and squeezed. Words tumbled out of her like a stream that had flooded its banks. "I do not know if I can remain calm. I am so frightened for him. You should have seen the state he was in when he left. He went to London determined to find the men who had tricked him. But I do not think he will be able to. Such men as that?" Her mother shuddered. "They are the very worst of society. The dregs, the scum of the earth."

"Mama, I cannot agree with you more," Georgiana said gently, meeting her mother's gaze. "But now all we can do is wait. I know how hard that is. But if anyone is capable of finding him, it is Edward."

"And Montrose," Elizabeth said from the doorway.

Georgiana turned to her sister. "I beg your pardon."

"The Earl of Montrose," Elizabeth said. "He went after father." A blush stole across Elizabeth's face. A moment of happiness, quickly replaced by the pain of the present. "You see, he has been staying in the area, and he and I have been… Well, he has been calling almost every day. We…we admire each other very much."

Georgiana could see the hints of affection on her sister's face, and she was heartbroken for her sister that the feelings between them had been so brutally interrupted by this affair.

Elizabeth winced. "And when news of Papa's disappearance came to us, Montrose offered immediately to go in search of him. I hope because he left so quickly after we discovered Papa missing that he will be able to find him with haste."

Surely, Montrose and Edward would be an unstoppable force in the finding of her father. "There," Georgiana said. "All will be well with two such fine men searching for Papa."

Her mother nodded, though nothing would likely convince her until she had her husband with her again.

Methodically, Georgiana stood, cleared away her mama's writing tools, and said in a voice that booked no argument, "Mama, you must have a bath. It will relax you and we shall prepare hot tea and toast for you."

She eyed her mother's frame, which looked as if it had shrunk considerably in but a few weeks. "And you will take a bit of broth."

And they would wait together, for it was the only thing that they could do.

• • •

Edward and Montrose checked every tavern near the dockside. When they proved fruitless, they then headed into the more dangerous warrens of East London.

Much to Edward's surprise, Montrose knew of Bly's misfortunes, for he had been staying near the family for the last month. His affection for Elizabeth apparently more than a passing fancy.

And Edward's friend had ridden from Yorkshire with the devil on his heels in hopes of finding Mr. Bly. Together, they'd find him, no matter what state he was in.

Despite his abilities, Edward was damn glad his friend was with him on this harrowing hunt. It felt as if both their futures depended on the outcome, a feeling which dogged their every step and failure.

Bottles of gin and pints of ale were bought for all the thirsty tavern-goers at The Maiden's Legs, The King's Head, The Mermaid's Tail, and The Rose and Thistle in the hopes that someone had concrete word of Mr. Bly.

All these hopes were to no avail. Mr. Bly had gone well and truly missing. Worse, it seemed his father-in-law did not wish to be found. Edward prayed he would not need to contact the morgues and ask if a body had been discovered in the river or on its banks.

Desperate men were known to take to its unforgiving tides.

But... There was a single thread of hope.

Rumors of a drunken old man weaving from hellhole to hellhole, blathering on about how he had destroyed his family's life had been whispered to them by a costermonger. But Bly's location was yet to be found.

Edward wanted to thrash the man.

He wouldn't. But the man's need to run away was causing anguish.

He paid every pickpocket, every street urchin, and every light skirt for a bit of information until finally, *finally*, a young boy who swept the streets to protect rich men's shoes from mud rushed up to him on the crowded alley and hollered, "Oi found yer bloke, Yer Grace. He be livin' in a room up above

Madame Quick's."

Madame Quick's indeed, he thought.

Of all the places of ill repute Mr. Bly could have found, he'd managed to find the worst.

The knowledge captured Bly's life in entirety.

The poor man seemed to fall from mud puddle to mud puddle to sewage pit. If he was still alive, it was a miracle he hadn't been skewered by a tough. It was even more remarkable that a man such as that had managed to have such daughters like Georgiana or even Elizabeth.

Poor Montrose was just as driven to find Mr. Bly as Edward. For the Scot kept muttering on about Elizabeth being in a state of distress. Edward understood.

The look on Georgiana's face haunted his every step. He did not know if he would ever recover from his part in it. Unlike the vast swaths of humanity, her face was one that he could now easily read, and the pain upon it had struck his heart like a dagger's blow.

This was his fault. There was no circumventing that. He'd given Bly the money to spend, and he had not thought to give him any guidance.

Bly was a foolish man, and foolish men needed a great deal of guidance.

Over the years, Bly had proved again and again that he was incapable with his finances. And much like giving a man prone to drinking gin a large cask, who then drinks it all in one fatal go, Bly had spent every penny that Edward had given him. What a fool Edward had been, something he was entirely unaccustomed to being.

Now he knew the only path forward. It had repeated in his head like a never-ending drum beat. He would develop a plan to save Mr. Bly from himself, not for his father-in-law, but for Georgiana and her family. And for all the people who had been hurt in his carelessness.

If he was honest, he supposed he did have an element of sympathy for the old man, too, who desperately wished to be the equal of far more sensible and wealthy men.

Alas, Bly was incapable, left to his own devices.

Edward and Montrose stormed the crowded alleys and into the dangerous closes of Seven Dials.

Various street sellers hocked their cakes, street gin, wilted flowers, pasties, and second-hand clothes. Everything one could imagine was on sale on the back streets of London.

If one turned the wrong way in the cacophonous area, they could have their throats slit as fast as they could have their tail tickled. Edward knew this from long experience.

Unlike many of his peers, he avoided these parts of town. So many lords adored them. They loved to go slumming in the misery, the raw life that was lived in poverty.

Edward found nothing entertaining about the sorrow of the people who lived and died in these parts, who often only escaped in a cheap wood coffin.

No, his entire life had been spent on measures passed in Parliament to improve the state of affairs here. It was troubling beyond measure to see that Mr. Bly had fallen in amongst the most desperate of

England's populace.

At last, they came upon the rickety building that dated back to Tudor times. Home of Madame Quick's worn rooms that were often let by the hour. Somehow, the crooked house had survived the great fire and it was evident. The plaster which covered the waddle work was missing in spots and the place looked as if it, too, was drunk on sulfur-laced gin.

Edward and Montrose beat upon the dusty door.

It opened on creaky hinges that screamed in protest.

A black-toothed old woman stood in the dark frame, her gnarled hands fisted upon stained skirts. "Why, Yer Grace," she cackled, "Oi've been awaiting yer man of business. But ye've come yerself!"

Edward wasn't surprised that Madame Quick knew him on sight. His face often appeared in newssheets or in caricatures that were posted in shop windows, making him recognizable to almost anyone in London.

"I'm here for Mr. Bly."

"Mr. Who?" she repeated with a wink.

"Madame Quick," he growled. "Do not keep me waiting. My gold will prove more fluid if you choose speed."

She held her dirty, wrinkled hand out, and without hesitation, he placed a golden guinea in it.

"Third floor," she said. "Second door."

"Thank you," he replied as he and Montrose made their way past her and into the dank hall.

They bolted up the stairs, feeling an urgency that did not bode well.

It was a wonder the stairs did not collapse

beneath the weight of both of them. It had sustained three years in London, though, he supposed it could sustain the weight of a duke and an earl.

As they headed down the moldy hallway, he heard the dubious sounds of various activities through the paper-thin walls. He paid no heed and marched to the second door.

He did not bother knocking. Edward simply shoved the rickety door open with a good slam of his shoulder. Mr. Bly sat at a broken table with a chipped mug of sludge like tea before him. Not wine.

For the first time that day, Edward was filled with surprise. He had thought to find Mr. Bly deep in his cups. Oh, no. The man sat in his stained shirtsleeves, his head hung at his chest, the most tortured look upon his old face.

Bly's gaze snapped up and he nearly choked on his own breath when he caught sight of Edward.

"Bly, what the devil are you doing?" Edward demanded.

"Your Grace," Mr. Bly said, trying to stand, but his legs seemed unable to support him and he sat with a *thud*. "I am so terribly sorry. I—"

"Don't," cut in Edward. "There is no point in it. You needn't lacerate yourself any further. I can see you have been doing so for days. But this self-pity will do no one good."

A great racking breath shook Bly's frame. "But I have destroyed everything."

"Everything?" Edward countered gently but firmly. "A great deal? Yes. But not everything. Your family awaits you."

"They can never forgive me for what I've done,"

he wailed like a small boy.

Edward had no time for such things and asked instead, "Why didn't you come to me?"

"I was too ashamed, Your Grace." Bly drove his hand through his unkept silver hair. "I thought I would be able to lift myself up, to bring myself to be worthy of your station. And I trusted men—"

"Och, you trusted sharks," Montrose corrected.

Edward gave his friend a fast glance, hoping to keep any harsh words silent. "Bly, you are a trusting fellow," he said. "And that is the most that can be said about you."

Bly's face crumpled. "Many people have lost their entire fortunes because of the scheme I have put myself in. I wish that I was not alive."

"You wish to never see your wife again?" Edward asked softly, not willing to drive the man further into despair. It would do no one any good to do so. "You wish to never see your daughters?"

Bly closed his eyes. "Not as I am now."

"No, not as you are now," Edward agreed. "But we can't have this. This is not the end. Not for you, not for those people."

Edward drew in a deep breath and crossed to his father-in-law. For once, he did not hesitate and placed his hand on the older man's shoulder. "You shall make amends to every single one of them."

"How?" Bly railed, lifting his gaze to Edward's. His worn face gaunt. "How shall I ever do it? I have lost all of the money you gave me and more. The house that my wife lives in, it shall be taken, too. And my uncle shall never wish to—"

"Bly," Edward said, "I have more money than I

could ever hope to spend in a lifetime, or in three or four generations. We shall find a way to repair the damage. Do not worry on that score. But I shall not give you such unguided freedom again."

Bly grew silent, his eyes wide as he tried to make sense of what Edward said.

Montrose stood quietly, watching the whole affair, though it was obvious he was holding himself in check.

"I made a mistake," Edward explained, willing his friend to support him. "I should have assisted you in more than a gift of funds. I should not have shunned you and left you aside simply because you and I did not see eye to eye on the way to navigate this world. From now on, you shall be by my side and I shall assist you."

Bly said nothing.

Edward crouched down and locked gazes with the broken man. "You are not alone."

Tears slipped down Bly's cheeks.

What Edward promised wasn't something he was looking forward to, particularly. He didn't like Mr. Bly, but he loved Georgiana. And so he would help her father. He would not simply brush his hands of him because he found the man distasteful. No, he would do his duty. And he would take care of his family.

And that he looked forward to very much.

"Bly," he said, "put yourself into my keeping, and all will be well. In time, you will be able to lift your head again, because you will do the right thing."

Bly stared at him with amazement, tears still slipping down his cheeks. "You do not hate me, Your Grace?"

"Why should I hate you?" Hate was not an emotion he allowed in himself and he was stunned for a moment that Bly asked such a thing.

"Because I have brought great shame to you."

Edward knew he had to choose his words carefully. He couldn't lie or the man wouldn't trust him. He'd insist on staying in his own misery because he would not believe there was another way.

So, Edward said with every bit of the love he felt for Georgiana, "I knew the sort of man you were when I met you. You're a gregarious soul who wishes to please everyone and thus pleases no one. It was my mistake, not yours, to have left you to your own devices in this. We shall make a plan *together*. Do you see?"

Mr. Bly swallowed, and for one moment, hope replaced his self-loathing. "I do not know what to say."

Montrose finally crossed the room and clapped Bly on the back. Both men realized that Mr. Bly was on the edge of not being able to bear living with himself.

Montrose looked down at Bly, his chest expanding in a great breath. "The only thing you need to say right now is that you give me permission to marry Elizabeth. Your daughters are remarkable women, and we shall find a way for you to be worthy of them."

Edward smiled at Montrose, and was then struck by how often he was smiling now, something that had only happened because of his marriage to Georgiana.

Montrose was a damned good man. His words

were perfect and seemed to have their intended effect.

Bly nodded, a great sob racking his body. "Of course, I give my permission. Thank you. Thank you, Your Grace. Thank you, my lord. Indeed, I shall do everything I can to lift myself up. I—"

"Do not make grand declarations just now." Edward stood and offered his hand. "You shall show them, day by day, bit by bit, and we shall help you."

Thankfully, his father-in-law took his hand, and with help, rose from his chair.

CHAPTER TWENTY-EIGHT

After ensuring that her mother had taken her hot bath, consumed nourishment, and was tucked into bed with a sleeping draught, Georgiana walked the halls of the house, unable to sleep.

She could not bear it.

Edward's words before they were married kept ringing through her head. He had been so disdainful of her family. So disdainful of her father, disdainful of their position. She'd loathed his arrogance…

But he had not been mistaken.

In fact, she was the one who had been mistaken. Edward was neither cold nor distant. His "arrogance" was a protective mask hiding the depth of his kindness.

In the last days she'd felt the change between them. It had filled her with so much hope. Hope that he would love her…just as she had come to love him.

Dear God. She did.

She loved him.

From the way he spent so many hours ensuring that the most minute details of the new roofs on his estates would be perfect for his tenants—he had spent a good hour showing her the figures—to the way he had shown his aunt daily kindness, he was a good man.

He improved the lives of everyone around him. Despite the pain he had learned to live with over the years. He had not grown bitter as some might. And

while the world did not understand him, Georgiana
did.

How could she bear knowing that the Blys would
be an eternal disappointment to him?

Would he turn from her now, denying the closeness they had forged?

She was his wife, but how, *how* could she look at
him with the same confidence as before? How could
she face the *ton*, for they would peer at her and
whisper behind their hands that she was the daughter of *that man and wasn't it a shame what Thornfield
had to endure*?

It wasn't she who had done it, she knew, but
Edward was still forced to carry the weight of her
father's misdeeds.

It wasn't fair to him. Life was not fair. She knew
it. But oh! What must he think of them?

Georgiana pulled her tangled hair over her
shoulder and took to the stairs. Nothing could distract her from her sorrow or her fear that something
terrible had happened to her father.

Truly, nothing mattered. Not until she knew he
was well. Not until she had seen Edward again and
looked into his eyes to see if he could ever love her.

Georgiana folded her arms about her, wishing
she could find solace in a book. But she could not
even read. She had tried novel after novel. None
could hold her distracted, desperate mind.

Without thinking, she walked through the sleeping house and slipped out into the purple light of a
Yorkshire dawn before the sun had crested the horizon.

The first rays of morning were coming up over

the fields, leaving the landscape painted in dramatic hues of lavender, sapphire, and butter yellow.

Her heart sank. Even that glorious sight couldn't lift her spirits, or alleviate the fear she felt for her father. She drank in the cool morning air, willing her fear to dim.

She searched the horizon, wishing, wishing beyond all measure that she could see her father and see that he was well, that he was still his bouncing self, not broken by the weight of his errors.

She wished in vain.

There was no miraculous sight of her father. Nothing but mist rolled in over the dales. But then the sun broke over the horizon, bathing the grass in its golden hue. The fog began to burn away and the first rays of late summer sun touched her skin. The lark sang, its joyous tune filling the air.

She walked out into the meadow, her heart finally feeling a moment's pause at the promise of a new day.

Could her life be as the dawn? Could she and her family come out of the darkness? She did not know. It was impossible to know.

Just as she bent to touch a cheerful-faced daisy, horse hooves thundered over the hill. She drew in a shuddering breath, turning toward that sound, and there upon his black mare, she spotted Edward.

He rode through the fog, his great coat flying out behind him. Montrose rode just a length behind as they tore up the road.

The light of the sun skimmed over them, and for one fanciful instant, they appeared as knights of old. Her breath caught in her throat at the moment Edward spotted her. He raced before her and in the last moment, he hauled up the reins and Antigone reared high on her rear legs and then drove her front hooves to the earth.

Antigone danced as if the ride from the South had been nothing. Edward jumped down before her and allowed Antigone to graze and rest.

Montrose paid them no heed but rode straight on toward the house.

Edward hesitated, raking his gaze along her frame, before he observed, "Montrose cannot wait to see Elizabeth."

She felt herself trembling as she stood before him, waiting for news.

"I found him. Your father is well."

Relief swept through her with such force, she couldn't speak. Until this moment, she had not understood how her every sinew was taut, how her stomach was coiled in fear, or how her mind had been consumed by the possibility of the worst possible outcome. At Edward's words, all of that began to ease.

At long last, she swallowed and asked, "I almost can't believe it. Where is he?"

"He is in a coach coming behind us, but I had to ride ahead to give you news. I did not wish you to wait. Aunt Agatha is with him. No doubt she has plied him with tea and practical words of comfort throughout the entire journey."

She closed her eyes and said a silent prayer of gratitude. But then she looked upon her husband who was studying her with uncertain eyes. "Thank you, Edward. I cannot thank you enough. Especially since you knew all along that something like this would happen—"

"Georgiana," he said. "Please, I behaved terribly in the past. And I can see that behavior has given you grave pain. The words I spoke before we wed—"

"The truth," she said, "you spoke the truth. And I cannot escape that."

"Yes you can," he said quickly, locking his gaze with hers. "We are not our parents. We are not our past. I am here today, this very morning, to tell you I love you. I did not go after your father because of a scandal. I sought him out because I couldn't bear your pain. Your happiness means everything to me."

"What?" she gasped.

"The moment I left you I was determined to find him, because I understood my responsibility in his state of affairs."

"Your responsibility?"

"Yes, Georgiana. He fell true to his nature, just as I have often fallen true to mine. But because of you, I made an attempt to be different, to practice affection, to practice love," he said. "Would you agree that I have done it?"

"Yes," she said, hardly able to grasp what was transpiring. "Every day you have shown me."

"And so, too, your father can change," Edward said confidently. He tilted his head down, gazing at her with an impassioned plea. "Georgiana, I promise never to let my arrogance or my sense of superiority lead me to hurt you or your family again."

"I don't understand," she said.

"I love you," he declared softly. "I love you more than I have ever loved anyone or anything. Please do not retreat from me now, because you have shown me how to have so much more than just a quiet life alone where I merely survive."

"Edward…"

He shook his head. "Before you make answer, I want you to come with me, because there's something I wish to show you. Will you come?"

He held his hand out to her and without hesitation, she took it.

With that, he swept her up onto Antigone.

She held to her husband tightly, trusting him not to let her fall as they rode into the dales, across the wild, green, rock-strewn moors and toward Thornfield Castle.

Though she said nothing, her heart soared with the possibility that all was not entirely lost.

He loved her…

Did she dare believe it?

• • •

Antigone raced up to Thornfield Castle and Edward pulled the reins gently, knowing the horse needed a little encouragement to stop.

When they had reached the top of the gravel drive, he jumped down and helped Georgiana to her slippered feet. She looked worn and he wanted to wrap her up and take care of her, but first…first he needed to show her something.

Quietly, he led her up the limestone steps to the castle. He took her in through the foyer that had seen kings and queens, ignoring the astonished looks of his butler, Forbes, and the other staff who had not been expecting them.

He took her quietly through the halls, leading her

to his private study where it had all begun. For it was in that study that their lives entwined forever.

He opened the door and led her in.

"Do you see something?" he asked, awaiting her observation with a nervousness he had not felt since boyhood.

She quietly looked about the room, at the crackling fire, and then she stopped. She looked exactly where he hoped that she would. There was his chair, the chair she had refused to leave, the one that had forced him to insist he would kiss her if she would not go. And beside it was another one, exactly the same.

"Is that…" she murmured.

"It is for you," he said, eager to explain his intent. "Your chair, beside mine. This study is yours now. It is *ours*. You will never be forced to leave this room, and you have a chair of your own."

She turned to him, tears filling her eyes. "When did you do this?"

"A week ago," he said. "The day we went to my stables, the day I introduced you to Beatrice, the day you accepted me for who I was. I saw it in your eyes, Georgiana. I saw then that you did not mind my past any more than I mind yours now. I love you," he said. "And I will always love you, and I want you beside me."

"I love you, too," she said. "I think I've known it for some time now, but I didn't know how to tell you because—"

"Because I'm a strange fellow?" he said.

Her brow furrowed and then she laughed. "You are teasing me, Edward."

He nodded. "So, you did not tell me because I

am strange."

"Because one never knows how you might react to things."

"Thank you for tolerating me."

"I don't tolerate you," she insisted. "I love you. I wanted to be yours from the moment that you talked about flight. I knew then that you were the man for me because you viewed the world with a sense of adventure and hope."

"My goodness," he said, a brow arched. "Who would have thought such a thing, that a little chat about science could cause you to fall in love with me?"

"It's the truth," she said, gently touching the chair he'd had made for her. "Though, if I'm honest, I think I began to fall in love with you from the moment you insisted that I get out of your chair."

He leaned down toward her, his heart beating with far too much joy for its own good. But he did not mind at all. "I think I fell in love with you from the moment you told me that my name was not written upon it."

She laughed. "I truly did think you were a servant, you know."

"I do know," he replied. "Now, come here. I wish to kiss you."

Georgiana's eyes danced with mischief. "Not to make me leave?"

"No, my love. To make you stay."

And as he pulled her into his arms and she relaxed against him, safe, he knew she would stay with him.

Always.

EPILOGUE

When a duke decided to do something, very little stood in his way.

It was a thing which still amazed Georgiana. The power her husband had. But unlike so many, Edward also had an imagination.

And so it was that Bly's Bookshop came into existence. Edward held out a circular ring of keys, his face all but beaming with an excitement heretofore nonexistent.

Oh, he still peered down his nose at others, and he still needed time alone. He still chose his chair in the evenings before balls. And he certainly was still a master of drawing long, deep breaths.

But she had noticed that in her presence there was a lightness and a joy to him, especially in moments where he was doing something he knew that would please her.

And this moment was beyond description.

While his great houses and estates were something to behold, this shop meant more because… It was for her and her interests, and her family.

They stood together on the pavement in front of the shop in West London. The coach, a large affair with six horses and a host of servants to operate it, had caused quite a stir. They ignored the growing crowd. A crowd which was quite common when out in the ducal conveyance.

"It is yours. The deed is in your name," Edward said, extending the keys to her. "Your father, with your permission, of course, shall have the name of manager. He shall be able to greet customers whenever he wishes, invite whatever authors he pleases, and feel that he has a good place in society. It will give him a feeling of importance."

"But you shall be married to a merchant," she protested, delighting in the fact she felt so free to tease him now.

"Do I look as if that bothers me?" he queried most seriously—before he winked.

"No," she admitted. "But you often don't look as if anything bothers you."

"Usually, it doesn't," he quipped. "Besides I am quite proud of the fact that a bookshop is in the family."

Edward never lied. So, she took his words as true, and felt her heart soar for it.

Most lords would find such a thing far beneath him. But not her husband. Her husband treasured ink and leather and the wit it took to put the pages together.

She took the large iron keys in her hands, turned to the glass door framed with sapphire blue panels. She slipped the key into the lock, twisted it, and pushed the door open.

A bright jangle from the bell overhead danced through the air.

Together, they crossed the threshold and she let out a sigh of pleasure.

Row after row, after row, after row of empty oak shelves waited to be filled.

Just like the years of their lives to come.

She lifted her gaze upward toward the balcony where she knew her father would be able to make himself a lovely office, a place where he would belong, a place where he would be able to read, gaze down at the customers, and indeed feel a sense of importance.

It would be far better for him than hiding away at home.

The last months had been a slow recovery for him, for her mother, and for their place in society.

But bit by bit, with Edward there every step of the way, they were making that climb.

She looked back at her husband, who was in fact the opposite of arrogant. How could she ever have thought he was unkind or distant?

The Duke of Thornfield was the most thoughtful man in the world, especially when he put his mind to it.

She shook her head, her heart overflowing. She touched her mid-section, which was now impossibly big and round, and realized that the tears filling her eyes were no doubt as a result of the babe who would be born any day. She had been a veritable tumble of emotions for months.

"I do not think I could love you more now that you've given me a bookshop," she said tearfully.

"I rather thought as much," he said, wrapping his arms about her. He placed his hands over her swelling belly.

The last months he had been alarmingly attentive. She'd never seen more lists or preparations in her life. Edward had made certain everything was in place.

She had never thought to be a mother, and at first the idea had been quite harrowing. She was grateful he was so capable and full of excitement. For she had been most overwhelmed in the first months by the changes that had occurred whilst their child grew inside her.

But now she could not wait to meet the little person inside her who often made so much riot that she was certain he was destined for the front benches of parliament.

Here in the peace of the book shop, she felt... love. So much she hardly believed she was capable of it.

"Shall we place Tom Jones in the front of the shop?" he asked playfully, kissing her neck. "Or Mrs. Radcliffe?"

An intense pain pulsed through her and she let out an involuntary cry. It was so sharp, her knees bent and it was all she could do to stay upright.

"My deepest apologies, my love," he laughed. "We shall fill the shelves with whomever you please, of course."

"No...Edward..." She gasped at the sensation that was so foreign and yet completely unmistakable. "I do not care about Tom Jones."

He cuddled her closer, nuzzling her neck. "I know he's a challenging character."

"Much as I love literary debate, take me to the coach please."

He frowned and pulled back ever so slightly. "You wish to go already. I thought perhaps we could explore the rooms toward—"

This time she let out a groan so fierce she thought her strong, stoic husband was about to suffer the vapors.

"I think it is time," she said, breathing deeply, grateful that she could stop waddling wherever she went.

His usually bronzed face went a strange shade of pale. His eyes widened and he echoed, "T-time?"

"Do you need smelling salts, my love?" she asked.

"M-me?" His voice broke.

"You look most unwell."

"It is you that is unwell!" he cried, starting for the door, but then he clearly realized he had left her standing alone in the center of the empty shop and he pivoted back to her. He swept her up into his arms, cradling her against his chest.

"I am in the best of health," she informed, doing her all she could not to be simultaneously amused and infuriated by his reaction to the imminent occasion. "I am simply having a baby. But we should go home. And you should call for my mother."

Her husband nodded.

For the first time in her life, she realized that the all-powerful duke was completely lost.

"Edward," she said gently. "All will be well."

A look of sheer panic crossed his face. "But what if it is not?"

She circled her arms about his neck and forced him to meet her gaze. "Look at me."

He did as she said. "This is going to be the most exciting day in our lives. Are you ready for it?"

"I am," he breathed. "And I shall not leave your side."

•   •   •

Four hours later

Henry Micheal Montrose FitzPatrick Stanhope, Marquess of Brookhaven, entered the world in a hurry, waiting for no man or schedule.

In truth, given the London traffic that particular day, it had taken nearly an hour to arrive at the town house. And Edward had nearly suffered apoplexy at the state of the roads. He may have yelled dire threats at various hackneys.

Despite all his planning, the doctor had not arrived in time for the birth. Certain that it being Georgiana's first, he could finish his game of whist or…two.

The doctor had been mistaken and was fortunate to still be breathing.

Like so many things, Georgina had chosen to give birth boldly.

And quickly.

Luckily, all had gone well.

Edward was in such good humor, holding his small but mighty son, that he would not run the rather overconfident physician out of town.

Between Greggs, who looked as if the sun and moon rose and set with the baby already, and Mrs. Bly, Georgiana had given birth with a great deal of wailing, strength, and the demand to know why the devil it was taking so long.

It had not actually taken long, as he had later been informed. But it had been particularly vigorous. When the baby had all but popped into this world, Edward had caught him in his own hands. It was a most shocking beginning for a future duke. There had been little pomp or ceremony.

But there was one true thing—the boy was loved by every person in the room.

Edward looked down at his wife who, though exhausted upon their bed, looked as if happiness was the only possible emotion left in this world.

Captain sat on the floor as near as he could physically be without leaping atop the counterpane. The wolfhound kept his vigil, guarding them all, bursting with canine pride.

Edward had never experienced so much emotion and so much peace at the same moment.

Gazing down at the tiny, impossibly delicate hands of his son, he had to agree with his wife's general air of joy.

He thought of the night that he and Georgiana had met.

That night had changed his entire life.

He was desperately grateful to the young lady, whose name he could not recall, who had flung herself most mercenarily into the muddy ditch. And he was very glad he had done the noble thing and gone in after her. For if they had not done their individual parts, he wouldn't have needed to change his breeches.

He wouldn't have strode furiously into his study.

And Georgiana never would have mistaken him for a servant.

"Whatever is going on inside your head?" she asked, her eyes full of adoration.

He leaned down and kissed her softly. "Only that a pair of muddy breeches can lead to remarkable things."

ACKNOWLEDGMENTS

A huge thank-you to Lydia Sharp and Jill Marsal. You two guided me along this process with so much kindness! Lydia, you are a rock star. Jill, you really were a great partner who supported me at every moment! Thank you to the entire team at Entangled for all the hard work for our book. My gratitude truly knows no bounds. A huge thank-you to Matt, Kelly, and Coochy for keeping me sane and promising me I COULD meet my deadlines. I love you three and am over the moon you're in my life. For Julie, who kindly and firmly told me during the last rounds of edits that the only way is through. My three gorgeous little boys gave up several hours with their mommy, and I am so grateful for their support, cheering, and pride that I am a storyteller. And last, you. Without you, none of this, not one little bit, would be possible. Thank you. I'm so full of gratitude for this adventure. And I'm ready for the next.

*Looking for another sexy and hilarious
Regency romance?
Turn the page to start reading!*

THE
RAKEHELL
OF
ROTH

AMALIE HOWARD

CHAPTER ONE

Was it peculiar that she didn't *feel* married?

A forgotten glass of warm champagne in hand, Lady Isobel Vance, the new Marchioness of Roth, peeked up at the towering, silent gentleman beside her as they stood on the balcony. The Marquess of Roth could be a statue carved from marble instead of flesh and bone. Starkly beautiful. Impenetrable. Impossible to read.

Her *husband*.

A thoughtful frown limned his full lips, turning them down at the corners, and his gray eyes held less warmth than shards of flint. Hardly a doting bridegroom. Other than the exchange of vows, he hadn't said more than two words to her since they'd left the chapel. Isobel swallowed past the thickening knot in her throat and the feeling of unease growing in her belly.

Shouldn't a bride feel a modicum of happiness on her wedding day?

Then again, her nuptials to Lord Roth had been rather abrupt. Over the past few months in London with her aunt and uncle, the marquess had treated her with polite courtesy and charming indulgence. He wouldn't have found her disagreeable in looks, she knew. Most men didn't. Her sister, Astrid, had always bemoaned her beauty as a curse, but Isobel well knew that men craved beautiful things. In their world, beauty was coveted, much like pedigree.

And the Marquess of Roth was of exceptional pedigree.

Heir to the Duke of Kendrick, he was well-heeled, handsome, and young. A desirable catch, by all accounts. And he wasn't the lecherous Edmund Cain, Earl of Beaumont, who was twice her age and had been trying to lift her skirts since the moment she'd been old enough to marry, especially after compromising her own sister. Poor Astrid had quit London, only to fend off his return as earl nine years later—and his vile pursuit of Isobel—by wedding the dreaded Duke of Beswick.

Isobel had attempted to take matters into her own hands to secure a husband who *wasn't* the earl, but it had only been with Beswick's help that she'd been able to avoid the earl's trap altogether. Astrid's scarred duke had not only persuaded the Prince Regent to favor Roth's suit, but had also procured a special marriage license.

Gratitude didn't begin to cover what she felt.

She'd escaped Beaumont's clutches and secured an enviable match with a marquess. A man who was both beautiful and heroic. Noble and honorable. The perfect gentleman. Already half-enamored, girlish visions of a blissful future had danced in her head, full of laughter and joy, family and children. They would be rapturously happy.

Despite a few vague rumors of his aversion to matrimony, their wedding had been a boon, and what had caused him to propose hadn't been of interest to her, only that he *had*.

Now, however, Isobel frowned.

Why had he decided to settle down?

Roth didn't need her dowry. As far as she knew, he was in line for a very solvent dukedom. She'd heard the gossip that the marquess had the reputation of a notorious rake, but which young gentleman wasn't a bit of a rogue? Her aunt had always said that reformed rakes made the best husbands.

Isobel didn't know if that was the case with Roth, but she hoped his roué days were over. Her own father had been faithful to her mother, and though Isobel knew that many gentlemen of the *ton* kept mistresses, the idea did not sit well with her. Not that she would have any say in such things. A society lady was meant to do her duty and provide an heir, and even if her husband sought carnal diversions elsewhere, it was of no consequence.

With a face like his, it wasn't hard to picture the dashing marquess being surrounded by fawning, simpering women. She spared him a furtive glance through her lashes and promptly lost her breath. The man made the estimable Beau Brummell look like a shriveled toad. Tall, broad-shouldered, and superbly fit, he was every lady's dream. Hers as well, if her galloping heart had anything to say about it. Even in profile, his sharply edged masculine beauty made her cheeks heat. Sculpted lips, high cheekbones, thick, golden-brown hair curling into a wide brow, and glittering eyes the color of a glacier in a winter storm. His given name was fitting.

Winter.

Because at the moment, he embodied the frigid season.

Suppressing a tiny sigh, Isobel sipped at her warm drink and winced. She'd give anything for a glass of her sister's whiskey. Or some French brandy. Something with a little more bite to bolster her flagging confidence. Or ward off the chill of her iceberg of a husband. Perhaps he had other things on his mind, like matters of business?

She drew a bracing breath, determined to make the best of it.

"Are you well, my lord?" she ventured softly.

Slate-gray eyes fell to hers, confused for an instant as if he didn't know who she was or what she was doing there, as though she were some species of creature he did not recognize. But then they cleared, and recognition filled them. "Yes, of course. And you?"

"I'm well, thank you."

"Good."

Awkward silence spooled between them.

So much for brilliant conversation. Ducking her head, Isobel cringed and gulped the rest of her tasteless drink, her eyes darting to the revelry within the balcony doors. Lady Hammerton's ball was in full swing, and Isobel knew that Astrid would be there. A small comfort, at least.

"I…I suppose we should go in," she suggested.

The marquess gave her an unreadable look, though his mouth pinched with the barest hint of resignation. "Yes, the show must go on, mustn't it?"

She blinked in confusion. "The show, my lord?"

He leaned down to graze his lips over her cheek, the soft caress at odds with his mocking tone and taking her by surprise. Inhaling deeply as though scenting her skin, his nose drifted down the curve of her jaw until his mouth hovered over the corner of hers. Isobel's lips parted of their own trembling accord, in unspoken invitation, which he did not accept.

Kiss me, she wanted to beg.

She didn't. But shyly, she tilted her chin, trying to show him what she yearned for. With a muttered curse, the marquess reared back and stared at her with a strange blend of irritation and desire in those flinty eyes.

Isobel swallowed her disappointment. "Did I do something wrong, my lord?"

It felt like an eternity before that beautiful gray gaze landed on her, the brief hint of desire from earlier no longer present. Not one ounce of warmth came through his impassive regard. It wasn't irritation now, she realized, but forced indifference. *Why would he need to be indifferent?*

"No," he murmured. "This is simply new to both of us."

"Marriage?"

His lip curled. "Until death us do part, love."

The sentiment and endearment should have eased her, but the cynical way he uttered those words did not sound like the commitment and union they were meant to represent, though rather more of a curse. But then, once more as if in contradiction of himself, he lifted her hand and brought her knuckles to his lips. Ever so slowly, he brushed his mouth over her gloved hand, until she could feel her heartbeat throbbing in each fingertip. The gentleness of the caress undid any worry she had.

If he touched her like this, they were going to be just fine.

• • •

Winter sat back against the velvet squabs of his coach and settled in for the ride to his father's ancestral seat in Chelmsford, his family home and the only place he could take a wife.

Bloody hell. Not *a* wife. *His* wife.

God, how his sister would have cackled to see the great Winter Vance leg-shackled.

I shall never marry! His twelve-year-old self had puffed his chest. *Girls are annoying, just like bratty little sisters.*

Prue had paid his male posturing no mind. *Then I shall curse you, my favorite brother, to marry the most beautiful angel in the world!*

And here he was.

Married to exactly that.

Winter forced himself to focus on the task at hand. He couldn't go to his private estate, Rothingham Gable, for obvious reasons. For one, that particular abode was not prepared for a Lady Roth, given the week-long house party that had just been hosted there.

He had not even been in residence. Rutland and Petersham and the rest of their fast set had run the show, desperate for some wild country fun to offset the terminal boredom of the season. While he missed them from time to time, those days of endless dissipation were over. They had been since Prue's death. Not that anyone actually knew...or had noticed. People believed what they wanted to believe.

Winter slanted his new wife a glance. Her attention was caught outside the small window, her face held in pensive thought. Her profile was exquisite, perfect in its symmetry from the classic line of her forehead to her delicate nose and pink rosebud pout. Isobel was young, fresh out of the schoolroom, but he couldn't deny her exceptional beauty…or his irritating and inconvenient attraction to her.

Christ, he wanted to debauch that mouth right there on the balcony—take it from virginal pink to passionate red. The urge had taken him by surprise. The honeysuckle scent of her satiny skin had been an aphrodisiac. When he'd grazed the corner of her mouth and seen her undisguised longing, the bolt of lust tunneling through him had nearly brought him to his knees.

Just like it threatened to do now.

Ripping his gaze from her tempting lips, he let it drift down the elegant line of her throat. He imagined tasting the skin there, nuzzling her fluttering pulse beneath his lips, and inhaling more of her sweet, flowery smell. Winter bit back a groan. He would no doubt sample both later…when he'd be expected to do his marital duty. *Hell*. He'd have to hold himself in check. Make it perfunctory. And most of all, quick. The act was a necessary obligation, nothing more, because he had an inkling that this woman could be the end of him.

"Did you enjoy seeing your sister?" he asked, his voice rough edged. They'd called in at Beswick Park after leaving Lady Hammerton's. Her rousing entertainments had gone well into the dawn hours.

His wife startled, attention flying to him. "Yes, of course, my lord. Thank you for arranging the visit."

"Call me Winter," he said.

She flushed. "Winter."

His wife turned the full force of those ice-blue eyes on him, and for a moment, it felt like his skin had been seared by lightning. But that gaze also shone with no small degree of infatuation. It didn't take much to interpret the shy glances and the soft blushes whenever she thought he wasn't looking.

This was why it could never work.

He wanted sex and a warm body; she wanted sonnets and his soul.

The plain truth was that he'd needed to marry. An expedient wedding was the answer to Winter's problems *and* hers—and he'd jumped at the solution. His father's recent codicil stated if he wasn't married by his twenty-first birthday, he wouldn't get a finger on the rest of his inheritance until he was thirty. That was over a decade away! The social club he'd opened with his best friend, the Duke of Westmore, using the first portion of his inheritance, was in its infancy. Anything could happen.

Which was why marriage was a lesser evil—it paid to be prepared.

And Winter didn't have to court anyone, endure evenings at Almack's, or worry about matchmaking mothers, fortune hunters, and the like. Isobel Everleigh was the perfect choice for a quiet, dutiful bride. He did not intend to be another casualty to fate, love, or beautiful women. He'd seen too much of what marriage and dependence had done to his own mother and his sister to ever want that deadly yoke for himself. Love made people weak and foolish, and drove them to madness or worse.

And Isobel—as perfect a bride as she might be—was no exception.

Reluctant amusement built in his chest. Oh yes. His sister definitely would have laughed herself silly at his predicament that he'd gone and gotten himself wedlocked to a jejune, enraptured debutante with romantic starbursts in her eyes.

She's just what you deserve, Win, she would have teased. *The angel to your devil.*

Right now, his devil wanted to strip the angel bare. Make her writhe and moan. Corrupt her with sin.

"What's your home like?" Isobel asked, interrupting his depraved thoughts, her sweet voice flicking against his senses. He'd much rather hear that soft voice screaming with pleasure, head thrown back and eyes glazed, golden curls tumbling down…

Damnation. Stop.

Winter cleared his tight throat. "Kendrick Abbey is much like Beswick Park, I suppose. Rolling hills, manse, ornamental ponds, a lake, tenants, the usual." He waved an arm, guessing that she might share her sister's penchant for horses. "You can ride to your heart's content."

"I don't care for horses."

A frown creased his brow. "You don't?"

"One threw me when I was a girl," she explained with a pretty blush. "My sister insisted I get back on, but I was much too timid. They frighten me, really. To be honest, mounting such an enormous, powerful animal makes my pulse race."

Winter stared at her, his frown deepening as *his* pulse kicked up a notch. Was she being facetious? At his look, his wife bit her lip, and his stare swung to that moistened, plump roll of flesh when she released it. Hell if he didn't want to taste it. Winter tore his gaze away and focused on the delicate slope of her nose. Yes, that was a safe bet.

When had it gotten so hot in the carriage? It was bloody sweltering.

He tugged at his collar. "What *do* you enjoy doing, then?"

"I like balls," she replied shyly, and the ones in his pants throbbed in approval even though they had nothing to do with the event in question. "I liked dancing with you at Lady Hammerton's very much."

"Did you?" His voice sounded choked, even to his own ears.

Nodding, Isobel's tongue darted out to wet her lips, and Winter dug his fingers into the bench. Everything she did and said was so artless and yet so deeply erotic he felt it in his bones. *Christ*, he needed to get in control! Oblivious to his deteriorating composure, she warmed to filling the silence with conversation while he descended into silent torture.

"I also enjoy playing the pianoforte, though I'm not very adept, I'm afraid. My sister accuses me of pounding the keys too hard at times."

Oh, bloody hell, there was no way she didn't know what she was doing to him with those provocative words—*mounting, balls, pounding*—but her pretty face remained earnest and sincere, not an ounce of artifice to be seen.

It was just him then, lost in the mire of obscenity.

Control, for the love of God, Roth.

"Anything else?" he managed politely.

She brightened at his interest. "I enjoy embroidery. It's a wonderful, ladylike pastime. Though I do not enjoy getting pricked."

Winter made a strangled noise. It was no use. He was going to fucking *die*.

● ● ●

The carriage ride had been an absolute disaster. A complete and utter calamity. Despite Isobel's efforts, once more, to have a mature, adult conversation with her husband, she had failed spectacularly. The marquess had glowered at her as though vacillating between tossing her bodily from the coach, wanting to incinerate her with his eyes, and staring at her as if she were his next meal.

The last had made her uncomfortably hot.

Was this what her wedding night would be like? Hot, uncomfortable, and impossible to predict? While she wasn't in the least experienced, those hungry looks had awakened feelings in her she didn't even know she had—a choked sensation in her breast, overheated skin, blood that felt like thickened honey, and the outrageous need to throw herself across the coach and scale his huge body like a monkey on a tree.

Without a stitch of clothing.

Thank God her thoughts were private, though she was sure that some of them might have been visible on her face, given the tightening of his brow and his restless shifting on the opposite bench.

Twice, out of the corner of her eye, she'd seen the heel of his palm grind into his lap, but she hadn't dared to let her eyes drift anywhere below his chin. It simply wasn't proper. At least her behavior was beyond reproach, even if her thoughts weren't.

Because those were *beyond* shameless.

It was a miracle Isobel had been able to keep her composure intact when they finally arrived at Kendrick Abbey.

"Are you well, my lady?" Winter asked after the footman helped her down in the well-kept courtyard. "You seem…flustered."

"The coach was rather warm," she replied, grateful for the bite of the crisp early evening air. "And I'm nervous to meet His Grace."

"Don't be. Kendrick isn't here. He's in Bath. He spends most of his time at his estate there, taking the waters. With any luck, it will just be Oblivious Oliver." At her questioning look, he shrugged. "My brother."

"Oh," she said. Isobel didn't know he had a brother, but there were a lot of things she didn't know about her new husband. She had years to learn, however. Grasping his gloved hand, she smiled up at him. He gave their joined hands a quizzical look but did not pull his away. Isobel took that as a good sign as she surveyed her new home and its occupants.

The servants were all lined up to welcome their new mistress, and she greeted each one of them, from the butler to the housekeeper to the footmen, with sincere warmth.

She would get to know each of them more later.

For now, Isobel followed her husband up to their suite of rooms, taking in as much as she could of the abbey's impressive interior, from its vaulted ceilings to its meticulously polished furnishings. Isobel was no stranger to fortune, but this took her appreciation of wealth to a new level. Her husband's chambers, though not the master, had a sumptuously decorated interconnecting bedroom. The decor was just as lavish as the rest of the house.

"Are you hungry?" Winter said. "I've asked Mrs. Butterfield to send up a tray for an early supper. I've also rung for a lady's maid to prepare you a bath." He paused at the threshold, his gaze unfathomable. "In the meantime, I must find my brother and take him to task for not being there to receive us properly. I'll return shortly."

Isobel gave him a soft smile, grateful for his thoughtfulness and equally glad he did not insist she accompany him. She was a bundle of nerves as it was, knowing their wedding night was forthcoming. A bath and a meal would help.

Hours later, she'd finished both, and despite eating the delicious fare alone—Winter had yet to return—Isobel couldn't relax. It was her first time in a strange place and finding herself eased was impossible. After changing into her night rail, she'd climbed into the huge bed. Would Winter prefer her under the blankets? Above them? In bed at all? In an attempt to distract herself, she tried to read from a book she'd packed in her things but couldn't concentrate. Her nerves were much too frayed.

Where was her husband? Would he come to her?

Stretching restlessly, she inched out of the bed

and went to the window, where the full moon cast its silvery light over the gardens visible from her room. She and Astrid used to pretend to be fairies dancing under the moon when they were little girls. Like then, she had the urge to run outside barefooted, feel the grass beneath her toes, and spin around in circles until she collapsed with dizziness. The whimsical recollection made her smile.

The skin on her nape prickled and she whirled around, throttling a scream in her throat.

The Marquess of Roth stood at the connecting door, watching her.

Isobel blushed, realizing that the moonlight through the windowpanes rendered her filmy night clothes nearly invisible. She crossed her arms over herself, only to be stalled by Winter's rasped, "Don't."

Obediently, Isobel dropped her arms. Her nerves returned in full force when he approached, only stopping when he was an arm's length away, dark, tall, and foreboding. The moonlight caught his face, too, casting his angular features in silver shadows. He was dressed only in shirtsleeves, she realized breathlessly, and her eyes traced the strong neck disappearing into the opened collar. His shirt was untucked from his trousers, his feet scandalously bare.

"I was waiting," she murmured when he didn't say anything.

"I trust everything was to your satisfaction?"

Isobel nodded, suddenly shy. "It was. Thank you, my lord."

"Winter."

She bit her lip, unable to say his given name in so

intimate a setting. He stared at her for what seemed like forever before closing the gap between them, and she gasped when his hands closed over her waist. One large palm slipped down to caress her hip. Sensations flooded her untried body, pebbling her nipples beneath the lacy night rail. She clenched her jaw hard. It was that, or give way to the vulgar moans clambering up her throat.

"Do you know what to expect?" he asked. "Did your sister or mother advise you of the wedding night?"

"Yes, my aunt explained," Isobel whispered. She would not admit the guidance she'd received from her Aunt Mildred was thin at best, though she had a general idea of the act and what it entailed. He would undress her. Impale her. Fill her with his seed. Even in her head, the process sounded awful. She swallowed hard, her muscles locking.

"Don't be afraid," he told her.

With that, he untied the ribbons at her throat and wrists, and the flimsy garment pooled to the floor. Isobel held her breath, fighting her blush, as he took her nude body in, his face hard as if hewn from granite. A muscle jumped in that rigid jaw.

"This first time might hurt," he said. "But I will try to make it as painless as possible."

In a show of effortless strength, the marquess scooped her up and carried her to the bed, and she scrambled backward before he shucked off his own clothing and climbed on top of her. There wasn't enough room to get a good view of anything, but good gracious, she could feel the hot brand of him on her thigh. Instead of making her frightened, it made her ache.

Was her breathing supposed to be this shallow? Her heartbeat so fast? The sharpness of all the combined feelings was making her light-headed. Her muscles tightened again, though this time it wasn't because of dread but excitement. Isobel had no time to process any of it before he bent toward her, his parted lips settling on her neck. Nerves forgotten, her skin burned at the erotic contact as his tongue swept over her flesh.

The slow sensual lick was vastly different to the chaste, perfunctory peck he'd given her in the chapel, or the almost-kiss on the balcony, but she wasn't complaining. He bit her earlobe, sucking it into his mouth, and her entire body shuddered. Good Lord, this wasn't even kissing, it was…it was…*devouring*. The idea of his mouth trailing down her body in a similar fashion nearly made her eyes roll back in her head.

Would he?

As if she'd demanded it, he continued his journey south of her jaw until Isobel moaned, her hands climbing up to wind in her husband's hair as she succumbed to his skill. Heavens above, she'd never felt more alive, more on *edge*. Every muscle in her body strained and shook as he reached the valley between her breasts, his lips wet and warm. She felt faint from the pleasure coiling in her stomach, her brain a muddled mess. Could a person die from such sensation? Surely it was possible.

One more lick, one more dangerously sinful bite, and she'd be done for.

A whimper broke from her. "Winter."

Cool air blew against the damp skin of her body when he broke away, a stormy gaze boring into hers. Was he going to stop? Pull away? He wouldn't be so cruel, would he? He'd *told* her to use his given name!

But with a fraught growl, his mouth descended to where he'd left off and kissed its way down her body, lingering over each of her breasts until she was certain she'd go mad. By the time he lifted himself above her, she no longer had a rational thought in her head. She was a blinding mass of need and raw desire. When his body finally slid into hers, it pinched, but his careful preparation had soothed the way.

"Hold still," he rasped, his voice hoarse with strain as his breath sawed out of him. "Get used to me."

It wasn't his words as much as his thoughtfulness that melted her. Once she'd adjusted to accommodate him, Isobel sucked in air as he began to move, withdrawing almost all the way before easing back in.

"Is this too much?" he asked.

"No, you're perfect."

Winter stilled, but she didn't have time to feel embarrassed by the blurted admission before he repeated the motion, making her gasp. With each pass, it felt better. Sensation upon sensation built inside her with every stroke until he reached between them to caress a spot that made her see stars and she cried out as pleasure took her.

A few short thrusts later, and Winter groaned what sounded like her name, though she couldn't be sure, his huge frame withdrawing completely from her and then going rigid with what she imagined was the culmination of his own release. Breathing hard, he slumped forward, his large body blanketing hers. It was strangely nice, though the moment did not last.

Her husband lifted off of her. For an unguarded moment his eyes met hers, a flare of shock evident before he rolled away. Isobel did not feel slighted when he stood and reached for his trousers. She could only remember the tenderness of his touch, and the kindness he'd displayed with her inexperienced body. Her husband *had* to care to be so gentle and considerate.

Isobel draped herself in the warmth of everything she felt and smiled to herself.

One day, perhaps soon, she would tell him she loved him.

CHAPTER TWO

Oh how she hated that bloody, black-hearted jacka-napes!

The brisk morning wind teased the pins from Isobel's hair, blond tendrils lashing into her face as she galloped at a breakneck pace across the moors. She was in a fine froth, and she pushed her mare Hellion to go even faster. Faintly, Isobel heard a voice calling out from somewhere behind her, but she couldn't turn back now. Nothing but a grueling ride would cool the heat in her veins.

According to the newssheets she'd read that morning, her husband was up to his disreputable exploits in London again, while she, the poor, pathetic—and any number of other uncharitable descriptors—country mouse of a wife remained at home in pious, devoted silence.

Devoted, my furious foot.

Her maggot of a marquess had abandoned her here.

After their wedding, Isobel had assumed she and Winter would live together in Chelmsford. It was his father's ducal seat, after all, and his family home. Old bitterness, buried down deep, spilled through her. How foolish and utterly naive she'd been! Her *caring* new husband had bedded her and then left her.

That. Same. Night.

She'd gathered—albeit after a lot of weeping and the shattering of her rose-tinted spectacles—that her husband might not have held as grand an affection for her as she'd had for him. That what had seemed so special to her had not meant a thing to him at all, because right after he'd done his duty, he'd absconded like a thief in the dark.

Isobel snarled out an oath as her mare's hooves pounded the dirt, putting much needed distance between them and those dratted newssheets at the manor. It was a beautiful day with not a cloud in the sky, but Isobel hardly took notice, so intent she was on outrunning her fury.

In the beginning, she had thought Winter's absence would be for a day or two. She had waited like a besotted fool for weeks before Mrs. Butterfield had taken pity on her and explained that the marquess was very busy with his business in London and very rarely came to Kendrick Abbey. And if he did come to the country, he had his own estate in Chelmsford—Rothingham Gable.

Even then, she'd been so sickeningly naive, wondering why a husband would choose to leave his new wife at his father's ducal residence instead of his.

Perhaps he was performing restorations.

Perhaps he wanted to surprise her.

Perhaps, perhaps, perhaps.

She'd learned the unpleasant answer a few months later from a loose-lipped maid—her heroic, honorable, noble husband was apparently renowned for hosting wild house parties at Rothingham Gable. Bacchanalian revels, the maid had confided with

suffocated giggles. Of course, that had all been long
before he'd been married, the maid had hastily assured her.

Of course, a heartsick Isobel had echoed.

Now, three years and five months later, with the
barest minimum of correspondence from the marquess, she learned more about her vagabond
husband from the London gossip rags than from
the man himself. Isobel had had enough. This time,
he'd purportedly engaged in a dawn duel. Over an
opera singer of all things.

She scowled as she slowed and dismounted,
letting Hellion cool off and graze.

How dare he disrespect her so?

As the Marchioness of Roth, she'd held her head
high and pretended her callous husband wasn't such
an empirical ass. She'd been patient. Honored her
vows. Respected his wishes. Brushed off his antics as
youthful folly. Buried the hurt that his coldhearted
desertion had caused. Told herself that eventually,
like all highborn gentlemen, Winter would come to
his senses and require an heir. Then she would have
a family, even if her rakehell of a husband did not
want to be involved.

Someday.

Someday had never come. Swallowing her bitterness, Isobel paced back and forth, the rich smell of
grass and earth doing little to calm her down. Even
the cheery sound of laughter from the children of
the tenant farmers down the hill didn't make her
smile.

As year after year passed, she convinced herself
that she wasn't bloody miserable each month she

spent cooped up like some forgotten mare put out to pasture, with only her pianoforte and her useless accomplishments to keep her company. Isobel remembered with acute shame what she'd primly told her sister years ago: *a young lady should be accomplished in the feminine arts. Music, and dancing, and whatnot.*

Well, she was eating a large serving of crow and *whatnot* at the moment. No one had ever explained to her younger and vociferously green self what *whatnot* had meant. If it meant dealing with a husband who had dumped his wife in Chelmsford while he gallivanted in London and pretended he was an eternal bachelor, then she'd be an expert in the matter.

"He'll grow out of it, dear," Mrs. Butterfield had told her. "All men sow their wild oats."

So she'd let him sow. Acres and acres of it. But this was outside of enough.

A bloody duel. Over someone who *wasn't* his wife.

Isobel clenched her fists together, staring mindlessly over the tops of the tenant cottages to the spire of the village church in the distance. Clarissa, her dearest friend and lady's companion, had suggested that some of the accounts of gambling and indecent revelry might be false—salacious stories sold newspapers, after all. But even *some* stories had to have a modicum of truth to them. Isobel thought she'd become desensitized to her husband's antics, but clearly not.

Rage and hurt bubbled up into her throat.

"Damnation, woman!" Clarissa wheezed as she

reined her horse to a lathered stop where Isobel stood at the edge of the rise overlooking the lake. "I never should have taught you to ride."

Her sweaty best friend dismounted, her dark mess of curls sticking out in every direction, and her green eyes knowing, full of sympathetic anger. Isobel's own eyes were dry as she greeted her. She'd shed enough tears for that pigeon-livered rogue of a husband. He did not deserve another drop from her, not a single one.

"I take it you read the newssheets," Isobel said. No need to beat around the bush. There was only one reason that her friend would follow her mad dash from the house.

Clarissa nodded and remained silent. After three years of shared confidences, particularly about the subject of the Maggot of Roth, she well knew when to let Isobel vent. She had enough opinions of her own about Isobel's scoundrel of a husband, but at times like this, she was the more level-headed of the two of them.

"They exaggerate everything," Clarissa said in a soothing voice. "You know this. Those abominable liars write what they want to write."

"Then why wouldn't Roth dispute them, if that were the case?"

"Perhaps he thinks them amusing? Men don't worry about those sorts of things."

"Those sorts of things," Isobel repeated. "He fought a *duel*, Clarissa. Over Contessa James of all people."

Clarissa pulled a face. "Maybe he's acting out," she suggested mildly.

"He's a grown man. How much acting out does he need to do?"

"Men mature differently than women," her friend replied with the patience deserving of a saint instead of her usual speak-first-think-later temperament. "And he's never recovered from his sister's and mother's deaths—you also know that as well as I do. Everyone knows that it left him in a terrible state. It's the reason he and the duke don't get along."

"Grief shouldn't make a man an absolute steaming arse-rag."

Clarissa's eyes sparked with reluctant approval, her mouth twitching at the inventive slur. "Shouldn't have taught you to swear, either."

"You shouldn't have taught me a lot of things."

Clarissa was the daughter of the Duke of Kendrick's private solicitor, Mr. Bell, and the youngest of six, the other five all boys. From the moment she and Isobel had been introduced nearly three and a half years ago, they'd been inseparable, and everything Clarissa learned from her rambunctious brothers, she'd taught to Isobel.

And that meant *everything*.

Isobel had been so sheltered that when the incorrigible, boisterous, and entirely too bold girl had asked her with a saucy grin if she was *up the pole yet*, her eyes had gone wide and her mouth had gaped. "It only takes one time, you know," her new friend had said knowingly. "To get with child."

"No," a scandalized Isobel had stammered. "I don't think so."

"What were his kisses like?" A curious stare had followed. "Did you stick your tongue in his mouth?"

"No!"

"Then you're doing it wrong."

Isobel had stopped blushing after the first life lesson—one involving how babies were made. That had been eye-opening, to say the least. Not that she hadn't had a thoroughly erotic introduction to marital relations with her own clodpole of a husband, a union which had not borne any fruit of the newborn variety. By design, she'd learned since, as the marquess had withdrawn and spilled in the sheets. Perhaps, that, too, had been a blessing in disguise.

Though deep down, Isobel did not deny wishing for children of her own and a family to care for one day, blessing in disguise or not.

Thank God for Clarissa, the only light in what had promised to be a lonely and dismal existence. From then on, her self-ordained best friend had encouraged her to ask her anything, as in *anything*. And since it was much too shameful to voice certain inquiries out loud, Isobel chose to pen secret letters to which Clarissa provided answers in lewd, graphic, and gleeful detail.

After the first letter asking about what it was like to truly kiss a man, the impish Clarissa had replied with a scandalous masterpiece dedicated solely to the vagaries of kissing, including tongues, spit, and fish-faced puckers that had made the two girls dissolve into irreverent giggles.

Eventually, what had started out as naughty but instructive letters between friends had turned into a surprising windfall. Isobel's sister Astrid, an authoress herself, had taken one look at the stack of scandalously frank correspondence, burst into laughter, and sent them off to her publishing man of affairs. While Astrid mostly published essays about women's rights with the steadfast support of her own husband, her visionary publisher had seen opportunity with the *Dearest Friend* letters. That had been the start of *The Daring Lady Darcy*.

All anonymous, of course.

Said publisher didn't want to go to prison.

Lady Darcy's instant success had taken them all by surprise. As it turned out, wicked advice to ladies of quality had been a shocking novelty, and the modest publication had risen to instant notoriety. From recipes to fashion to needlepoint, to physical and emotional intimacy, to scandalous erotic advice, there was no stone left unturned, no subject left untouched. The frank periodicals flouted decency, but readers were greedy for more.

"I should write Lady Darcy a letter on disemboweling unsuspecting husbands," Isobel said, then with a grin, she added, "And hiding a body without getting caught."

Clarissa cackled, eyes sparking with glee. "I'd have to do some research, but why not? I bet our readers would love that. What do you think of 'A Lady's Guide to Mariticide'?"

Isobel laughed with her friend, the hottest part of her anger draining away. She could always count on Clarissa to make her smile.

Thundering hooves interrupted their amusement.

"Your ladyship!" A panting groom rode out to meet them.

Isobel schooled her features into calm. "What is

it, Randolph?"

"His Grace is in residence!"

Oh, good Lord, she had completely forgotten her father-in-law's arrival!

Strangely, Isobel had developed a fondness for the duke over the years. Having lost her own parents in a terrible carriage accident, she had gravitated to the stoic man. Besides her sister, who had her own life, Kendrick was the only family she had. Eventually, they had bonded over a shared love of music as well as their common bedsore of a connection—his estranged son and her equally estranged spouse.

Isobel stepped over to where Hellion was grazing. She glowered at Clarissa. "You could have reminded me," she accused without much heat.

"How could I when I forgot as well?"

"Some friend you are. Come on."

Clarissa shook her head. "Not a chance. You enjoy the Duke of Derision by yourself. He positively loathes me. Besides, I need to cool my horse and my sore behind after chasing your shadow for the last half an hour."

"He doesn't loathe you."

Clarissa's eyebrows shot upward. "He called me a witless pest, Izzy." Her eyes widened as she clutched at her chest with dramatic flair. "*Witless*. Me? Doesn't everyone know that I am the undeclared Goddess of Eternal Wit? For shame!"

Isobel snorted. "That's a mouthful."

"Well, you know what they say about more than a mouthful."

"No, Clarissa," Isobel said, her lips twitching,

"what *do* they say?"

She tapped her lips with a finger. "Something I might need to consider for our next batch of letters. Speaking of, I should get started. 'More than a Mouthful' is a memorable title, don't you think? Or perhaps, 'Ladies Gobbling Bananas.'"

"*Clarissa!*" Heat flooded Isobel's cheeks. Sometimes her best friend was too much.

"What? It's a natural part of life, or so my brothers declare in secret. All men enjoy it, I bet." She wrinkled her nose. "Even the duke. Perhaps we should send him a copy and see if we can get him to crack a smile?"

"You wouldn't!"

Isobel pinned her lips between her teeth. If the duke had any inkling of her secret life as Lady Darcy, he would implode. As much as he cared for her, Lady Darcy's intrigues weren't the *done thing* for a lady of quality. The duke was a fastidious man who was a stickler for decorum.

That said, most people didn't appreciate her father-in-law. Underneath all that aloof, brooding reserve, he had a heart that beat fiercely for his sons, even though his firstborn seemed to be convinced the duke was the devil. From what Isobel could garner from the tight-lipped upper servants, they'd been on the outs since Winter was a boy...a divide that had only worsened in recent years.

Isobel sighed and mounted her horse. She wasn't sure she was up for company, but she turned Hellion around, stroking the mare gently. Hellion was the foal of her sister's prized thoroughbreds, Brutus and Temperance, and had been a belated wedding present from the Duke and Duchess of Beswick. At first, Isobel had been terrified of the horse, but the truth was she'd been so lonely that she'd learned to ride out of sheer necessity.

At least the mare had stuck around.

Because Hellion was *loyal*, unlike a certain fickle, spineless marquess.

Arriving at the stables in short order, she slid from the horse with a soothing word and a caress, and threw the reins to a waiting groom, before dashing toward the kitchens. With luck, she would have a few minutes to freshen up and change before greeting the duke.

"Goodness, watch out!" a voice exclaimed as she barreled to the stairs.

Isobel slowed, narrowly missing a collision with one of the Fairfax twins. Violet and Molly had shown up six months ago with a note from their late father's solicitor citing the duke as their guardian. Kendrick had read it without blinking and told Mrs. Butterfield to take care of it. He'd ignored his wards ever since, though he hadn't batted an eyelash at allowing them to stay. At two-and-twenty, they were only two years older than her, and Isobel suspected he might have done it for her sake. Outside of Clarissa, female company was in short supply.

"Sorry!" Isobel caught her breath before climbing the stairs at a more sedate pace. "I forgot the duke was back today and with everything this morning, I'm a mess."

Violet pulled a face, lifting the hem of her black bombazine mourning dress to follow Isobel. Molly, never a far step away, appeared beside them. "He doesn't look happy. He never looks happy. Maybe he saw those awful scandal sheets, too."

A fist clenched around Isobel's heart, mortification rushing through her. She couldn't deal with anymore pity, not even from the one person who could possibly understand. She and the duke had shared a lot over the years, but this was painful new territory.

"Honestly, you can't believe a word of it, Izzy dear," Violet said when they reached the landing. "The papers reported that I was an unremarkable, plain spinster, after two unsuccessful seasons, while Molly here was the rose of the hour, when we look *exactly* the same. How am I not a rose as well? No, no, I'm some anonymous, hideous weed." She exhaled a peeved breath. "My name is *Violet*, for heaven's sake. *I'm* the flower."

Molly rolled her eyes and gave a shrug that made her brown ringlets bounce. "Everything isn't a competition, Violet. But maybe if you were less thorny and more flowery, that would help your prospects."

"I am not thorny, you beast!"

Despite being identical, the twins couldn't be more like chalk and cheese, always at odds with each other. It usually made for good fun, but right now, Isobel had other things to worry about. "For the love of all things holy, stop bickering you two and help me change!"

After a quick sponge and spray of honeysuckle-scented water, it didn't take her, the twins, and two maids long to switch out of her riding habit to a pale green muslin morning dress. Her hair brushed and re-braided, Isobel made her way down the stairs to the duke's study.

With a calming breath, she knocked and entered.

In terms of coloring, the duke looked nothing like his eldest son. His hair leaned toward black instead of brown, and his eyes were blue instead of gray. However, the family resemblance was stamped in his high forehead and that proud nose. Not that she'd seen enough of her husband of late to compare otherwise. For all she knew, Winter Vance had put on ten stone and developed a set of jowls better suited to his excessive lifestyle.

"Your Grace, you've returned earlier than expected." She greeted him from the open doorway, watching as the tall, elegant man rose to his feet from behind the desk.

"We had good weather and made excellent time." The Duke of Kendrick frowned, a concerned expression on his face. "How are you faring, my dear?"

It was only then that Isobel saw the rolled-up newssheets on the desk, and all of her brave composure unraveled.

"I could shoot him in his rotten legs," Isobel muttered, bursting into tears. She'd sworn no more, but her body shook with the effort to contain them.

"Get in line," the duke said, offering his handkerchief. "Though I suspect you'd have much better aim than me."

Isobel dabbed at her eyes with a laugh. He'd been the one to teach her to shoot and bought her a pair of pocket pistols for her last birthday. She composed herself and took a seat, pouring a cup from the nearby tea tray instead of the bottle of brandy she wanted.

Kendrick eyed her. "You need to go to London."

"I cannot go to London."

"He refuses to see me," he pointed out. "He won't refuse his wife."

Isobel sighed. "We've had this discussion, Your Grace. I won't go and be publicly cast aside. We both know that Roth is more than capable of doing that. I won't set myself up for such a public rejection."

The duke flinched. A year ago, the wretched marquess had cut his own father—*a duke, no less*—dead at a ball. It hadn't done anything except pour salt in an old, raw wound between the two men, and the rumor mill had put it down to family intrigues that weren't as rabidly exciting as Lord Roth's other deliciously devilish escapades. Like his races in Hyde Park, bare-knuckle boxing, outrageous gambling, and illegal duels over opera singers.

"You must."

A slight frown drew her brows together. "Why do you want me to go so badly? I've been content here in Chelmsford."

She cringed at the lie. *Content* was a ludicrous stretch of the truth. If she didn't have Clarissa, and more recently, the twins, she would have gone mad ages ago. But Isobel had long convinced herself that her situation was better than many other *ton* marriages that ended in disaster. She couldn't hate her husband if she didn't actually see him, could she?

She silenced the voice screaming an emphatic *yes!* and turned back to her father-in-law.

"I would like to hold my grandchild before I die," the duke said.

Isobel's brows rose at the turn in conversation

and tried to hide the instant ache his words brought on. "You do realize that your son needs to participate for that to happen." After years of fruitless waiting for her marauding husband to come to his senses, she'd long squashed that yearning, but it rose to torment her all the same whenever the duke mentioned grandchildren. "And you're not going to die."

"I will someday," he said. "My son is far from happy. And I believe his happiness starts with you."

She felt a twinge at the sadness in his voice. "He doesn't even *know* me."

"Not yet," the duke said. "But *I* do, and you are perfect for him. He needs a woman like you. Someone with a backbone who won't take his shit."

Isobel gasped. Kendrick *never* swore. Perhaps he was as fed up with his son's antics as she was. She sipped her rapidly cooling tea and contemplated the stern-faced man sitting across from her. "And you think that's me?"

The duke studied her for a long moment. "What is it you want most out of life, Isobel?"

The question was one she'd put to herself many a lonely night abed. Isobel considered the answer. She wanted an enthusiastic, dutiful husband, and someday, a loving family like her sister and the Duke of Beswick had. She wanted companionship and friendship in a partner. She wanted a bit of adventure, passion, and maybe the chance to experience something new. And all of those things were out of her reach.

They would continue to be so long as she stayed in Chelmsford. Isobel fisted her hands in her skirts. Confronting Winter in town was daunting, but she knew she had to make some sort of stand. She deserved to be presented to society, not hidden away like some mistake. A part of her wanted to shake her odious husband until his teeth rattled, and then show him just what he'd been missing all these years. Flaunt her presence in his face.

Raise the daring Lady Darcy in the flesh.

Make him grovel. Make him sorry. Make him *beg*.

The thought made a dark thrill course through her veins. How often had she fumed to Clarissa about getting even? About pulling her husband up to scratch? This was her chance, and now, she even had Kendrick's blessing.

Isobel's hard gaze met her father-in-law's. "Very well, I'll do it. I'll go."

Because damned if she wasn't going to make him regret making a fool of her for so long.